WIS

ROBERT M. COATES was b̲_____
Yale in 1919 and worked as a writer for a newspaper syndicate and wrote
pamphlets for the United States Rubber Company before deciding his
"heart was not in it". In 1921 he went to Paris and later became part of
the expatriate set that included Ernest Hemingway, Gertrude Stein and
F. Scott Fitzgerald. His first novel, *The Eater of Darkness* (1926), which has
been called the first Surrealist novel in English, was originally published in
Paris and republished in New York in 1929. Coates returned to New York
in 1926 and wrote book reviews and features for *The New York Times* and
other papers before landing a full-time job at *The New Yorker* with the help
of his friend James Thurber. He would go on to work at *The New Yorker* for
decades, publishing over 100 short stories and serving as the magazine's
art critic. Besides *Eater of Darkness* and *Wisteria Cottage* (1948), Coates is
also remembered for his nonfiction book *The Outlaw Years: The History of
the Land Pirates of Natchez Trace* (1930). Coates died in 1973.

ROBERT M. COATES

WISTERIA COTTAGE

Introduction by Mathilde Roza

VALANCOURT BOOKS

Dedication: TO BOO AGAIN

Wisteria Cottage by Robert M. Coates
First published by Harcourt, Brace & Co. in 1948
First Valancourt Books edition 2020

Published by Valancourt Books, Richmond, Virginia
http://www.valancourtbooks.com

ISBN 978-1-948405-60-7 (*trade paperback*)
Also available as an ebook.

Set in Dante MT

INTRODUCTION

Wisteria Cottage: A Novel of Criminal Impulse was published for the first time in 1948. Although more than seven decades have passed, the novel has lost nothing of its remarkable power of taking the reader into a disturbed man's world. Robert M. Coates's chilling rendition of protagonist Richard Baurie's mind—derailed by suspicion, misogyny, and a messianic obsession with power and control—continues to be as sinister as it is compelling: "I could make you remember," Baurie thinks, and, "I could make you forget, too." *Wisteria Cottage* met with rave reviews when it came out. *The New York Times Book Review* hailed it as a "brilliant tour de force," while *The New York Herald Tribune* praised Coates for his "superb imaginative excursion into the mind of a reluctant murderer." *The Saturday Review* credited Coates with touching "top peaks of terror" and proclaimed the novel a "Grade-A Psycho-thriller." Republished in 1985 for the last time, this book certainly deserves to be in print once again.

The novel tells the story of Richard Baurie, a former mental patient who is incapable of forming healthy human relationships. Richard worms his way into a lower middle-class family, consisting of a middle-aged mother and two young adult daughters, and pins all his hopes for a much-desired harmonious family life on "Wisteria Cottage," an isolated summer cottage in the dunes along the Long Island shore. Richard discovers the cottage by accident and instantly knows this is the place for him: "It was a lovely place, all right, hidden, immaculate, secret, inviolate. It was a place where anything might happen." He does his utmost to persuade the family to rent it for the summer and succeeds. Over the course of the season Richard descends into ever more frenzied madness, with disastrous, grueling results for the family.

Highly effective today, *Wisteria Cottage* also strongly reflects the time in which it was created: with World War II barely over, and the Cold War just begun, American (popular) culture developed a great interest in the phenomena of violence, crime, mental disorder and suspicion. These themes seeped into American culture on a large scale; the 1940s saw a rising popularity of crime writing, detective stories and hardboiled fiction. Next to the massive outpouring of dime novels and pulp fiction, the era saw the rise of the American film noir, with its characteristic emphasis on violence, death, troubled men, "vicious" women and nihilistic emptiness conveyed through low-key lighting and ominous shadows. Indeed, the poorly-known filmic version of *Wisteria Cottage*, the black-and-white, low-budget movie *Edge of Fury* bears many noir characteristics. The novel (and the film version even more so) also reflects popular culture's deepening interest in psychiatry and psychoanalysis. The fragments of the "Psychiatrist's Report" which form part of *Wisteria Cottage* clearly hint in that direction, as does the detailed description of one of Baurie's dreams—an element reminiscent of Hitchcock's inclusion of a dream, famously animated by Salvador Dali, in his noir movie *Spellbound* (1945), likewise concerned with murder and psychiatry.

Robert M. Coates (1897-1973) had published three novels before publishing *Wisteria Cottage*, but given the heavily experimental style of these books, most people knew him through his long association with *The New Yorker*: not only did he review books and visual art for the magazine, many of his short stories were published there. Coates's stories of the 1930s and 1940s tended to be dark and violent, especially "One Night at Coney" (*American Mercury*, May 1934); "The Fury" (*New Yorker*, August 15, 1936) and "The Net," a study for *Wisteria Cottage* which appeared in the *New Yorker* on January 27, 1940. Indeed, Coates had always had a keen interest in the darker recesses of the human mind—his first work, for instance, called *The Eater of Darkness* (1926), revolved round a futuristic "x-ray machine" which kills dozens of people. His best-known work today is his historical work on the bloody and violent land pirates of the Old Southwest, *The Outlaw Years* (1930), which continues to be in print today.

Although Coates was aiming at a wider audience with *Wisteria Cottage* than was usual for him, the writer's penchant for experimental writing is visible here too. The writer structures his narrative by Richard's moods and thought processes, and suggests his psychological states by the rhythm of his sentences, as well as by repetitions, rhyming patterns and associations. Also, there is the occasional bout of Coates's signature use of parentheses, colons and semi-colons to convey the scattering impact of the city on the human mind. In chapter three, for instance, this style serves to convey how the noise of the Third Avenue Elevated, dismantled in the 1950s, weaves itself into Richard's already restless mind as the trains rumble right past his tenement room window.

To readers familiar with serial killer lore, the name "Wisteria Cottage" might ring a bell; the novel's title refers to a killing committed by the notorious murderer Albert Fish, who, among many other crimes, choked a girl to death in a deserted house that was referred to in the press as "Wisteria Cottage." The case received extensive newspaper coverage in 1934, six years after the original killing, when Fish started sending anonymous letters to the murdered girl's family, and is unlikely to have escaped Coates's attention. In terms of plot, however, *Wisteria Cottage* is patterned after another murder case that took place in the early spring of 1937, when a psychiatric patient named Robert Irwin strangled his ex-landlady and one of her two adult daughters, and killed a male lodger with an ice-pick. The case inspired Coates to think about how to describe an act of killing in a literary work: "I began wondering," Coates told his close friend Kenneth Burke. "If, I wondered, it's hard for a person to kill just one person, what must it be like, in the sense of physical and mental strain and long-continued effort, to kill two or three?" In relying on actual murder cases, and including material such as the "Psychiatrist's Report" in his novel, *Wisteria Cottage* anticipated the "true crime" genre, made famous by Truman Capote's "non-fiction novel" *In Cold Blood* (1966). But Coates did not surrender his art to a clinical search for "truth:" what turns *Wisteria Cottage* into such an engrossing work of fiction is the great skill with which Coates conveys Richard's distorted mind and sinister worldview. His rendering of Baurie's deteriorating grip on reality, never hysterical but always low-key, is frighteningly genuine and constitutes the book's most memorable aspect. Impressed with the quiet confidence of Coates's approach, *Commonweal* noted: "No tiled asylums, no mental bedlams are employed to wring the reader's emotions. *Wisteria Cottage* is simplicity itself, as direct and frightening as the uncoiling of a serpent."

MATHILDE ROZA

MATHILDE ROZA is Associate Professor of American Literature and American Studies at Radboud University Nijmegen, the Netherlands. She is the author of the literary biography *Following Strangers* (University of South Carolina Press, 2011), the only available book-length study of the life, career and literary works of Robert M. Coates.

I

From the Psychiatrist's Report:

"It is usually difficult to determine the exact moment when a criminal intention first enters the subject's brain. But in the case of Richard Baurie it apparently was at least adumbrated, even though faintly, the first time he saw the house called Wisteria Cottage. . . ."

Richard didn't know the cottage by that name at first, of course. He had been on a three-day walking trip at the time, a thing he often did when he could get time off from the bookshop where he worked—and he was rapidly learning that he could get time off more or less when he wanted it, by simply taking it. And this time he had taken the train at random out Long Island, getting off again purely on impulse at a likely-looking station that turned out to be the village of Smithtown.

The time was late April, but already the weather was warm. He wore shorts, a brown jersey, a beret, and an old pair of heavy climbing boots. He had a rucksack and blanket roll; and quite unmindful of the slight stir of interest he caused along his passage—or if momentarily mindful, he smiled his thin, indrawn, taunting smile and ignored it—he struck east on the town's main street and then north along a side road that promised to be less traveled; since he'd started from the city that morning early, it was still only mid-afternoon when he reached the sea.

It was the Sound, of course, and the section where he first came upon it was the cluster of little islands and inlets around Setauket; the sea that day, as far as eye could reach, was absolutely calm and lake-like. It was so still that it bothered Richard a little. He had expected to find sound and movement, the pound and heave of surf and spray flying; that was what he had been in the mood for, and the almost listening calm of the water dis-

concerted him. It was too quiet, too secret, too observant; there
were times, as he walked along, with the sun sinking slowly over
his shoulder and the sea sleek and oily with the faint pinks and
yellows of sunset colors, when it seemed like a great glinting eye
aslant, watching him balefully.

It made him nervous, it troubled him, and with Richard nervousness always was a spur to action; there was once when he
walked right down to the edge of the water and yelled.

It was a narrow beach, and pebbly, that he happened to be on
at the time, and it was bordered by a broken-down breakwater
made of pilings, with behind that a roadway and bungalows. But
the place seemed deserted, and without really thinking what he
was doing Richard walked down to the brink, where the sea's
incessant faint stirrings were made visible at last in a soft, lazy,
wavering, fractional reaching and receding among the sand and
the pebbles, and yelled.

He yelled meaningless things at first, yowls and catcalls and
so on, and then an idea began to take hold of him.

"Hey!" he yelled, "HEY! Is anybody out there? Why won't
you answer?"

There might really be someone or something out there, he
thought, devils, maybe, or strange monsters, and they hiding,
and that gave him a sense of challenge; he cupped both hands
around his mouth and yelled straight out across the water till his
face grew flushed and the words he was shouting ran together in
a queer kind of rhythm of their own—HEYisanybodyoutthere
HEYisanybodyoutthere—and he grew suddenly tired of it.

He dropped his hands. He kicked a pebble. "All right, then. All
right," he said aloud, as if in answer to the commands of some
inner mentor, and then abruptly he whirled and looked hastily
along the row of bungalows behind him. He knew how often
and how shamelessly men—yes, and women too—spied on
others, and the thought had occurred to him that the watcher
might be there, silently observing him.

But there was no one in sight. The beach bungalows—there
were only about a dozen of them in the row, and they were
almost identical, shingle-sided in the Long Island fashion,
shut-windowed, their deep, shadowy porches bare of all fur-

niture and windswept-looking—all stood silent and deserted, gazing bleakly past him out toward the sea.

"There you are, sirs," he said, and bowed slightly in the direction of his inanimate audience. "The poet. You have seen what the poets do when they're alone. Try to remember."

He smiled slightly. *I could make you remember,* he thought. But he did nothing about it. He remembered what he had been told and he did nothing about it, and after standing awhile looking carefully along the row he walked slowly on his way again. He had come almost to the end of the row, where the beach ran out into rocks and sedge and the shore line curved sharply inland; he had lighted a cigarette and he was breathing easier when, without warning, a small truck appeared around a bend in the road at the last bungalow and came rattling toward him.

Without hesitation, Richard made his way up the beach to the roadside and hailed it.

"Were you waiting around back there?" he said.

The truck was a made-over Ford, loaded down with pipe and other plumber's supplies, and the driver, a small, worried-looking red-haired man in overalls, looked down at him curiously.

"Waiting? Where?" he asked. "You mean down at the Piersons'? I ain't been there yet." And then something in the incongruity of Richard's appearance seemed to strike him. "You got something to do with the Piersons?" he said.

"Piersons? No," said Richard. It had flashed across his mind at first that perhaps this man had been the watcher he had suspected; perhaps he had been parked in his truck around the bend in the road, waiting, listening, grinning cynically; he knew how often such things could happen.

But now the man's manner was beginning to reassure him. He was either very clever or very simple, and in either case Richard decided he didn't want to go into the matter further. After all, all he wanted was peace, and a chance to do a little walking. "I'm just out for a quiet little walking trip," he said. "And I thought maybe you'd heard me calling. And I thought . . . Have you seen Johnny Guinan around here?" he added suddenly. "He's the one I was calling for."

The driver now was leaning down over the wheel, his red knuckles clamped around it, as if he couldn't quite believe what his ears were telling him. He was clearly puzzled, and as his puzzlement increased Richard began to enjoy the encounter. "You say, calling?" the man said. "What's that name again?"

"Johnny Guinan," said Richard.

" 'S he live around here?"

"Summers, he does," Richard said. The name had simply popped into his head. It was a name he had read in the newspapers or had heard somewhere. Now he added another. "Is this Weldon's Point?" he asked abruptly.

"Weldon's Point?" the man repeated, more puzzled than ever. "You sure you got your names right, bud?" Then his glance became a little wary. He was being kidded, or something, and the trouble was he couldn't quite figure out why; and the uncertainty made him uneasy. Richard recognized the signs, he knew the symptoms, and as the fellow's uneasiness grew his contempt for the man increased. He had always hated fearful people, women or men, and the trouble was that there were so many of them. But if he showed any evidence, it was only that his eyes grew more somber.

"I think that was the name," he answered mildly.

The man still stared at him. Richard was twenty-eight, not as tall as he thought he was, or as slim or as boyish, but as blond; he was actually rather stocky, of medium height, square-shouldered and heavy-thighed, with an expression that was at the same time impassive and slightly derisive, and to the man looking down at him as he stood on the lonely beach in his shorts and jersey and blanket roll he must have seemed something of an apparition. "Well, you're on the wrong track somewhere," he said, this time brusquely, as he slipped the car in gear. "There ain't no Weldon's Point around here."

Richard stepped back smiling and bowed ironically, as a signal for the truck to proceed. "It doesn't matter," he said. "I was just walking." Then he smiled more brightly than ever. "You know, doctor's orders. And I just thought . . . I remembered a friend of mine . . . But it may be I'm in the wrong locality."

"You're on the wrong track somewhere, bud," the man

repeated, and drove off. Richard watched him go, then walked on a short way and looked back again. The truck was drawing up before the farthest bungalow, and as it came to a halt Richard dropped down behind the breakwater and, just peering over the tops of the pilings, watched it.

He saw the man get out and stand for a moment or two looking back up the roadway, as if wondering where Richard had gone. Then, apparently, he dismissed the problem. (I could make you remember, though, Richard thought.) But he seemed in no hurry to start about his work. The one moving figure in the rather barren vista, he walked slowly around to the back of the truck and let down the tailboard, stopped awhile then to light a cigarette and gaze out to sea, and then, lazily, took out some tools or something—it was too far away for Richard to distinguish clearly—and walked up the steps of the bungalow.

There was a glint of sun on glass as the door of the bungalow opened, then the man disappeared inside. But he came out again almost immediately, this time to fetch a length of pipe and some fittings, and again went back into the bungalow.

This time he stayed. He was at work, apparently, somewhere in the silent, winter-dusty bungalow, doing whatever he had come there to do. (And across Richard's mind there flitted swiftly, glancingly, a vision of the tools on the oilcloth floor and the man in his overalls bending, preoccupied, by the sink; it would be in the kitchen, musty and dusty from long shut-upness, and as Richard crept through the door there would only be the faintest creak of the flooring to betray his presence. But it would be enough to make the man turn, and see, and shriek. God! What shrieks! *I could make you remember,* Richard thought. And then the limp, salt-soused figure, the face oozing blood, and the blood sluicing off on the waves. "I could make you forget, too," he said.)

But there were no waves. He did nothing. He waited, watching the truck, the bright stretch of roadway, the houses diminishing in line; he waited until he was ready to move, then he got up and walked quickly around the bend at the last bungalow and on up the road.

★

It was only an incident, and in the end Richard felt that he had come out the better in it. But from then on he followed the inland roads, more or less away from the shore and the sea.

It was not that the shore wasn't quiet. It was. Week-ends, maybe, at that season, people came down and opened up their houses for a day or two; there were signs, here and there, of a kind of pre-summer awakening—in a half-painted rowboat turned bottom side up on a pair of sawhorses at the side of a bungalow, or a partly spaded-up garden, or a lawn that had been carefully fenced off with twine, after seeding. But perhaps just because of this there was a feeling of desertion about it now, a sort of waiting stillness that troubled him, and that was heightened by the watchful, too quiet sea.

He preferred walking inland, along the roads that twined lazily from inlet to inlet, a little way back from the coast. Here, too, there was little activity. Now and then he would come upon a farmer planting a field with potatoes, or plowing, or harrowing, and there would be a thin smudge of dust blowing with the wind from the trail of the plow or the harrow. Now and then there would be a group of laborers working on a road, or a truck gardener out cultivating his early peas.

But for the most part the feeling was of that purposeless, tentative time, between spring and summer, when things seem to grow by themselves without human attendance; the wild grapevines along the roads and the trees that stood over them were just coming into leaf but in no hurry about continuing; the greens everywhere were fresh, shyly yellowish, transparent and unassertive.

He could walk as he wished—and Richard loved walking— without fear of observance or spying. He loved walking, as indeed he loved movement of any kind; the mere fact of being transported from place to place was a source of almost physical exhilaration for him, and in the city, even when he was in his darkest moods, a bus ride or a ride on the Elevated was enough, often, to restore him to good spirits again.

But walking was the best of all. It gave a sense of adventure, in addition to the magic of movement; and now, freed of observation, or at least undisturbed by it—there was something companionable, *innocent*, really, about the easy, comfortable, rustic life hereabouts—he could throw off the restrictions that everyday life in the city imposed on him; he could walk as he liked, hop occasionally, skip, run a little, do all the impulsive things that seemed so natural to him and so strange, apparently, to everyone else.

Once he walked for a hundred yards or so in the German goose step, and in the excitement of finding himself doing it (he had fallen into the step without really realizing it, because of some connection with whatever he had been thinking), he soon found himself talking away like mad to an imaginary onlooker.

"Oh, yes, you. I saw you," he said aloud. "Did you think I didn't see you? And I know what you're thinking, too. You don't know it, but I'm right there inside you; I'm a Hitlerite, that's what you're thinking. Well, maybe. Only the war's over now, long ago, in case you didn't know it. And besides, Hitler never asked me. And you know, or maybe you don't know it, but I'm the kind that has to be asked, and by the chief of them all, the highest Chief of Chiefs." And then, for fun, he made his little ironic bow. "*Compris*, now? Or maybe I should have said—but I don't know the German of it."

Then he laughed, at the silliness of it all. "Yes, the Chief, or the Super-Chief. Listen in every Wednesday and Friday, same time, same station."

He was happy, that was the truth of the matter. He'd been bored, cooped up there in the city, working all day every day in the bookshop. Old Jennie Harm-Nobody Carmody couldn't know that. She thought selling books was the beginning and end of existence. She didn't know that a man wanted more than that—freedom, freedom really from the endless pushing constrictions of people around him, and light, movement, air, the sense of distance and emptiness.

Even Elinor didn't quite understand, really—though, good girl, she tried to. Perhaps no woman could ever really understand that the one thing a man *didn't* want was constriction, encirclement, envelopment; and yet it was just what they were always, eternally, trying to draw him into. In a way, of course, it was part of their charm. But in a way, too, it was the devil in them.

But here, anyway, he was happy. He felt free, expanded, expansive. ("And expensive?" he thought. "Extensive?" And then: "Well. No. Not that.")

He felt completely in touch, and completely in control. He had dinner in a roadside diner on the outskirts of the town of Port Jefferson, in a mood quite above the investigating glances of the locals around him. He slept the night in his blanket, quite cozily, underneath some scrub pines in a cove a few miles farther down the coast; and although he awoke slightly depressed—but that was usual with him; he was almost always depressed in the mornings—the mood of reasonless melancholy soon passed.

There was that calm sea, of course, still there to trouble him; the first thing he noticed upon awakening was the eerie, inquisitive glint of it, through the low pine branches. But he was beginning to realize that it wouldn't be calm forever. As was his custom on such trips, he had bought sandwiches and fruit and a quart of milk at a grocery the night before; he heated milk and powdered coffee over his Sterno on the beach, and as he sat there munching and crunching, it came over him that he really controlled the sea too.

He could, and did, outstare it. He could throw pebbles and stones at it, to disturb it, and the wide, ring-like ripples that spread after each stone's fall were as pure and appealing as a smile; when the larger ones lapped against the beach—for as he grew interested he threw larger and larger pebbles, real rocks even, but he didn't let himself get excited—they made a sound that was curiously plaintive and appealing, too.

"Please don't hurt me. Don't hurt me," they seemed to be saying.

But he didn't let himself get excited; and though thereafter, when he found himself following the coast, he occasionally threw a pebble out into the water, it was done absent-mindedly, as one sometimes continues an action after the impulse that originally prompted it has been forgotten. It was about noon of the second day when he came upon the lonely cottage.

★

He was in dune country then, and because of that he might well have missed seeing the place entirely, for it lay in a sandy hollow that was deep enough to hide all but its rooftop and chimney from the paved road that he had been following. But there was a road—hardly more than a double wheel track, really—that led down to it; and because he was bored with the traffic along the highway he did turn down it; he had walked only a half-mile or so, up one slope and then down it, and up another, before he found himself face to face with the hidden cottage.

That, of course, was its principal charm, its hiddenness. It was not a large cottage, apparently, though Richard realized that its looks might be deceptive, for he had come upon it from above, when a house always seems smaller than it is, and it was dwarfed further in appearance by the mass of the dunes that rose around it.

Actually, it was a story and a half in height, with two large dormers projecting from the roof on either side, and a small attic window, framed in red, just under the peak; and it was built upon concrete piles, so you could look right beneath it at the slightly slanting floor of sand over which it stood.

The piles were painted white, quite fresh, and the red trim around the doors and windows looked fairly fresh too. But the walls, which were shingled, had been left unpainted, and the color they presented now was the wood's sheen only, greenish gray for the most part, shading off here and there almost to silver.

There was a screened porch, and the darker and the more mysterious because it was screened. There was a sort of small shed at one side and slightly behind it, and behind that a tiny outhouse. And around the whole place, front, sides, rear, ran a neat little picket fence, scarcely more than a couple of feet or so in height, but with each picket meticulously painted, and painted, like the foundation pilings, white.

It was an odd little fence, for it served no purpose, really. It was too low to act as a barrier, and it could hardly have been meant to be a boundary, for it enclosed the same ground, sparsely grassed and sandy, that lay outside it. It was just there, a fence, and what it did was to give a feeling of compactness to the cottage.

Without the fence, the place might have sprawled. As it was, it just sat there, the house, the yard, the little shed at the back and the outhouse beyond and the fence around all, an entity; still and small and lonely as it was, in the waste of sand that surrounded it, it was somehow complete and quite self-sufficient.

Richard stood for some time looking down at the cottage. "Peace. Just peace," he thought. He had been walking, he felt tired, and that may have had something to do with it, but at the moment the house, in its deep, brooding emptiness, its almost sullen isolation, held a dreamlike invitation.

"Peace—and calm," he said, savoring the words, and the words themselves had never seemed lovelier. Beyond the cottage the dunes opened out in a wide, sloping **V**, leading down to a little bluff or cliff overlooking the beach; and for once the calm sea, rising levelly up to the horizon like still water in a vessel, made a perfect background.

It was the thing that was needed, the one segment that made the whole ring of quietness and isolation complete. You could do what you wanted to do here; you could do the most secret things and be undisturbed, you could be yourself completely and the place would contain it all. It looked innocent, and wise. It was a place that had seen everything, and despite all its freshness there was a vine by the side of the porch, cut back now, and just coming into leaf, and with a trunk that was almost as big as his arm, that showed how old the house really must be.

"I know you seaside places," said Richard, and he nodded at the cottage sagely. There had been naked parties here: girls and men trooping drunkenly down to the beach and then rollicking around in the sand; running screaming from the porch and the screen door slamming behind them, and then caught, the arm circling the eager, bare flesh, and then the pair of them sinking on the sands together, laughing. "And who would know?" he said, thinking of the bare dunes around, the town a mile or so at least up the road.

God would know. But to people like that . . . Murder, rape— and then next season, perhaps, an old couple sitting rocking on the porch, or a family of children calling to each other from room to room. The little cottage could contain them all. "And even storm," Richard thought. There was a thought beneath all his other thoughts that he wouldn't yet let rise to the surface, but it was there, and it made his heart beat faster.

"Even storm," he thought. It would be a testing-place then, all right, a place where honest relationships could be forged, if they could be forged anywhere. He was standing on a slope overlooking the cottage, and the road he was on ran down to it to end in a sort of rough **Y** in the sand where the cars of previous inhabitants or their visitors had been parked or been turned around to head back up the road again. In the middle of the **Y**, on a post driven into the sand, there was a sign FOR SALE OR RENT, and then the name of some real-estate dealer.

For the moment Richard hardly noticed either. For the moment he had let his mind fill the hollow below with the harsh surge and suck and then surge again of the waves and the wind; he saw it clearly as in a movie—the storm—and in the midst of it the cottage, its white fence and white pilings whiter still in the thunder darkness, its roof crouched against the rain and the spray, lights shining perhaps in a couple of its windows. And then the dark pile of clouds disappearing, the bright sun shining waterily through. . . . Storm would make the place cleaner, he thought. Storm would purify.

It was a lovely place, all right, hidden, immaculate, secret, inviolate. It was a place where anything might happen. He was walking down the road to the cottage, and it was after the storm now, the sky was clear, the sun was shining, sand and sea were clean, and yet he and the storm still were one. He was walking down the road and the sun was shining; it was then that he noticed the sign.

FOR SALE OR RENT, the sign said, and then the name of the real-estate dealer, and the surprise was so great that for a moment he stopped and looked about him. Until now he had thought that the cottage was like all the other cottages he had seen on his journey, something glanced at and then passed by, and perhaps remembered.

Now he saw that it was more than that. In a way, it was emptier than he had thought. It was ownerless, it was ownable; it was his, or it could be his, and he would make it so. He would tell the Hacketts—hadn't they asked him to look out for a summer cottage for them? And if he could get them to take the place, couldn't he share it with them?

He could, he could; whether they knew it or not, he could—and from then on he walked about the place, trying doors, peering into the windows, with something the air of a proprietor. It was, already, the place he had chosen; already, he owned it.

2

From the Psychiatrist's Report:

Richard Baurie was under observation for nearly two months at Willetstown State Hospital before his case finally came to trial, and during that time we had a number of talks with him. He often mentioned his discovery of Wisteria Cottage; he would come back to it frequently in his conversations, and although his very definite flair for self-dramatization had to be taken into account in analyzing all his utterances, there can be no doubt that there was also some symbolism involved.

"I knew right from the start the thing would have to be worked out right there," he would say.

And again: "It was the end of the road. That had something to do with it, I guess, because it was the end of the road too, for me, you know. And with that tight little fence around it . . . I knew that whatever happened, it would work out all right there."

And he added, "But then things got so mixed up later on. God knows, though, I tried to help them."

Richard Baurie was a short, rather thick-bodied man, with light-blue eyes that had a noticeably fixed expression, a high, bulging forehead, blond hair, pale skin, and a small mouth and chin. He could be extremely engaging at times, and had clear consciousness and dependable memory. But in general he presented a typical schizophrenic picture—was withdrawn and preoccupied a good part of the time, particularly when alone, while his mood could change at other times to one of potential or real destructiveness, depending on the circumstances and his opportunity. He was not always approachable.

"And then, well, you know, the city," he said on another occasion. "You know, what have you got? You're too crowded there. There's no room to expand, to let your soul expand, and your spirit. What you've got is a room, or an apartment. Well, I had a room, and the Hacketts had an apartment, and there we all were, in the city.

"But the trouble is, you're always being watched, and spied upon; you can't act naturally.... And I was in the room, and Elinor was in the apartment. And the rest of them—that old harridan, the mother; and Louisa, no better—just polluting the air she walked in."

He seemed troubled for a moment. "I never minded about Louisa, though, really. I saw through her from the start," he said. "But I was a long time seeing through the old woman."

He got up and walked over to the window of his cell and walked back again, and his hands began clenching and unclenching in a way that usually preceded an outburst. There were times when it was physically dangerous to enter Baurie's cell, and we had wondered, that day, if this was to be one of them. Now we wondered still more. But there was nothing to do but sit quietly, and in the end he came back and sat down peaceably enough.

"You've got too many people above you in the city," he said. "That's the trouble. Now, the Hacketts, you know ... Did you know, did you know that was only a third-floor apartment they had? In a ten-story building? I never told them, because I knew they would laugh at me if I did, but I used to think it, if they only lived higher, on the top floor, maybe...." He looked down at his hands and went on a little shamefacedly, as if uncertain how we might take what he was about to say. "They'd have been that much nearer to God," he added solemnly.

"I knew I had to get them out of there, anyway. Especially Elinor," he went on. "And there I was, at the end of the road...."

"You mean, that day when you were walking?" we asked.

"That's right. Golly, I used to love walking." He glanced around the cell and then leaned forward to look at us earnestly.

"*You* know; you *must* know they can't keep me here much longer, can they?" he said. "Why, good *Christ!*" he exclaimed. Baurie rarely swore; it was a curious survival of his early training, and when he did it was with the awkward vehemence of one unused to profanity. "Don't they know they can't afford it, with a man like me? Don't the damn fools *know* that? Don't they? You can *tell* them, anyway, can't you?"

He inched forward a little on the cot where he was sitting, facing us. "Can't you *tell* them?"

And again, but this might have been pure fabrication: "And there were clouds that day, you know. And then the sun struck through, just as I stood there, and it lit directly on the cottage. I saw the ray myself, and I knew then that it had to be there. If I was ever going to do anything for them, it had to be there."

He had some difficulty convincing the Hacketts.

There were three of them in the family—Florence Hackett, the mother, a tall, well-preserved woman of about fifty, with dark eyes and abundant dark hair, who had come from Virginia originally and who was a partner in an antique shop in the middle Fifties, and Louisa and Elinor, the daughters—and they lived on East Forty-ninth Street, only a few blocks away from where Richard lived on Third Avenue.

And he loved them, especially Elinor. And he hated them, too— or he feared them, rather, which was much the same thing—for they were so much above him, so much what he wanted to be. And somehow, very soon after he had come to New York, he had gotten involved with them. He had met Mrs. Hackett one day, buying groceries in the neighborhood A & P—"He picked me up," she sometimes said, coquettishly, "right there among the lettuces"—and then one thing had led to another, and now lately he had come to have the run of the apartment.

He had dropped in there, in fact, the night before starting on his trip, and they had said, or at least Mrs. Hackett had said, ". . . And if you see a nice place for us—not too large, you know; something we could take for a month, perhaps—or if it was near enough to trains and things; I shall have to get into the shop occasionally, even in summer, and I suppose Louisa . . ."

She had a way of letting sentences trail off like that, or of getting them so involved with stray clauses and things that in the end she would have to stop, and start over. "I mean to say, we might take it for even longer. And then you'd have to come down for week-ends, and so on. That is, of course," she had finished, "if you *do* see something."

And now all he wanted in the world, at the moment, was to have them rent the place for the summer, and for him to spend the summer there with them. It was the right thing, the perfect thing; more than that, it was the *just* thing for them to do. It would straighten them out, quell the evil forces that were working among them; it would—well, this was something he'd never dare mention to them, they'd be too sure to laugh at him; but out here on the wind-swept dunes, alone, he could think it—it would bring them nearer to God. He spent the next hour or so, once he had discovered the cottage, just prowling around the place and the dunes that surrounded it, studying it, enjoying it, loving it; and throughout most of that time he was telling himself—rehearsing, so to speak—what he would tell the Hacketts about it. For there were forces at work against him; he knew that, and he knew he would have to move carefully.

"It's the cutest little place, all white and gray and shingled, and red-painted windows," he said to himself once, experimentally. "And with this wonderful, utterly useless little fence!" But that mightn't do, either, he thought.

It was Louisa who would probably decide things in the end, he realized, and she didn't go in so much for the "cute" or the "useless"; that was more in Florence's line. Louisa was the older sister, and to his way of thinking a bitch. But she was an actress who played small parts on the radio—"bits," she called them—and the real money-maker of the family; and for that reason, principally, she would have a good deal to say about any arrangements they might make for the summer. And for all her air of breezy casualness there was a good deal of practicality about her. She would probably snort at a "useless" fence, whereas for him it was one of the main charms of the cottage.

She was tall, like her mother, with the same abundant dark hair and rather haughty profile, but of course she was nowhere

near so full-figured, and her eyes were a brownish hazel. She
was pretty, all right, Richard had to admit, and beside her Elinor
looked stocky and short and rather pudgy. Louisa was the real
beauty of the family, with the sort of long, racy-looking legs,
small hips and high, rounded breasts, full, wide mouth and
direct, almost challenging gaze that you saw in the fashionable
advertisements.

She had in fact been in the advertisements herself, having
modeled for a time while she was breaking into radio, and she
had the same sort of crisp self-assurance that the people the
advertisements were meant for had—or that Richard assumed
that they had, for of course he had never met any of them in his
life. And she had beaux all over the place; she was "dated" constantly, and the places she went to were the kind of places that
Richard had heard of but had never dreamed of going to—"21,"
the Stork Club, the Rainbow Room. (And what she did with the
fellows who took her there Richard didn't know, but he could
well imagine; men just didn't spend that kind of money on any
girl for nothing.)

She was the main source of evil, all right, especially in her
influence on Elinor. But he mustn't let himself think too much
about Louisa now, here at the cottage. The thing to do was just
not to bother about her; she was too unpredictable, he decided.
The thing to do would be to play up to Florence. Florence, he
could manage, and Elinor.

"It's sort of rambling, but small, and it's shingled," he said,
aloud. "And it has this wonderful big screened porch."

The porch screening, he noticed, was rusted away in spots,
here and there. But he could fix that, he could fix that.

"And there's something about the setting. Those big dunes,
you know, so hidden. And the sea . . . There's a sort of cliff just
beyond, only it's sand, that you have to climb down to reach the
beach, and a gap in the dunes leading out to it. And when there's
surf!" The sea was calm now, as it had been the day before,
but in his mind he could imagine the rightness of what he was
saying. "I don't know. I suppose it must be the way the beach is,
or something, because you get these long, easy rollers!

"Lord!" he said. He was still talking as if to the Hacketts. "It's the place for you, really, if there ever was one. You'll have me down occasionally, I hope." He bowed and smiled with ironic humility. "Or we might work out some sort of arrangement. I don't know if you know it, but I'm quite good as a handy-man." Looking in at the living room windows, he had seen a long wicker sofa, some tables, a Morris chair, all the usual furnishings. But the porch was bare. But he knew there must be some furniture for it somewhere, so he made it up. "Nice old rockers," he said. "And one of those wonderful old-fashioned swings— you know, the kind that goes back and forth?"

Now that he had made it up, he could see it; it would be for him and Elinor, dreaming together through the long summer evenings. But for the moment, strategically, he was willing to give it to Mrs. Hackett. "I can just see you, Florence, lazy you, sitting propped there, reading a book!"

No, he thought, it was perfect; they *had* to like it; the thing now was to get the matter settled. He had a couple of sandwiches left over from breakfast—it seemed so long ago!—and he sat in the sun on the porch steps eating them and already savoring a feeling of proprietorship; there was literally no one around at all. Then it occurred to him to look up the real-estate agent.

He found the name and address—J. Debevois, Broker, Mount Sinai—and as soon as he had finished the sandwiches he started out to find the man. "Mount Sinai!" he exclaimed to himself. "What a name! What a wonderful name!" He knew Elinor would appreciate it.

He knew the town too, he was sure of it; it was the pleasant little village he had passed about a half-mile back up the road. But as he walked he began hurrying a little. At the cottage he had felt the place was so wholly his that it had hardly occurred to him that others might want it. But now, away from it, he felt differently. It was a prize, there was no doubt of that, and now anyone at all—someone walking like himself, someone motoring and noticing the chimney, the rooftop from the road; anyone—might stop by there and see it and claim it.

He had to hurry. "Mount Sinai," he kept repeating to himself, and when a little while later he passed a couple of men at the roadside—they were telephone linesmen, obviously, and one of them was just strapping his climbers on, while the other, with a loop of wire hung on one arm, was staring judicially up the pole—he called over to them questioningly, "Mount Sinai?"

They looked slowly around at him, startled, and then pointed in the direction he was going. He kept walking, though it occurred to him now that they must have been surprised to see him in so much of a hurry. A second or two later he heard one of them call something after him. But he was too far away now to distinguish the words, and he kept right on walking. There was no harm for them, once, to see a man who was really going somewhere.

"It's the place! It's the place for you really, darlings, if there ever was one!" Richard was saying. He was sitting, next evening, in the Hacketts' living room, and it was just as he had foreseen it, only maybe better—the three women grouped around, docile, gentle, attentive, and he sitting in the one big armchair; he, the returned traveler, the adventurer, holding, controlling them. And beneath it all, the feeling of family; he felt like son, father, and husband rolled into one. For the moment, he truly loved them.

"It sounds lovely, all right," said Louisa. She was sitting propped up among the pillows on the red sofa in the corner, with one long, slender leg dangling over the edge and the other tucked under her so that the round of the knee showed out. She had had no program that night, and no dates, and that was what had made the circle complete, and her voice, as she spoke, was casual. But Richard thought that he recognized a challenge in it.

"It *is* lovely," he said, and for once he looked straight at her. She was touching up her nails with an emery board and didn't catch his glance.

"I know," she said. "I just wonder . . ." And there, turning her attention back to her nails, she seemed willing to let the matter drop.

Richard still watched her keenly. Here she was, spoiling things, right from the start, and he couldn't keep a certain irritation from creeping into his voice.

"You wonder what?" he demanded, and this time she looked up at him directly.

"Well, I wonder if it's just the thing for us."

Richard threw back his head and laughed loudly. " 'For us,' " he repeated, and in spite of himself he found himself mimicking her a little. " 'Not for us.' Well, maybe. But you haven't even *seen* the place yet, for one thing. And for another, it does seem to me you ought to speak for yourself, about things like that. There are Florence and Elinor to be heard from too, you know."

Louisa stared at him for an instant, and then bent to her nails again. "Why, of course, kid," she said. "That goes without saying, I'd think. It's for all of us to decide."

Yes, thought Richard, for all of *you*. And no business of mine to butt in, I suppose; and he glanced over at Florence and Elinor to see if they had noticed the insult he had been offered. But if they had they gave him no sign, and—he knew he was getting excited, but he couldn't help it—he decided that if she wouldn't say it he'd say it for her. "And no business of mine to butt in, I suppose," he said to her.

And she looked at him. They all looked at him. "Oh, my God!" Louisa said.

"Richard. *Richard!*" said Florence. "Don't just act like a child, my dear. Don't be silly! And you too, Louisa," she added, just to make things equal, and Louisa looked up at her once and looked down again. "Has it got a good beach? " she asked.

"Has it got a good beach!" Richard almost shouted. And then he told them about the rollers, how they came in, and broke, and pounded, filling the whole hollow with sound. "And you've got to remember, it was a calm day when I was there; they just came in lazily. But in a storm . . . Well, I guess there's no telling *what* it would be like in a storm."

He ended lamely, a little; it had occurred to him that too much storm talk might frighten them. "But it's sheltered, you know," he went on. "And it's calm, too, of course, sometimes. Or so the real-estate man told me. . . ." He'd had a feeling for a moment that he was getting off the track, somehow, but now he brightened. "Did I tell you about him? Did I? Mr. Debevois? Of Mount Sinai? (And don't you love that name?) Because really he was really something."

He told them about Mr. Debevois, and he did it well, too, he thought; he was really in control again. "Little dark wiry man, white hair, skin like leather. He looks more like a fisherman than a businessman, and I guess really he is; when I came in he was sitting in his little office, around the side of this lovely old white house—the whole village is lovely, really—" He couldn't help glancing at Louisa, satirically, when he used the word "lovely," but she took no notice. "And I hope to die if he didn't have fishing boots on; just come back from putting a boat in the water, he said. But anyway—well, you can tell he can't be much of a businessman, only five hundred dollars for that lovely cottage, and—well, darlings, you'll just have to see it."

"Mmmmm," said Mrs. Hackett, mildly. She was mending a parchment lampshade she'd brought home from the antique shop. No one bothered to "entertain" Richard; he was "one of the family," as Mrs. Hackett put it, and when he was there they all went about their usual tasks. "Not *too* cheap," she said.

"But not too expensive, either," put in Richard quickly. "And if you'll permit me"—he made his little bow in her direction—"if you'll just let me use that little shed I told you about, I'll be more than glad to contribute a share of it."

In his prowlings, he had noticed that the shed at the back of the cottage had been fixed up roughly as a sort of guest house; the walls had been whitewashed inside and there was even some furniture, a cot, a chair, and an old-fashioned marble-topped commode. "Just for week-ends, of course," he added. "I wouldn't want to be underfoot all the time."

He had expected some sort of protestation ("Oh, Richard!"—a chorus of voices—"Of course we'll want you, and not just for week-ends, either!") and in the lack of it the slight pause that followed was dreadful. Mrs. Hackett had held out the shade at arm's length and was inspecting it narrowly.

"Trains?" she said, in her languid voice. "Did you think to look up the trains?"

"That I did, ma'am," said Richard shortly. Did they think he had gotten the cottage, his lovely cottage, just to hand over to them, he wondered. Did they think they could freeze him out?

"Because I'd need to get in to the city, you know, at least now and then," Mrs. Hackett went on, not noticing. "We'll be closing up the shop for August, certainly. And even through July things will hardly be very active. But I shall want to keep some contact. And Louisa, naturally . . ."

"Yes, Louisa," said Richard. He looked over for help to Elinor. But Elinor just smiled. "Well, I did look up trains, and there are plenty. And the station—Port Jefferson, it is—is just a couple of miles away. You see, I myself—"

He was going to add that he himself had some business interests in the city. But again someone cut in. Louisa. "And how do we get from the station to the cottage?"

Richard glared at her. "A bus, darling," he snapped. "Or taxis. There's a regular bus line, just up the road from the cottage. I looked up trains for my own sake, partly," he added clearly. If Elinor wouldn't help him he'd have to take control of things himself. "Because I thought," and this time his bow was really ironic, "if you'd be kind enough to have me on the terms I suggested, using only the shed, and week-ends only too, of course. I wouldn't want to be underfoot all the time. . . ."

And this time, gloriously, it came. Mrs. Hackett looked over at him, smiling. "Richard. Richard," she said, gently, chiding. "So formal? Don't you know that you're one of the family? If we do take the place, and mind you, nothing's been settled . . ." For a few moments after that, Richard literally was deaf to what she was saying.

"If you take it . . ." he said earnestly. He looked at Elinor, and she too was smiling. They all were smiling. "I'll write. Really, I'll write," he said. "I know you all think I'm just a waster. But down there . . . Oh, don't think I didn't think that little shed would be a perfect place for me to write in!" Mrs. Hackett was saying something but he paid no attention. "And you, Florence," he said happily to her, "in that porch swing I told you about—or did I tell you? Anyway, there is one. And I can see you there, lazy you, sitting there with a book in the sunshine, swinging. . . ."

He was so happy that he even wanted to include Louisa. "No, the beach," he said, and the fact that he brought up a subject that they'd already almost clashed about was itself intended as a subtle peace offering. After all, he thought, maybe she hadn't meant what she had seemed to mean before. "It's a wonderful beach; it is, really. Just wonderful. And so lonely. You'd have it all to yourself, you know." He knew what she would want, of course, with her dates and her necking parties, and he was so happy now that he was willing to yield it to her. He was looking directly at her, and his glance was meaningful. "You could do just about anything you wanted to do on that beach, I guess, Anything."

But Louisa refused to accept his peace offering. She looked startled for a moment and then she just burst out laughing. "Honey, what are you getting at now, for God's sake?" she demanded. "What on earth would I want to do on a beach, except swim—or sun-bathe, maybe?"

Richard gave a dry little chuckle. "Well," he said. As usual, she was making things embarrassing. "Isn't that what I mean, darling? Only, there . . . well, I mean, when you girls are on the beach alone . . . or when there's been a party. You've had some friends down for the week-end, maybe, and then later, in the evening, if you feel like a swim . . ."

He was getting excited, in the way that Louisa could always get him excited; right now, for example, he wanted to say to her, pull down your skirt, don't you know your knees are showing? And at the same time, for a moment, he had actually seen the white bodies, Louisa's among them, running shrilly down that **V** between the dunes to the cliff-top and the beach. . . . He could feel his face flushing a little.

But he knew too that he was going too far. Mrs. Hackett had raised her head to listen, and Louisa was staring at him; he was afraid that if something didn't stop him, if she didn't turn aside that stare, he would go right on talking, talking, and in the end he would say something he shouldn't. And he mustn't. . . . In the end, it was Elinor who saved him.

"I know what Richard is talking about. He means bathing nudey, that's all, only he's too shy to say so, poor thing," she said suddenly, with that wonderful mixture of frankness and innocence that was always hers. And she got up and patted his cheek with her hand. "Don't you know everybody does that now, darling?" she demanded. "There's no reason for getting all gawky about a little thing like that, you know." Then she picked up their highball glasses and started toward the kitchen.

"I think I'll make us all another drink," she said. "Don't you think? And then Richard can tell us more about this cottage. I think it sounds wonderful."

And in the end he put the thing over. Louisa, the recalcitrant, settled her share of the matter by simply withdrawing. She'd be busy with her programs most of the time, she said, and they came at such odd hours that the best thing to do was to make up their minds without her; whatever Florence and Elinor decided would be O.K. with her, she said. She'd come down only week-ends, probably, anyway, and the rest of the time she would stay in the city at the apartment. But there was no reason, because she'd be tied up so much, that the others shouldn't have a good summer.

Richard let her get away with it. He knew perfectly well what was in her mind, probably, and the only thing that bothered him was that Florence, her mother, didn't seem to see it too; it showed a lack of maternal concern that disturbed him a little. Because all that Louisa wanted was to have the road clear and the apartment empty; she had her dates, heavy dates, and if she could get the place to herself—well, then, the sky would be the limit. He said nothing, however, because for once what *she* wanted fitted in so well with his own desires.

But he sometimes wondered, could a mother be so blind, or so foolish as Florence was, and not see what was going on, prac-tically under her eyes? Or—he wondered, too, sometimes—did she know, or suspect, and either just didn't care, or was too lazy and easygoing to do anything about it? After all, he thought cyn-ically, at such times, Louisa *was* the family's meal ticket. But he said nothing.

And that, anyway, was a development that came after Flor-ence had come down with him to see the cottage. She went down there, and Richard went with her, letting Miss Jennie Car-mody and the book shop once more go hang.

And in the end, after haggling over such matters as rent, and furnishings, and so on, until Richard was almost frantic, she signed the lease; Richard stood beside her in Mr. Debevois' quaint little office, watching her sign. Then, and later, going back in the evening train to New York and the long wait—but now a confident one—until June first when they might take the cottage over, he felt more and more like a son to her, and more grateful than he had ever felt before.

"I'll write, this summer," he told her. "You'll see, Florence. I'll really write." And it was like the promise of a child to a parent, as if he'd said, "I'll work hard, Mother. I'll really try to pass those exams."

But Mrs. Hackett had chosen that moment, or the moment after, to be coquettish. They were in the train by then, headed back to New York. They were seated side by side in the yellow-lit little day coach; and the train had stopped, and started, and stopped again (and the conductor had called out a name—was it Sunny Brook or maybe Stony Brook? Anyway, it had sounded familiar; had he walked through that town, on one of those days when he had been walking?) In the midst of it, suddenly, he felt a faint mood of depression settling upon him.

He had done enough for one day, he thought; all this traveling, all this cajoling. He was tired, and he wished he were back in his room and alone, and instead he was conscious, a little unpleasantly, of the soft, flesh-intimating sag of her hips against his, as they sat side by side, jostled now and then by the movement of the train. He had opened a copy of *Life* that he had bought in the station.

"Well, I must say, Richard, you're not being what I'd call *galant*," he heard her saying. She was using French words, and the purpose, he felt, was to put him in his place a little. "Or is it the custom, perhaps, in your part of the country, for a gentleman to read while his lady companion sits beside him?" And he looked up and saw her, saw her plain; saw the carefully made-up, slightly uneasy, falsely supercilious, malicious, worried, aging— oh, aging, malicious—sagging-skinned face; saw the toothed, teasing smile; and it was suddenly, horribly, as if his own mother, back there and a long time ago in Topeka, instead of comfortably smiling had been grinning and leering at him. "Can't you think of something bright to say, Richard?" Florence demanded.

Suddenly—and the train was stopping again, and the starting and stopping gave a feeling of tedium to the voyage; it would be a long time, and late, before they reached New York—he wished he was on his way far away from Louisa and her and all the Hacketts, and from all their involvements, that he knew (he was tired: he knew) he would never be able to understand completely.

3

That night, back in his furnished room (on Third Avenue; and the El, and the trains going by. Even in his sleep he heard them: and each one the long faraway rumbling; the (growing, the) feeling of menace, and the wolflike, bright, flashing-toothed, almost-enveloping roaring as: passing, and then (dying) the long hungry-hunting sound trailing after. That night) he had a dream.

Richard was a man who often had dreams, and tormenting ones, and this one was no worse than a good many others of his had been. And yet somehow it bothered him. He woke thinking about it.

It may have been because it was too close to reality. The train scene with Florence was in it. He was again in the train, and it was the same dozing, jostling day coach and Mrs. Hackett was sitting beside him. And again she kept nudging and jostling him. He was looking at a book that was a book of his poems; he was surprised that the book was so nicely printed, and in a way he was surprised at the poems themselves.

They were poems that he himself had written. He knew that because the title page said so. POEMS, BY RICHARD BAURIE, it said, but as a matter of fact the title page was about all he could read, because trains, other trains, kept passing; and the noise and the light from their windows passing falling on the pages confused him, while his own train's jostling—and beside him the insistent light nudging and crowding of, who was it? Mrs. Hackett?—kept his mind just that much more uneasy and distracted.

He kept turning the pages distractedly, seeking for something he could understand. (And outside the window the trains, other trains—with a rising deep roar and a sidelong flash and a long, departing, warning screech—and beside him, Florence Hackett.) Florence had begun reading his poems now, too, reading them aloud and looking over his shoulder. She read rapidly and with complete assurance, but all she said was gibberish, and as the train's noises grew her own voice grew louder. In the end she was shouting, while people all down through the coach turned around to look and then glanced at each other and smiled. And the conductor, when he came in the gusty door to call out the name of the next station—only he didn't quite finish calling it; he got part way and stopped—"Mount . . . Mount . . . Mount . . ." he called, and then he broke down too and laughed; he was staring straight at the two of them, Florence and Richard: she fat, shameless, shouting, and all Richard could do was just sit there, angry and embarrassed; he knew suddenly that he must disavow her.

"She is not my mother!" he cried. It seemed important to tell them that. "She is only a friend. She is Mrs. Hackett, Florence Hackett." And he pointed, and knowing already before he pointed: he pointed. "There's my mother!" he cried; and there, sure enough, surely, surely, far back down along the linked train corridor he saw her, his mother, as if enshrined, nichelike, in the last of the series of diminishing rectangles made by the successive car doorways. She was at the end of the vista, and he was running now, back along the aisles from car to car toward the last car of all where she sat or she stood looking calmly out at him.

Lights, of stations, of towns, of houses, alone or in clusters, winked along beside him; trains kept screeching, flashing, passing. But they passed him more slowly now. He was going in the same direction that they were going, and it began to seem almost that he was keeping pace with them; and when the conductor began crying, "Mount . . . Mount . . . Mount . . . Mount . . . Mount . . ." monotonously behind him again he had the feeling that if he could only run a little faster he might outrun that too—like the man in that passage of, what was it? some book?

his poems? who went away from the earth so fast that he went backward in time as well, and (he was waking now: "I must tell Elinor," he was thinking, and) suddenly it was not his mother he was running toward at all.

"Elinor," he was thinking. It was Elinor standing there, purely, sadly, benignly; naked (she was naked, and innocently unconscious of it) and she was reaching down gently toward him; she was as innocent of her shame as, who was it? her mother? had been unconscious of hers. Suddenly, overpoweringly, there was a sense of pursuit.

He heard the yelling. Mob noises. The terror. "Mount . . . Mount . . . Mount . . . Mount . . ." the conductor was chanting. (And behind him the swelling, the voices; the trains, flashing, passing.) Richard found himself yelling too.

"I can cure you. I can remake you. I can make you whole again," he yelled. He was yelling to Elinor. He was close to her now. He was close enough, almost, to touch her, and the mob, too, was close enough; he could see their hands reaching, clutching. "If they touch you," he yelled. "If they touch you . . ." It was clear that she hadn't heard. She stood, calm, serene, holy, and beautiful—and the conductor, still shouting . . .

He woke, sweating, and for a moment he didn't know where he was. That was not unusual; frequently, on awaking, there was a blind, empty, helpless, dizzying time when he didn't know who or what he was, and he would lie in his bed, waiting passively, rather pleasantly, for some hook or tangent of the whirl of reality to come past and come close enough so that he could seize it and haul himself back into himself again. Or some sign . . .

Cloudily, still half-dozing, he heard an El train go past, but too late, when he heard it, for him to be able to tell if it was going uptown or downtown; all he heard was the confused sort of rumbling, dying ponderously—or rather not dying, really, but spreading out overlappingly into the other sounds of the city, so that it seemed to swell out and grow fainter in all directions at once, in a wide and ever widening circle around him. . . .

"Third," he said, and then the memory of a woman's voice came to him. "I don't know why it is—" the voice was saying. A fat woman it was, with a round, soggy face, and a striped dress and wearing an apron—"but there is always a breeze on Third Avenue. I don't know if it's the Elevateds passing or what it is. All I know is it ain't like Second, or First. There is always a breeze."

That would be Mrs. L., Mrs. Loomis, Gloomy Loomis, his landlady, when she'd been showing him the room, and there was a breeze on Third Avenue now; he could see the curtains stirring. He was on Third Avenue, in New York City. "I must tell Elinor," he thought. He had remembered about Elinor; she existed and he had dreamed about her, and it was something about running backward. But the reasons for telling her—what?—dropped away again as soon as they had arisen, and meantime it was the room that was orienting him.

It was a room, his room, it was the place he lived in. Bare and plain as it was; like, as undoubtedly it was like, the rooms above and below and beside it (and, too, shadowily, the people in them; they were forming around him too. Mr. Brinkley, tall, spare—wasn't there a Mr. Brinkley, who listened? And below him the little grumbling man with the dog? Or had that been another city?)—the room still had its place in the city's structure, and if he could place himself firmly in the room, and the room in its place in the city . . . Or if he could just find Elinor.

Elinor would guide him. The world around him was getting peopled with people—the spry, prying Mr. Brinkley, even now doubtless listening behind his partition; the little man with the dog; Mrs. L., Gloomy Loomy Mrs. Loomis; and beyond them now sprinklingly twinklingly hundreds of others . . . the bright, buttery-face man (was it in (Dave's?) the sandwich counter?), and the bald, brownish, in the cigar store; and Jennie (had he forgotten? Jennie) Carmody—dotlike, twinkling, they winked here and there.

Only he was obscure; he still hadn't fitted into place. Or rather, he was multiple; he might be anyone, anywhere, or himself, but still elsewhere, in Rochester, Topeka, Cleveland. . . . And then suddenly, without seeking further, he knew. He was Richard Baurie, poet, artist, artisan, traveler, courtier ("And general all-round knave," he added, laughing), he was lying in his bed in Mrs. Loomis's rooming house on Third Avenue—and the knowledge was like a great light pouring power and luxuriance upon him, and through him out on the world he lived in.

The room received its share of the illumination too. Humble as it was—the weekly peering, precarious, carious chest of drawers, the low, bowlegged table, the red-plush-covered chair by the window (and the curtains stirring; an El train went past)—there was a certain justness about it, and a radiance as well that came to it because he lived there. And if he were to rise—" 'I will arise and go now,' " he said—and go over to the window, he would see . . . He knew what he would see.

He would see the ragged, wrought-iron cornices, and the glitter of the El tracks, skating slanting past; and beyond the mean neighborhood that enclosed them (and which also, unfortunately, enclosed him; but that would pass, that would pass)—beyond that, rising, rearing, height to greater height: soaring, aspiring, the towers. . . . "The high towers he had come to the city to conquer. He, a poor starveling poet," he said, and then throwing himself back on the bed and laughing recklessly. ("And you may listen, Mr. Slinky Brinkley, or whatever your name is. You may listen.") "Oh, you fool, you silly, silly, lovesick fool!" he added aloud.

He had had a sudden vision, luminously clear and as factually vivid as a scene that might appear in a movie: of the city as it lay strewn and sparkling beneath the sun, and himself as the dressing-gowned poet leaning from his garret and poring over it; and then (the camera shifting) of the one roof among all the many other roofs beneath which Elinor, in her bed, in her room, in the hushed apartment, lay, probably, curled in cozy doziness, sleeping. . . .

And the dream . . .

The dream was love, too, really, if you thought about it. He was forgetting the details now, but he knew he had been riding on a train, and the train was crowded, and somehow, there had been Florence—the details were getting blurred, but there had been Florence, Florence shouting or giggling or something and somehow bothering him; he skipped that, because he didn't feel in the mood for unpleasantness now. They had been coming back from seeing the cottage, that was it—and then, somehow,

Elinor. Floating. Naked. And there had been a time when he had run, run to get away from the voices. . . . Had she floated through the train? And (impossibly) naked?

The trouble was, he couldn't remember, and then in the midst of not remembering he did remember—the pale body standing in its innocent serenity and around that, like an atmosphere, the suggestion of a shrine and (before that?) his mother; and the shock as, behind him, the voices . . . Suddenly, without transition, he found himself thinking of death.

The curtains stirred, and an El train came past; he could see the dark length of it slitting the window, bound uptown. "I am death," he thought experimentally. But that wasn't quite true, of course; he was much too full of life and richness and promise for that.

But then too, in another sense, weren't life and death identical? That at least was what the Hindus thought, with their Karma and their transmigration of souls and so on. Death, to them, was simply a way station, a stop on the long voyage to—wasn't it?—Nirvana. And if one could believe that, really believe it, then of course one might easily embrace death willingly. "To escape the jumble of Life," he said. "To reach Karma. . . ."

But there was something that lay hidden still deeper in his thoughts, and he mused a while, trying to recapture it. Had the train been full of Hindus, he wondered, and they all riding on serenely? And was that why they turned and laughed when he, the infidel, got up and ran—away from death, of course, as well as toward his mother and Elinor?

It had been an odd dream, anyway, and that touch about the Hindus would make it better. And it would be better to leave out the nakedness. . . .

"I was riding in this train," he would say when he told the Hacketts, and he pushed himself up a little higher against the pillows and smiled and nodded this way and that as he acted out the scene. "And the train was filled with all these white-robed Hindus." (There *had* been someone in a white robe somewhere in the dream, or hadn't there? There had been Florence. . . . But he would leave out Florence) "And at every station one or two of them would get out, only making no fuss about it, you understand; they would just get up and shake hands with their friends, and good-bye, good-bye—it was just like a commuters' train, really; all little stops and starts—and then the train would go on. . . ."

Yes, indeed, it would make a pretty picture, and he could see himself telling it, sitting there in the midst of them, in the comfortable chair: he, pale-browed, the poet. "Only, I got scared," he would say. "And when the conductor came in . . ." And then so on and so on—about the running, and the trying to outstrip the voices (for he mustn't forget about that, and the unconscious inventiveness of it; it would make an amusing little interlude), and then the tension, the feeling of pathos, when he came to the part about the shrine at the end of the train, and his mother, and the change. He would pause there dramatically.

"And do you know who my mother changed into?" he would ask. And then he paused dramatically, glancing from the table to the chair by the window and from there to the chest of drawers. And then, finally, focusing on Elinor. "She changed into—you."

It would be nice, told that way. He would leave out the nakedness, of course. But still wouldn't it be possible—there was so much that could be told in a glance, if the words were subtly phrased enough to carry their meaning—wouldn't it just be possible that even without his quite saying it she might understand?

"And I ran, I just ran," he might add. "And then, of course"— the wry touch—"I had to go and wake up!"

It would be nice. In a way it would be a sort of avowal, and for a moment, a long, delicious, half-dreaming moment, he lay basking anticipatorily in the light little secretly communicative grateful smile she might give him in return. For although he had never said anything to her or she to him, he knew she knew how tenderly, how fondly he loved her. Then a name like a weight descended on the scene.

Louisa. He had almost forgotten her. But at the shock of remembrance he glanced quickly toward the chair by the window, as if she might really be there where he had placed her, and smiling at him satirically.

At the Hacketts', she *would* be there. She would be sitting there sewing on shoulder straps or relacquering her nails or doing something of the sort, as she always did, that was deliberately planned to excite and humiliate him—as if he were a servant and so of no account, he always thought.

And with her there, there would be no possibility of a scene of the sort he had just been imagining. Romance, tenderness, love itself were the things that she always gibed at. "Why, how *sweet!*" she would say, in that voice of hers that implied it wasn't sweet at all. Or, "Why, Richard, how poetic! Elinor, aren't you flattered?"

And even Elinor, sweet and simple and innocent as she was, would feel the cuttingness of it—or what was worse, she would fear it before she smiled; she would know what was coming before it came, and instead of even smiling she would gaze at him with that mixture of reproof and anxious apprehension which in itself was a symbol of how deeply she was under Louisa's power, and was ruled by her, molded by her. By Louisa, the evil one. And still Florence, the mother, sitting there uncritically by the table, complacently watching. . . . "Damn it! Don't you see what goes on around you, all the time?" he cried suddenly, venomously.

It was a thing he just couldn't understand, that relationship. But he couldn't tell them the dream, that at least was the truth of it. And it made one more barrier in the series of barriers that had one by one been erected, largely by Louisa, between him and complete understanding, real familyness, with the Hacketts. For a moment, sheer hot rage swept through him, and he lay there with his mouth taut and his hands clenching and unclenching. "Death. Death. Death. Death," he kept muttering.

"Yes, Death," he said again, and he said it aloud, and defiantly, without caring where his thoughts might lead him. Death was clean; it was life that was the jumble, and the worst of it was that life messed things up further by constantly throwing the oddest people together.

Florence, silly and cynical. Louisa, evil. And then the innocent Elinor, trapped helpless between them—trapped there by the sheer accident of birth, and now locked there, in a tangle that only death could unscramble. While if Florence had been his mother, and still Florence; if he could just have been the son, so he would have had the power and the responsibility; if he could be at once husband and brother to Elinor, for she needed both. . . .

"I can remake you," he said. The thought had come to him suddenly from somewhere, and with an air of offering enlightenment; and as soon as he had said it he turned his most brilliant, most sardonic smile in the direction of Mr. Brinkley's partition. The thought had carried an injunction of secrecy with it, too, and yet he was sure now that, like a fool, he had spoken aloud. But that was all right, too; it had brought to him a feeling of power, as well.

"You may listen," he said, to the partition. "You may listen all you want to. I might remake you too, you know, if it struck me as advisable."

He was joking, of course. And yet, still . . . To re-make, to re-mold, to re-model . . . What a gift, if one had such a gift! And when you thought of the hundreds of sufferers . . .

But his mind slid away, and meantime other pulls were developing, toward the bathroom, toward closing the window, toward Dave's Lunch up Third Avenue where he usually had his breakfast, toward (inexorably) Books THE BROWSE SHOP Books where already, undoubtedly, Jennie Carmody, impatiently . . . For an instant a picture crossed his mind of Elinor dead, dead and bloodlessly pale, but the body still soft and warm and voluptuous, the body unperturbed by its nakedness and now infinitely vulnerable.

But he put the thought out of his mind at once. There were men who liked women like that, who could love them in no other way. But not he, and not Elinor . . . For a moment, a last long vicious delicious moment before getting up, he fell to baiting the putatively eavesdropping Mr. Brinkley.

"You, there," he said. He never used the man's name; in a way, that would be giving him too much recognition, and he spoke so softly that even if Mr. Brinkley had been listening about all he would have heard would have been a vague mumbling. "Are you conversant with the Hindu mythology, by any chance? Are you *au courant* with such matters? And do you understand all its ramifications, the relation between Karma and Parma, and Nirvana and Savannah, and so on? And their relation to the human relations, such as sisters and cousins, and mothers and brothers, and so on. . . ." And so on and so on, he thought. "Have I confused you enough, my dear, good, prying gentleman, the prying prior, the slinking stinker; have I confused you enough?"

Jennie Carmody later remembered that morning, not because Richard came in so late, for he did that frequently, but because he acted so strangely throughout the day.

She was a slight, graying-haired, rather bony woman, very Scotch, very matter-of-fact in manner, but also hiding beneath her brusqueness a certain timid warmheartedness that Richard, almost from the first, had unerringly sensed and made use of.

He had worked for her for nearly eight months, or from shortly after his arrival in the city; he had walked into the shop one morning and started looking around among the books, and he had been pale then, and lonely-looking, but he still had that air of arrogance and inner satisfaction that never quite left him. "Can I help you?" she had said, walking over toward him.

He had looked up as if surprised. "Do you have W. H. Davies's poems? Not that I can buy them," he had added, almost defiantly. "But there is a line . . . Well, I'd like to look into them. And you call this 'The Browse Shop,' don't you?" He had suddenly fixed her with a smile so bitter and brilliant, so full of a bright, hard, challenging assurance that it had struck somehow, instantly, to her very marrow. It had made him seem so defenseless. "'Browse,'" he had continued. "'To forage here and there. To nibble. To seek pasture.' But if one can't afford the price of the fodder . . ."

"Yes," Jennie had said, and—she had prided herself afterward on the gesture—she walked over to the poetry shelf at the back and pulled down the thin, brown-bound volume. "It just happens I have it," she said. It was an early edition, and rare, but she didn't mention that. "Go ahead and browse."

And then—well, then it had turned out that he was a poet, too, and like Davies something of a wanderer; he had traveled in the west and traveled in the east, and now he was working as a soda-fountain attendant in a drugstore on Eighth Avenue just off Columbus Circle. "A good soda-jerker—that's what they call us—can get a job almost any place," he told her. "Which makes it a good trade for a writer, I suppose, especially if he's a foot-loose one into the bargain. But it's dull, dull, dull." And he had looked around the shop and smiled at her, but more warmly, more gently, this time. "While, books . . ." he had added.

"It's dull here too, sometimes," Jennie Carmody had found herself saying.

But he just shook his head and looked at her. . . . The upshot was, she had hired him; sometimes, afterward, she told herself she might just as well have gotten a tiger by the tail.

This morning was an example. Like most middle-aged, soli-tary people, Jennie Carmody liked to sleep late, and one of the reasons for hiring Richard as her clerk—apart from, well, from the fact that it just happened—was that he should take away the onus of opening up the shop from her.

It was the one part of running the place that she truly detested, the early rising, the haste over breakfast, the chill, yesterday-smelling air of the shop when she unlocked the door, and the half-frightening feeling of having to start everything all over again that the emptiness gave her—and she had explained all this to him quite frankly. Richard had smiled at her and nodded, understandingly.

"I know it's asking you to do something I don't particularly want to do myself," she had said worriedly. Jennie Carmody was a woman with a conscience. "And I expect that's unfair, in a manner of speaking. But on the other hand . . . Well, for one thing, you won't have a great deal to occupy you in the morn-ings. There're only a few customers at that time, really, mostly office workers, coming in for the lending library on their way to work, and once you've done with them, you know, your time will be your own. You can read . . ."

And then an idea had struck her and she had gone on more happily. "Or why shouldn't it be a very good time for you to get on with your writing? You could, you know. Why, there's even a little desk I've got that we could fetch in from out back, if you wanted, and you could keep your papers on it, or whatever."

He had nodded and smiled through it all, and they'd got the desk in together, and placed it. For the first month or so—for two months or more, really—he had been most punctilious.

But it was almost as if he had been working himself into a position of security, in order to use it for his own purposes. He got to calling her "Jennie"; he learned her habits, her little idiosyncrasies, and it was as if he had wormed himself in, wound his way around her—as if, once he had gotten so he could call her "Jennie," he had gotten to be a member of the family, in a way, and so could permit himself to take family liberties.

"I must warn you. I may not be very reliable," he said once, on that first day when she had been outlining his duties. But he had said it so disarmingly that she hardly noticed. He had added, "At least, I've never been very reliable before. But among these books . . ." He had made such a wide, foolish, childishly embracing gesture toward the shelves that she had at first felt a little embarrassed. "I'll try, anyway," he had said; and then to get past the awkwardness of the moment they had both laughed.

Now, however, she sometimes wondered. It was as if, once he had gotten himself established, he had set out to take advantage of it—or as if, she sometimes thought, he had only gotten himself established with her *in order* to take advantage of it. As if, once he had made himself a member of the Carmody family, so to speak, he had set out to be as bad a one as he could be, and still not be disavowed entirely.

As for his reliability—well, she had wondered recently, she had really wondered, how in the world he could ever have kept a job anywhere, least of all in the drugstore where he had been working—and where they must have demanded punctuality— if he had let himself take even so much as one-tenth of the liberties he had taken with her.

This morning was an example. He came in at exactly quarter past ten, more than usually gay and cheery, and she met him with the prim, tight-lipped, disapproving look that, even as she'd grown used to using it, she hated using. The conversation followed the usual pattern.

"You're late," she said.

"Too late?"

"Well, late enough to be an annoyance."

He had been heading toward the rear of the shop, where the hat rack was, and there had been a look in his eye—as if he was not only estimating the degree of her annoyance but was already coolly working out methods to circumvent it—a look, anyway, that annoyed her still further.

"Late enough to go without your lunch to make up for it," she said sharply. "That is, if you've any sense of responsibility whatsoever," she added.

He deposited his hat on the rack, quite carefully, and came slowly toward her. For a moment there was something in his manner, something at once somber and calculating, that almost frightened her.

"I have plenty of responsibility, all right," he said quietly.

"I know you have," she said hastily. "But when you come here at all hours, Richard, when you take whole *days* off, and never even tell me—"

He went on almost as if he hadn't heard her. "That's a part of it, too," he said. "I'm at a bad time, Jennie."

"I know. I know. All about that cottage. But still, Richard—"

"Oh, it's more than that, Jennie. Whatever anyone else may tell you. But I have the will, too." She was not quite sure now what he was getting at. "I am not an inconsiderable person, Jennie Carmody," he added.

It was such an unexpected word to use that Jennie misunderstood him completely. "Oh, I know you're not, Richard," she said. "Or at least you don't mean to be inconsiderate. It's just sometimes—"

Then Richard interrupted her. "Inconsiderate?" he repeated after her. "Inconsiderate. Inconsiderable. Inconsistent. . . ." Then he widened his eyes at her suddenly.

"Jennie, darling," he said. "I love you. You say such wonderful things!" And he took both her hands in his. "Look, forgive me, just this once, won't you? And instead of all this wrangling about lunch, why don't we both have lunch together? Why not, Jennie? We'll just shut up the shop for an hour or so—we'll make it one o'clock, or maybe one-thirty; no one comes in much then anyway—and you, just you—" He held her hands wide apart and then brought them together. "You'll have lunch with me," he finished happily. "I've got so much to tell you, Jennie."

"No," she said, but she couldn't help bridling a little. "I really mean it this time, Richard. I really *depend* on you, you know. And we *can't* just have people coming by every morning and finding us closed. We'll lose customers. I think today, really, for punishment—"

"You wouldn't starve me, madam, would you?" he said. "Me, a poor, starveling poet?" He was still pressing at her, trying to cajole her, and she knew it, and yet she had difficulty resisting. And there was one thing about him, he was very easy about money. When she docked him occasionally for his absences, he never once protested.

"D'you know," she said suddenly. "I haven't yet seen one of your poems?"

"You will, Jennie. You will. I may have a book of them coming out shortly," he said. And then, with one of those abrupt shifts of thought that always confused her: "Listen, Jennie—and forget about lunch; you have lunch when you want; I'll stay here. I'll take my punishment—but do we have anything much on Hindu mythology?"

"Why, I think so. Yes," she said. And then, the oddness of it overtaking her: "Why?"

But he was suddenly opaque and uncommunicative. "I just wondered. Show me, will you? You know the whole stock better than I do."

She showed him, and—not entirely to her surprise, once she thought of it—he spent the rest of the day, to the practical disregard of their customers, reading Jennet's *Hindustan and the Hindus* and the Everyman edition of Lake's *Eastern Religions*.

What surprised her, really, was that, late in the afternoon—there was no one in the shop at the time, and she'd been going out back to the washroom—he glanced up at her suddenly as she passed and then jumped up and seized her. "Jennie! You're my aunt!" he cried excitedly. "Did you know it? But of course you couldn't possibly; I just thought of it myself, reading this. But it could be, you know! Everyone can be placed, and if they're not placed right the first time they can try it all over again. It's wonderful religion, really. Would you like it? To be my aunt?"

"I hadn't thought about it, really, Richard," she said dryly, and pulled against him a little to get her arm free. After all, she was only forty-one.

He must have sensed her feeling, for he added quickly, "I'm just joking, of course, Jennie; you know that. But still—do you know much about it? About Buddhism, I mean, and the transmigration of souls, and so on? I didn't either, till I started reading this. But it *is* a wonderful religion, Jennie; so much sensibler, sort of, than our old cut-and-dried ideas about heaven and hell, and all that. You can make up for your mistakes, for one thing. Or—you know what I've been thinking of, Jennie; something even *they* didn't think of?—suppose someone else, if he were good enough and really wanted to, could make them up for you. Wouldn't that be wonderful? If they'd had *that,* you know, it would really be the perfect religion."

But Jennie wasn't interested. "I'm afraid I don't hold much with that sort of nonsense, Richard," she said. "I was christened a Presbyterian and I expect I shall always remain one." And this time she did get her arm free.

Richard gave her such an odd look of mixed sorrow and (it almost seemed) commiseration that she remembered the expression and puzzled over it mildly afterward. "I thought at least *you* would understand," he told her.

From the Psychiatrist's Report: It would be unwise to say that a relationship such as had developed between the Hacketts and Richard Baurie, or between him and Jennie Carmody, could occur only in New York City, and yet it is true that New York was in many respects a peculiarly favorable place for it. In smaller cities the stranger may be welcomed freely enough, but he is also observed and commented upon, and the network of social relations in which he moves is so closely knit that in a sense his least action pursues him everywhere; if he shows any oddities of behavior or evidence of departure from the norm it will surely be noticed by someone, and through that someone be brought, almost inevitably, eventually, to the common knowledge.

But in New York, so to speak, all are strangers; and the city is so vast and its range of activities so scattered that the individual and his actions are always more or less lost in it. Even under normal circumstances a large part of any man's daily doings must remain a mystery, even to his closest friends; and conversely, the new acquaintance, the new friend, must be accepted more or less at face value.

This explains, in part at last, why Richard was able so quickly to establish himself on terms of comparative intimacy with the Hackett family and Miss Carmody. They simply didn't know all there was to know about him. In point of fact, Richard was, at the time of which we write, already a graduate of at least one mental institution—the Greenwood County State Hospital at Danville, Kansas, where he had been confined for twelve weeks in 1945—yet in spite of this, or possibly partly because of it, he gave at most times no sign of his unbalanced state.

In a sense, a man like Baurie lives always in enemy country, forced, at least when in the company of others, to conform to rules of conduct which are actually more or less alien to him; and like anyone else in such condition he had developed considerable agility in masking his own reactions and sustaining a façade of apparent normality.

Around the rooming house where he lived, for instance, he was known to be unusually secretive and suspicious, and he had once had a violent altercation with a fellow lodger, a Mr. Thomas Brinkley, whom he suspected, apparently without reason, of following him about in the streets and spying on him. In the neighborhood, his habit of occasionally talking to himself as he walked had caused some comment.

But these were isolated instances, and were little regarded. Mrs. Loomis, his rooming-house keeper, for instance, had long ago grown used to the crotchetiness of her lodgers, and to her he was only a bit more peculiar in his ways than were the others. Richard, too, when the situation demanded, could be disarmingly candid, charming, and convincing, and Mrs. Loomis, for one, never dreamed that there was anything abnormal about him.

"He had his little ways," she said. "But then so do they all.

Apart from that one time—and then I blamed the other as much as him—I never had the least trouble with him."

Meantime, ordinarily, Baurie could be extremely engaging. He talked freely, and though he tended with strangers to be a little awkward socially this was generally accepted as evidence of a boyish, and rather attractive, shyness. Otherwise, the very imbalance of his responses lent a certain lively unpredictability to his behavior. At the book shop, for example, he made up for his periods of unreliability by others of extraordinary activity, rearranging the stock, re-doing the window displays, and so on, in a manner that both impressed and a little overwhelmed his employer, Miss Carmody. The moods of depression which occasionally intervened were explained away, both by her and by the Hacketts, as being merely periods of "sulkiness," or of the discouragement natural to a young man struggling to express himself in poetry.

Mrs. Hackett was the first of that family to make his acquaintance. She met him, as has been related, at a neighborhood grocery store on Third Avenue, and Richard, later, talked freely about the occurrence.

"She used to say, 'He picked me up,' sort of joking, you know," he told us once. "You understand, I'd be there at the apartment, and some friends of theirs might come in, and for a long time the way she'd introduce me was, 'This is Richard Baurie, the boy who picked me up.' And she'd laugh. 'There I was, among the vegetables, and he picked me up,' she'd say. Or, 'We met among the cauliflowers, didn't we, Richard?' Something like that. 'I want to tell you, he's a quick trick with the girls,' she'd say. I didn't mind, though it seemed a little strange, you know, for a cultivated woman like her to be acting so, well, coquettish. All I did was to help her with the parcels, and then we got to talking, just like anybody might with an older woman.

"I thought nothing of it myself. I don't know why, but I never had any difficulty getting into conversations with women. And I didn't mind her talking that way, either, even in front of Elinor—at least, not till I realized the kind of woman she was. I was badly deceived there at first; badly. I had a glimmering now and then, but I just didn't think things through. I was too innocent. And then later, when I thought about Elinor . . . She was innocent, too."

It was rather a gray day when this interview occurred, and like most mentally unstable persons Richard's moods were directly affected by the weather; there was always a quite noticeable difference in the degree of his tractability on clear sunny days as against stormy or threatening ones. In this instance, he walked over to the window of his cell and stood staring grimly out at the drizzling weather. We thought an outburst might follow. Instead, his flair for self-dramatization took hold of him. He turned quietly, and smiled.

"If I'd only had a chance. If I'd only had a chance," he said slowly and with an indescribably theatrical air of self-commiseration. "I might have rescued all of them. I had a plan, you know."

Richard Baurie had been born poor, the son of an itinerant Scotch-Irish tailor and an English mother who had emigrated from Glastonbury, England, to Topeka, Kansas, and had failed there to better themselves materially. He had grown up the poorer because his father, when Richard was about five, had resumed his wandering habits and disappeared from the household, reappearing thereafter only occasionally, and then rather in the role of a visitor than of a husband and parent.

It is hard now to tell which of the parents was responsible for the separation. It is significant, however, that from the start Richard sided always with his mother; and the mother, who was apparently a strong-willed, violently emotional woman, seems to have used whatever means came to hand to win, and hold, the boy's sympathies.

She had been the daughter of a moderately prosperous Glastonbury tradesman, and there is no doubt that in allying herself with Donald Baurie, Richard's father, she had married "beneath her." But in the account she gave Richard both the magnificence of her life before—"till your father dragged us down," as she always put it—and its instabilities afterward were exaggerated to the point where it may fairly be said that for a large part of his youth she and Richard lived in a dream world of his and her making.

Richard left home when he was about sixteen, and in his second year at high school. He left, significantly, shortly after a reconciliation had been effected between Mr. and Mrs. Baurie, and the father had returned, supposedly "to stay," to the household; and there seems to be no doubt that his sexual attitude towards his mother had by that time become ambivalent. He felt himself to be as much husband as son to her—and her re-acceptance of the simple, rather stodgy man who was her real husband to her bed was in this sense, to him, a betrayal.

He left home, then, with his psychic confusions accentuated rather than resolved. Psychologically, he left it doubly homeless, and the underlying motivation of all his later actions was unquestionably a desire to find a new "home" for himself, to discover or construct a family for himself that would make up in security and warmth of affection for the lack of these virtues in his own.

In the Hacketts, Richard felt for a time that he had attained his goal; and he felt too, perhaps snobbishly, that he had taken a step upward in the world as well, though in this he was a little blinded by the force of his own desiring.

The Hacketts, though of quite decent middle-class background—both the father and mother had come originally from West Virginia—were neither so well-born nor so rich as Richard imagined them. The husband, Thomas Hazzard Hackett, was a consulting engineer of some ability, who went from factory to factory on short-term assignments, designing special machinery or devising processes to expedite manufacture. He returned home but seldom, and sent small and fairly irregular sums for the family's maintenance.

It was the elder daughter, Louisa, who in fact held the family together, both financially and—despite Richard's suspicions—morally as well. She was brisk, direct, glibly sophisticated, and neurotic enough to be a little avid in her pursuit of pleasure. But as far as can be determined the excesses which Richard attributed to her, and deplored—and was also, of course, fascinated by—were in great part imaginary.

Mrs. Hackett, by contrast, was far less direct than her elder daughter. It was she who presented the façade for the family, and this was, incidentally, not very far different from the façade that Richard's own mother had constructed.

Mrs. Baurie had been (always in her own imaginings) an English gentlewoman, and Mrs. Hackett had an equal tendency to aggrandize her own slightly higher social background and position. There were other similarities between the two women. Mrs. Hackett was beset by much the same problems as Mrs. Baurie had been—by the necessity of maintaining a household in spite of an unaccommodating husband; by the problem of governing a family single-handed; by the effort of preserving an appearance of ease and comfort in the face of occasional stringencies—and though these were all set upon a slightly higher plane than Richard had been accustomed to, they were still problems that, from long usage, he could understand and accommodate himself to.

The Hacketts, too, had a further advantage, quite important in its effect on Richard's thinking, of being more wise in the ways of the city, more knowing, than he was. They had lived there longer, they had achieved more stability, and the result to the homeless, disoriented youth was at once over-awing and enticing.

There were, however, complications, and their focus, as always, lay in the difference between "reality" as Richard pictured it, and reality as it existed. Once again, he was living in a dream world, and this time it was a more dangerous one. Mrs. Hackett, for one, was not the angelic "mother" he had at first conceived her to be. (Neither was she the creature of bloated, senile depravity that he later pictured her.) Louisa wasn't the schemer that he imagined. And—most important of all, in the end—Elinor was far too flesh-and-blood, far too willful, to fit into the passive sister-wife role that he had prepared for her.

4

Spring's a nice time, too, but it is nothing at all like summer. Spring is all offering, and no giving. Spring is promises, and the summer is the fulfillment. Spring is tentative; and summer fulsome and rich and rewarding. Everyone, almost, looks forward to it, from the child counting the days till the end of the school term to the family planning its vacation, and you have plenty of time to prepare for it. You have April and May, while the city grows hotter and heavier with its own expectation all around you; you have June, or a part of June—and then, suddenly, you are in the midst of it! For it comes with a rush when it does come; and the force of it, the heat, the completeness, are enough to sweep anything and anyone before it. . . .

For a while they had a delightful time at Wisteria Cottage. A new place, a new house—with furniture to rearrange, rooms to settle in, lawns, and grounds around to explore and accustom oneself to—in this sense, a new house is always an adventure; and if it's a summer place the feeling is heightened. There is a certain impermanence about everything that adds its poignance. It is summer, vacation-time, when nothing ends and, when, too, nothing lasts: you will be here, in these walls, in this setting, for two months or maybe a little longer, and then the walls will no longer enclose you.

Time, and you, will inevitably have moved on, and the house and the setting—the sea, the sand, the scraggly path through the dunes and the still more particular little place-markers: the big section of chimney-brick cast up on the beach, the bleached rock and the tree beyond, the poison-ivy patch halfway up the path, the water-faucet that drips and the hall-closet door that you have to press down on to open, the queer, musty-salty smell of the bedrooms—these, inevitably, will become part of your past; are, already as you see them, slowly receding. And meantime you must hurry, hurry, in the sun and the days that are already inexorably shortening, to drain them of all they can give you. For the summer, once begun, is as brief as the waiting for it seemed endless. It's a greedy time, swift and voracious, and the person who would enjoy it must be as greedy and swift as the season itself.

Richard had this sense of hurrying most of all. Richard—Richard was everywhere; from the first he was indefatigable. He went down to the book shop reluctantly, came back eagerly—sometimes Friday nights, sometimes even Thursdays; while there, though he slept in the shed, he had his meals with the Hacketts regularly; he was "family" really, now; and as the summer wore on he was as likely to stay over till Monday as he was to go back on Sunday—and while at the cottage he seemed irrepressible. He seemed to want to do everything at once, and he had hardly begun re-screening the porch before he dropped that in favor of painting the shed behind the cottage that he had taken over as his own—and then turned from that to start building a series of steps down the path to the beach. . . . Richard, for the first weeks at least, was beside himself, almost, with pleasure and pride and accomplishment.

He was having his own way, that was one of the things that delighted him, and he had the added feeling that he was having his way against resistance, so that he could measure the extent of his progress and his power. He was re-shaping, he was remolding; he was making new characters out of the old ones; and when Mrs. Hackett raised her head complainingly from a flower bed they had planted—"But my *back!*" she cried pathetically. "You don't *realize*, Richard! My poor, *poor*, poor back! What do I care about your morning-glories?"—and yet, when he still spurred her on, went on docilely weeding the morning-glories; when Louisa, even hard-boiled Louisa, handed nails to him while he braced up a sagging shelf in the hall closet; when dear Elinor stood beside him at the drippy little white-enameled kitchen sink, peeling potatoes for a chowder while he opened the clams he had bought on the way from the railroad station—at such times he had a feeling of power and rightness and resolution that was deeper and more satisfying than anything he had ever felt before in his life.

He was having his own way, and he was growing used to having it. Only occasionally was he crossed; and then it scarcely escaped his notice that it was by Louisa. Mrs. Hackett complained, but complied; Elinor was docile; but Louisa at times was caustic.

"Hur-ry, hur-ry, hur-ry, hur-ry," she said once, and she said it in the flat tones of a sideshow barker. They were down on the beach at the time, and Richard had set them all determinedly to work collecting stones for an outdoor fireplace that he had suddenly decided they needed. "Just a dime, folks, two nickels, the tenth paht of a dollah. See ol' Simon Legree workin' dem po' ol' Southern gentlefolks nigh to daith."

Then she looked at him and grinned, but the grin had an edge of exasperation. "What's the rush, kid?" she said. "We don't really have to get this damned thing done today, do we? And if we do, then what do we do with it?"

Richard looked at her. "Well, we do want to get it finished, don't we?" he said. He knew already that there was no use arguing with her. She had simply defied him, quit work, and lighted a cigarette. "And you know very well what we want to do with it."

"Yes, I know," said Louisa. "But what I mean is, we've got all summer, haven't we? Just don't ride us so damned hard, Richard, or me, anyway. I came down here to have some fun, among other things."

"Fun!" cried Richard, waspishly. But this time she ignored him.

Things were always coming to a crisis between her and Richard, and she herself didn't quite know why. "Me, I'm going for a swim," was all she said, and picking up her bathing cap she walked unhurriedly down to the water's edge and plunged in.

As usual, it was Elinor who saved the situation:

"*Well!*" said Richard, and for a moment he could only sputter, while his face grew as red as if someone had struck him a blow.

What Louisa had said had attacked him on a dozen grounds— on the fact that he was from the North and they from the South; that he was an outsider and a nobody while they were a family, a unit, and a close-knit, established one at that; that he was poor and a beggar, hardly worth a dime, the tenth part of a dollar; a meddler, fussy, cheap, ill-bred, overbearing, interfering.... For a while his mind really raced, as he tried to encompass all the challenges she had flung at him.

And the trouble was that the others just didn't see it. It was as if she had risen as suddenly as a snake and struck at him, not once but many times, and so viciously and fast that the two others, Florence and Elinor, couldn't even see the blows; they just sat there, the two of them, and all they did was smile foolishly-awkwardly, looking everywhere but at him. And meanwhile work was stopped, their companionship broken, his dream (the dream that he'd had of nights on the beach, and the three of them gathered around while he broiled the steaks or the hamburgers, and then afterward, cozily: that dream) shattered—and he now, he knew, looking foolish and awkward, too, squatting there with no fireplace to build, no more orders to give, no companionship any more.

For a moment, he hated them all. ("But I mustn't get excited," he told himself.) He knew even then that he couldn't let himself go as he'd like to; the worst thing of it all was that he still *was* an outsider, a nobody, and if he let himself go, if he really let them have a taste of his temper, it would only draw them closer together, and lead to worse disaster.

It was Elinor who saved the situation:

"*Well!*" said Richard again, and even he could tell that his voice was getting a little shrill. "I may be from Kansas. I may be just a nobody...."

"Now, now, Richard," said Mrs. Hackett lazily. She had been watching Louisa's white bathing cap, far out now and moving purposefully, and the glint and flash of her arms as they propelled it through the water. "Don't let's all have tantrums."

Richard still had a stone in his hands, a big flat stone that he had chosen with some care, thinking that it might make a splendid back for the grill. Now he flung it down petulantly on the sand. "Well, I *mean* it!" he said.

"Mean what, my dear?"

"Well, I mean ..." He looked almost piteously at Mrs. Hackett. "Don't you know? Don't you *know* what she was getting at—that I'm just nothing, Florence? That I'm somebody with-

out a dime, I've got no business being here, even? While she . . .
she . . . And then boasting about being a Southerner!" He was
going farther than he should, and he knew it. But he couldn't
help it. "As if being a Southerner meant anything!" He saw Mrs.
Hackett's eyes grow a little colder. "Florence, can't you *see?*" he
demanded.

But she *couldn't* see, that was the truth of it. "My dear Richard," she said, and he could tell that she had decided to be crisp.
She'll be being grande dame with me next, he was thinking.) She
was at least being matter-of-fact and, in her own way, motherly.
"Louisa didn't mean anything of the sort, and you know it. She
was bad-tempered, a little, and impolite, and I shall spank her
very soundly for it when I catch her. But she's not the sort of
person who'd say anything so rudely vulgar as the things you
impute to her, and why you read such meanings into it as you do
is quite beyond me. All she meant—" and here she let her voice
go out in a little sigh, as if she were tired of so much explaining—"all she meant was that she was tired of piling up rocks and
was going for a swim. Really, Richard, it was as simple as that.
And I must say, I'm tempted to do the same thing myself. We
don't have to get this all done today, you know. Or do we?"

Richard watched her. She was quitting, there was no doubt
of that; she was joining Louisa, she was siding against him. And
the trouble was that he was helpless; there was nothing at all
that he could do about it. But he couldn't resist one last gibe.

"Lazy Florence!" he said, and though he tried to say it
jokingly it came out in such a way that for once Mrs. Hackett
glanced at him almost angrily. "Manners, Richard. Manners,"
she said. "But you know, I *am* going in for a swim."

He watched her rise, rather stiffly, for she had been sitting for
some time. He watched her brush the sand from her seat and
her legs.

She was wearing a bathing suit that was almost as skimpy as
Louisa's, which was saying a good deal, according to Richard's
way of thinking. All it was—all that any of the women wore, for
that matter—was a sort of brassière over the breasts and a pair
of trunks, with a good deal of flesh showing in between, but on
her the flesh seemed more noticeable.

And the trunks were part elastic, so that they clung fairly close to her hips.... Richard watched her standing there, her back turned partly toward him; watched the crimson-nailed, bony, wrinkled hands going absent-mindedly, indiscriminately over the flesh and the cloth, over the slightly sagging, aging buttocks encased in the stretched, water-wearied cloth, and the bare thighs where the tan she had already acquired didn't quite conceal the little veinings and puckerings of the tired, unresilient flesh; and a feeling of disgust at the sheer unashamedness of it came over him. She might pretend to be a *grande dame,* he thought, but she wasn't one; she wasn't even a decent mother. Underneath all her pretensions she was as rotten within as Louisa was.

But he said nothing of that. He said nothing at all, and the silence would have become embarrassing if Elinor hadn't broken it.

"We'll be along too in a moment," she said. She had been scraping the sand away with a piece of board, trying to level off a spot for the fireplace. She had been sitting with her head bowed, as if she hadn't noticed anything, and when she spoke it was as if nothing had happened. But when Florence had gone she bent her head still closer to Richard's.

"Richard. *Don't* mind Louisa," she said. "Or Mother, either," she added. Her hair was darker than her sister's; she was shorter, and her whole body was at the same time frailer and more feminine. She was plumper and prettier and somehow more vulnerable, and when she spoke, kneeling there in the sand beside him, offering him her companionship and sympathy when both the others had denied it to him, it so fitted her very nature, her air of docile, nineteenth-century femininity, that Richard, for a moment—and out of happiness, mostly—almost wanted to cry.

Even the slight air of furtiveness she had about her fitted, too. She was a woman, and like all women, to Richard's mind, catlike a little, indirect, concealing. "Louisa ... Well, you know Louisa," she said. She was kneeling beside him, and Mrs. Hackett was halfway across the beach by now, but suddenly she felt it necessary to raise her voice a little.

"Have you still got that big flat stone?" she said. "Wouldn't this be a good place for it, maybe?"

And then, when he had brought it, she bent her head closer to his again. "I think she's having boy-friend trouble, or something, and that makes her sort of picky. Anyway, she's worried. And now, of course, Mother's worried too, about her." For an instant, without his quite meeting her gaze, he felt her eyes, pale and lamp-blue against the tan, look directly at him.

"Don't you worry, though, and go getting all picky too," she said. Then she got up briskly. "Let's go swimming."

It was balm, it was calm, it was peace, it was benediction. But it wasn't quite enough, all the same; underneath, Richard felt a little ferment of anger still working, and when the time came—on the beach, when he ran into Louisa a few minutes later—he had to let it go.

He hadn't stayed in the water long. He wasn't much of a swimmer, for one thing. He thrashed his arms about with great earnestness, when the mood was upon him, but he hadn't learned the proper strokes, and both Louisa and Elinor could beat him. And today he was still hot with the sense of his own humiliation. So he had just paddled around for a while and then come out, and there, coming out too, was Louisa. Mrs. Hackett was farther up the beach a little way and Elinor was still in the water; Louisa was alone, and he walked straight up to her.

"Look, Louisa," he said. And as if nothing had happened at all she turned and smiled at him.

"What's it now, honey-chile?" she said. "Isn't that water wonderful?"

He had had some idea of making friends with her, of tiding the thing over; it would have been more politic, he knew. But somehow the very sight of her was itself too much for him—the half-naked brown body, and the skin still glistening with the water, the breasts half exposed, and the breasts and the shoulders so close to him that he could see the tiny hairinesses, the little bristlings of gooseflesh that seemed at the moment to be the ultimate in careless obscenity—and before he could control himself his voice changed a little. He could feel his breath coming thicker.

"Oh, yes, wonderful—as you were the first to find out," he said sarcastically. The way she showed herself around him, he was thinking, you might think he wasn't a man at all. "I'm afraid my poor little fireplace won't be so wonderful, though, now that you've wrecked it."

She still smiled at him. "Oh, that! Well . . . Well, I'm sorry about that, Richard. But it really isn't wrecked, you know. I'll help you with it right now, if you're so set on making it."

But he was past wanting that kind of compensation. "I'm afraid it's a little bit late now," he told her. "And anyway, it's not your help or your lack of it that bothers me. It's what you said."

"What I said?"

"Yes, said." And then he let her have it. "Because if you don't think I know what you were getting at back there, darling . . . Well, anyway, just don't think it. Because I did. I knew everything. You may fool Florence, and you may fool Elinor. But, darling, *darling*"—he threw in the extra "darling," acidly —"don't ever get the idea you can fool me. I just know too much, don't you know that? Don't you know it? I know so *much*. I may be just a Kansas boy." He was getting excited now, and he knew it, but now he was enjoying it. "I may not have a dime, the tenth part of a dollar—only I have, I have. But I *do* get around, and—oh, well, darling, *you* know. . . . Shall we swim?"

He said the last words ironically, in the manner of one saying, "Shall we dance?" But if she had been willing to go into the water with him he might well have tried to drown her. All she did, though, was to look at him puzzledly for a moment.

Then she leaned forward and, dripping as she was—so chill-skinned that when she touched him he felt the cold of each finger separately—she gave his cheek a little tolerant, noncommittal pat. He knew her breasts would have felt as cold if he had touched them.

"Richard, why do you take things so hard?" she said. (And the smile! The smile!) And then she said something that he was to ponder over occasionally, later. "I know you've been around, all right," she said. "Haven't we all? But that's no reason for you to go off the handle so badly all the time, Richard, and for so little reason, really. It sounds funny, Richard." (And already he was asking himself: is she hinting at something, has she been finding out things? About the hospital at Danville, for instance?) "It sounds crazy."

But that was only an incident, and it floated away and sank from sight in the stream of sunny days that followed—sank or, like some waterlogged piece of timber, was at last submerged, and only bobbed up in Richard's consciousness occasionally, when he would find himself wondering: "Does she know? Does she know?"

Ordinarily, though, they all got on very well. Richard had his own little shocks from time to time, but at first they were pleasant ones, and in any case he said little about them. He was unused to women, and except for his mother and sister—and that had been in childhood—he had never lived with one; and the life at the cottage, where suddenly he was thrown into intimate contact with three of them, was a little unsettling.

And it was summer—and in summer, vacation time, everyone grows careless; in the heat, morals melt, everyone goes a little native. Richard lived in the studio, as he had come to call the shed where he made his quarters, and that helped a little. But in spite of that, in the cottage, since he was there increasingly as the summer went on, he had to grow used to things—well, to things that he never had been used to before. To the girls, either one of them, passing from bedroom to bathroom, or back again, in the flimsiest of costumes. Or to Florence, in a bathrobe over a nightgown, and still redolent of sleep, un-made-up, undisguised, unprotected as it were, sitting down to breakfast. To stockings hung over the towel racks, and girdles; shorts and jerseys just dumped anywhere, as their wearers had changed into bathing suits, or the wet bathing suits, as the same owners had changed back again. To all the other little privacies, intimacies of the toilette—jars and boxes of hand creams and face powders and ointments—all spread out before him on the wash basin's rim, in the medicine cabinet, often spilling their contents, as if to say, "Here we are. Now you know us. Now you know all our secrets."

But it was family, he kept telling himself. It was *family,* and if this was one of the embarrassments it was also one of the prides of it. For his own part, Richard did his best to live up to his side of the bargain. He was brother to Louisa, or he tried to be; he was son to Florence—and when he wanted to be, he could be wildly entertaining, with a touch of real madness about his fantasy that went perfectly with moonlight, and sunlight, and, well, with summer.

> *"Oh, Louisa, the sneezer,*
> *Got a cold in her beezer—*
> > *By which I imply, her nose.*
> *So she turned out a wheezer*
> *And nothing could please her*
> > *Except a new outfit of clothes.*

> *"Florence, too, caught a whiff of it,*
> *Started to sniff of it.*
> > *Soon she too caught a cold.*
> *But she hadn't the—"*

"No!" he said suddenly. They were all sitting on the screened porch at the time, in the evening, and once he had begun on that kind of doggerel Richard could usually go on indefinitely. ("You really ought to write popular songs, Richard," Elinor had once said to him earnestly. "You really ought to." And he had looked at her tolerantly.)

But there were times when it pleased him to break the mood, to change the subject suddenly, as if to prove all the more how complete his hold was over them.

"No," he said. "It's so silly, me jingling and jangling like this— with that moon, and that sky. And the sand . . . Doesn't it look just like water, the waves and waves of it? Florence, look; can't you see a boat coming over the crest of that dune there—pirates, maybe, or smugglers?"

"No-o-o-o. Not pirates, Richard," said Florence from her seat in the corner of the porch swing, and though she'd put on the shiveriness in her voice in part jokingly, Richard knew that he had touched her on her weak point. Florence, he'd discovered, had a fear of aloneness, of being unprotected, that amounted almost to a phobia. She drew the curtains at night, less against the prospect of being observed than against the very loneliness of the dunes around the cottage. She locked the doors when they went to bed, and though his thoughts had so far been vague it had struck him as a possible advantage, a key, somehow, something to be remembered.

"No smugglers, either," she said now, and he reached out and touched her hand briefly.

"Don't you worry," he said. "Not while I'm here, anyway." And again it gave him that family feeling; he was the protector, the one who soothed, reassured, who controlled things.

They got along very well, those first weeks at the cottage. And meanwhile, the nights, the days . . . The days lengthened into the nights, and then, inexorably, the nights lengthened in turn, shortening the days.

Summer is a happy time, but it is a harrying, hurrying time, too. It is a mixed time. Haste and laziness are mingled; it is a time when time seems to stand still, and each day is like every other day, and yet different; it's the time when the calendar almost, but not quite, supersedes the clock, and you think in terms of days instead of hours, of whole seasons instead of days.

You are closer to the sky in summer, or at least it seems so, and especially at the seashore; you are closer to the sun. You are closer, really, to nature—and at the seashore, in summer, nature is reduced to its most elemental, elementary features: a slice of cliff, a narrow rind of beach, dune contours, the endless pulse of waves, a slow daily progression of light, heat, coolness, shadow—and all this in a landscape so sparse that each fence post, each tree (almost, each spear of grass) has its separate accent; is itself a sort of sundial, and the course of its shadow, and the length of it, as the shadow moves across the hot sand beneath, are as good a time-teller as anyone needs, in the careless days of summer.

One can say, "Oh, we've got lots of time for a swim still. The sun is still over the trees."

One can say, "It must be lunch time now. The sun's right above the path."

One can say, "My! It's late. See, the cliffs are in shadow."

The seashore is a kind of jumping-off place, where nothing save the tenantless sea is before you and everything else is behind you; and the summer fits it perfectly, for the summer is a jumping-off time, a time when anything imaginable can happen. But the trouble is, it has to happen quickly, for the one bad thing about summer is that, somehow, it is always over almost before it has begun; and whether or not you think about it in that way, really—in terms of days' lengths, and solstices and equinoxes—there is something, perhaps something instinctive and elemental, that makes you realize it without even thinking.

Summer is the shortest season. June ends, and July begins, and passes in a haze of heat and lazy summer silence. But with August—and without your quite knowing why—the pace quickens: it is as if the earth itself had shifted position a little, and as the sun moves away, sliding south toward another hemisphere, all the shadows fall differently, stretch and lengthen differently, become steadily longer, larger, more all-covering.

Dinner time, that great punctuating point in the whole random day's length of summer—when at the Hacketts', at least, one was supposed to sit down to the table in more or less presentable garb, instead of the fragmentary raiment that everyone wore during the daytime—well, as August passes, shadows seem to encroach on the dinner time, too.

At first, eight o'clock, or even eight-thirty, is the dinner hour, and even then the long, hesitant summer twilight lasts long enough to light most of the meal. But as time passes, time also shortens; one must change and be dressed and ready for dinner by eight o'clock at the latest, by seven-thirty, finally, by seven—or the lights must be turned on, or the candles lit, the table moved in from the porch to the living room, the whole meal overcast with an ominous, autumnal formality.

And meantime, if the summer is to mean anything, if the season is to contain all the accomplishment one had wanted it to contain, one must hurry ("Hur-ry, hur-ry," Louisa had said), hurry, hurry, or all its magnificent early promise will be wasted.

Richard was a Kansas boy; he was new to the ocean and

new too to the summer in its seaside aspects; to him the beach
down the path from the cottage was a jumping-off place indeed.
It didn't matter that it was only the Sound that it led to, and
on clear days (on clear days only) he could see, over the level
waters, the gray, inch-high boundary that indicated the coast of
Connecticut; it didn't matter that, in actual fact, he was looking
back toward his native Kansas, instead of off toward the ocean
and Europe. The sea is the sea, and it is easy to imagine that it
rolls on endlessly; if you can't see the opposite shore, or can see
it only shadowily, it is easy to imagine that no barriers are there
at all, and the wave that breaks before you breaks breathlessly,
because it comes from so far, so far—from Spain, from Portugal;
from Cornwall, or Ireland, or the Azores.

So time passes, in such lazy imaginings. . . . Who has ever
known a summer when everything turned out just as he wanted,
and he managed to get everything he wanted to do done?

5

Richard was a Kansas boy. He was new to the ease and the casualness of seashore life; he was new to the laziness of summer.
He was new to its haste and its hurry. All he knew—and he
didn't know that very clearly, consciously—was that he wanted
to get something done, to make the Hackett family *his* family,
and to make himself part of it . . . and somehow to fit Elinor,
and Louisa, and Florence around himself as the core of it.

And meantime the days passed, and the nights. . . . In a sense,
Richard did grow into the family; more, at least, than he could
ever have done in the city. From the first, he had marked down
the shed at the rear of the cottage as his own, and early in the
summer, he had made a sort of studio out of it. It was done,
though he didn't know it, over Louisa's slight objection.

"Look, Mother," she had said once, when the Hacketts were
alone. "Don't you think you may be getting in a little too deep
with Richard? What I mean is, he's all right, and he's been helpful about finding the place, and so on. But we don't really know
much about him, you know. You don't want him just moving

in on us. But if you're going to let him have *his* room, and *his* house, and so on—well, that's exactly what's going to happen. You'll just have him on your hands all summer, or every week-end, anyway, and I wonder if you're going to like it. Why, it's getting so now he's even counting on having his meals with us. You don't want to adopt him, do you?"

Elinor only smiled, but Florence explained, quite amiably, that it wasn't a question of adopting anybody; she was interested in the boy, and he was certainly agreeable; as for not knowing too much about him, well, what *did* one know about most of the young men one met nowadays in the city? For the rest, he would probably be helpful; it was nice to have a man around, in the country. "And after all, dear," she concluded, "you have your problems, you know. Why not let us have ours?"

That was early in the summer, before the Hacketts had really transferred from the city to the seashore. It was a time of slight tension; and as always at such moments an ancient unresolvable resentment of Florence's for Louisa tended to come to the surface—unresolvable, because it arose from the fact that it was the income from Louisa's work that kept the family going, and at the same time Louisa's financial independence that took her away from Florence's domination. And the family perceptions, each to each, were so acute that from the very way Florence had said "dear," Louisa knew there was no point in arguing any more.

Instead, she shrugged her shoulders. "O.K., Ma," she said. "Ma," too, was a symbol in the family. The girls, Louisa especially, used it half-derisively, at moments, because they knew it had a sort of backwoods connotation that she despised. "It's up to you. I won't be down there a great deal, anyway."

So Richard, as Louisa had put it, moved in, and he did it so determinedly that it would actually have been difficult to dislodge him. The little shed had apparently been some sort of a workshop, originally; the beams were heavy and the floor was concrete and easily scrubbed, and once Richard had cleaned it the place had a certain bright neatness about it that he found particularly charming.

It looked "old world," he thought. It looked cottagey, and at the bookshop he talked a good deal to Jennie Carmody about it, expatiating on its simple rusticity. "I swear, Jennie," he once told her, "if it had a thatched roof, and a hedge, and a garden gate, I bet you'd think it was some place in Scotland. You really would!"

And he bought some red cloth for the window curtains; Florence sewed them and Elinor helped him string them on the rods and put them in place. He found an old pine table in one of the bedrooms that he could use for a desk, and laid out pencils and paper to work on his poems. He even had a sort of housewarming, when all the fitting-up had been completed.

He had it on a Saturday night, and the family all came over, including a young man whom Louisa had brought down for the week-end. The whole thing went off very well, too—though it began a little nervously.

Richard had insisted on a certain formality about it. He had asked them for nine o'clock, and explained that he'd need a half-hour or so before that to get things ready—but since he was also to have dinner with them all first, that meant complications. It meant, specifically, an early dinner, and that, unfortunately, is not always the simplest thing to arrange in the casualness of summer.

Florence, prodded on by Richard, did her best to help, and tried too to make the others conform. She left the beach before six, to begin her cooking, and the last words she said as she started up the path toward the house were, "Don't forget Richard's party now, the rest of you. I want you all to be at the table by seven."

Richard went up soon after. But when he went over to the Hacketts' at seven precisely, there were Elinor and Florence, waiting—but no Louisa and no Mr. Crosby, which was what Louisa's young man's name was.

It was Elinor who had seen them last, but all she could report was that when she had come up from the beach they had said they would stay for just one more swim and then follow her. But instead they had just disappeared, it seemed, and there was nothing at all the others could do but wait—Richard, fuming— until they put in an appearance. It was nearly eight o'clock before they turned up, full of explanations and apologies, and of course still in bathing suits. For the first and last time that summer Florence broke her rule about dressing, and let the two of them sit down at table without changing, so they wouldn't delay things any further.

As for Richard—Richard sensed a rebellion. He saw a plot, he saw his party ruined, and solely because of Louisa's spitefulness. He hardly spoke to them when they sat down at the table, and he bolted off to his own place only a few minutes after they arrived.

But surprisingly, when they all came over to the party, Louisa was niceness itself.

Richard often remembered that evening, lovingly—later, longingly. In a way, though neither he nor the Hacketts realized it then, it was the high point of the summer for all of them; though there were to be good times later, many of them, there were none with quite the warm, simple, friendly togetherness of that one.

For his own part Richard had really done things rather elaborately. He had cleaned off his desk and set it against one wall of the room, and put out on it his two bottles of Scotch, one opened and one not, and the ice, and the glasses, between a couple of lighted candles. (The ice and glasses he had gotten from Florence, but the candles and the Scotch he had bought himself, at Port Jefferson.) It was the first real party that Richard had ever given in all his life, though he would have died rather than admit it, and he was intensely anxious about its outcome.

He knew too that in a way the whole thing was an elaborate make-believe. What he was "housewarming," really, was not a house of his own but a sort of glorified guest room, and he apprehended that he might be open to all sorts of mockery if anyone happened to be in the mood for it.

But when they all came in, dressed with just enough extra care to make things seem festive, and with that shining, cleaner-than-clean look that people have at the seaside, as if a little of the day's refreshment of sun and ocean still clung to them, giving radiance to their bodies and sleekness to their hair—as soon as they came in, he could see that they were with him and not against him; everything was going to be all right.

"Why, Richard!" Louisa exclaimed. There was a good deal

of chatter going on on the part of everyone, but he heard her voice most clearly. She was pointing at the table, and he glanced around at it too, a little suspiciously.

"What's the matter?" he said.

"Nothing, darling, nothing's the *matter*. Only—well, what I mean, two bottles! And Scotch, too! You really did set out to throw a party, didn't you?"

Richard tried to make his voice sound offhand and casual, but in spite of himself he found himself beaming. "Well, I wanted to be sure there'd be enough," he said.

"You certainly did that, honey-chile."

"I've got sandwiches, too," he told her. He was conscious of his duties as a host, he had made up his mind not to forget them, whatever happened, and now even as he spoke he had picked up a glass, slipped in some pieces of ice, and was pouring her a drink. "But I don't think I ought to bring them out now, do you?" he asked. "Maybe later."

"That's right. Save 'em," she said, as he handed her the glass. She stood looking at him a moment, smiling. "It's going to be a swell housewarming, keed," she said suddenly, and there was something in the way she said it that made it seem almost as if she understood all his anxiousness and inexperience and, quite marvelously, didn't think it was funny at all.

It embarrassed him a little, but it pleased him, too; Louisa *can* be sweet when she wants to be, he thought. But all he did at the moment was to turn away a bit self-consciously. "It's time I saw to the others," he said, and seeing Louisa's young man looking in his direction he picked up a glass and raised it toward him inquiringly. "You, Mr. Crosby?" he said.

And it was like that all through the evening; there were moments when Richard could feel his heart literally filling with joy that his own place, *his own place,* should be so graced, so honored. For it was his own place, wasn't it?—in the sense that he had discovered it, and imagined the life that would go on in it; in a way, created it? As the evening went on, and the others seemed cheerfully determined to corroborate his ownership, all his early uncertainties evaporated, and he saw the little house as his own, unassailable and inviolable. His own.

All three of the Hacketts had been involved in one way or another in his furnishings and his refurbishings. But now they all pretended a little that they hadn't; and Florence exclaimed over one thing and Louisa and Elinor over another, and even the young man, though he seemed a little bewildered by it all, did his best to admire and praise with the others.

He was about Richard's height, but much slenderer. He had something to do with the technical side of radio, and Richard, privately, found him rather unpleasant. (One of the nicest things about the way the evening was going was that it allied him, Richard, with the Hacketts and so placed the other fellow at a disadvantage.) He was well put together, though, and wiry; he was a good swimmer, Richard had noticed, and good-looking, too, he had to admit, in a sort of hair-parted-in-the-middle, blunt-featured collegiate way. And he had an odd, rather pushing manner that at times bordered on the insolent. He came up to Richard once, later in the evening, and stared at him curiously.

"Don't you have any nicknames, Baurie?" he demanded. He always stood a little too close to people when he talked, a thing that Richard particularly detested. "My name's Richard, too, you know, but it's I don't know to Christ how long ago since anybody ever called me that. It was always Dickie or Dick when I was a kid. And now it's Rick. . . . What I mean is, does everybody always call you Richard?"

Richard handled it gracefully, though; after all, he had his duties as a host to consider. And the fellow was swaying a little even as he talked; he was tight, or he was getting so, and Richard could look down at him tolerantly from the heights of his sobriety.

"I'm afraid they do," he said evenly. "Should I mind?" And then, without waiting for an answer, he took Crosby's nearly empty glass from his hand. "Let me liven this up for you, won't you, old fellow?" he said. It had occurred to him that it might be fun if he got Crosby really drunk.

For once, too, it didn't matter that Richard's strict plans for the evening got a little bit out of hand. What he had planned was something cheerful, but quiet and conversational—a little talk about his poetry, their projects for the summer, schemes for

outings; maybe something, toward the end, a little more serious, about religious theories, maybe, and the mystical beliefs of
the Hindus that he had been reading about lately. But before he
knew it, things changed. Something almost explosive was in the
atmosphere; it was as if everyone had just been waiting for a
party, and without his quite realizing it he was affected too.

They stood, or sat, and talked, for a while. But the feeling of
explosiveness was in the air, and before Richard knew what the
others were up to, Louisa and Rick disappeared and came back
from the Hacketts' carrying the radio; they pushed the bottles
and the candles aside and put the radio on the table; they shoved
the chairs against the wall—and from then on some or all of
them were always dancing, or else hanging over the radio and
twisting the control buttons, trying to tune out talking and
tune in music; and the sound of the music, sometimes velvety
and sometimes brassy and harsh, underlay all their movements
and all their voices, making them all talk a little more loudly
and more disjointedly, and giving a certain air of excitement to
everything they did or said.

Richard loved it. He wasn't a good dancer, while Crosby was;
but that night he flung himself into it gallantly, dancing first with
Florence (as befitted his duties as a host), and then with Elinor
and then with Louisa, and then with Elinor again. "I can see
now why Louisa likes Crosby so much," he said once to Elinor.
They were dancing and so were the other two, and he had, as he
watched them, a moment of pure admiration—almost, even, of
gratitude, for after all it was in his house that they performed—
for the grace and smooth accustomed assurance with which
they moved. He nodded toward them as he spoke.

Elinor didn't look. She too was not really a good dancer. She
was a little too stocky for that, and she hadn't the same easy
natural feeling for rhythm as her sister. She danced close and
followed carefully, yet—for Richard at least—she was more
appealing as a partner, more exciting, really, than Louisa.

Louisa, sometimes, was so light in his arms that she seemed
almost not to be there at all. But with Elinor he was always conscious of her body, and there was something excitingly honest
and intimate as it strove, awkwardly but so eagerly, to follow

his. Now, however, she had been dancing abstractedly, with her head turned away as if she had been thinking of something else, and she didn't reply for so long that he began to think she hadn't heard him.

"Why?" she asked, finally.

"Well, because he's such a wonderful dancer. She is too, of course. But so is he. I've been watching."

"I see you have," said Elinor, and then she added, "Well, I'm glad you think Louisa's such an awfully good dancer."

"Oh, she is. She's wonderful," Richard said. And then almost accidentally—because he himself set no particular value on dancing—he continued, "I like your dancing better, though, you know."

"Do you, Richard?" she said. She turned her face up to his, still dancing, and at the same time drew it back a little, as girls do when dancing—as if to see him better. Her lips were smiling, and her eyes were smiling, too. "You know, they say that people who make good dancing partners get along well in other things too."

He got closer to Elinor that night too, in a way, than he had ever gotten before.

They all went down to the beach together, later. That was when Richard had brought out the sandwiches, and by that time it was after midnight. Richard really had thought the sandwiches would be a signal for the party to break up; he had an idea that Florence expected it, and besides he was getting a little bored himself with all the dancing.

But the spirit of hilarity was still upon them, and instead the idea of something to eat merely gave the party a new form. Again without even consulting Richard, Rick and Louisa swept the sandwiches into a basket, dumped a bottle in and some glasses, and soon they were all straggling—un-surefootedly in the sudden darkness, and laughing about it—down the path through the dunes to the cliff and the beach.

Only Florence at first objected, and then only for her own sake, and not about the idea in general; she had simply had enough, she said. "I've *had* my party," she explained, "and I've enjoyed every minute of it, too. But as for getting me down to that cold, cold beach, in front of that cold, cold ocean, and at this hour ..." And she shivered daintily. "No, darlings. Quite simply, no." It seemed to Richard that the efforts of the others to make her change her mind were merely perfunctory.

Richard, though, had a feeling—in a way, it was almost panicky—that she *must* come along. It wasn't only that he felt she *ought* to be there, as the two girls' mother, though he felt that too. He was beginning to worry about the whole fabric of his party. Things had gotten out of hand a little before, when instead of just sitting around and talking as he had expected the others to do they had all started dancing; and although that had turned out all right in the end this was a further divergence, and it might be a more dangerous one; he wasn't sure now what might happen down there on the beach, and whether or not he could handle it alone, and for a moment or two all his old, vague distrust began rising; he wasn't sure but that there mightn't be some strange, secret plot in the making against him.

Perhaps something to do with the beach and the darkness. . . . He might *need* Florence, he felt obscurely, and he urged and pleaded—"We'll build a fire, Florence," he promised. "We'll keep you warm, we'll bring along some blankets. Florence, you've *got* to come! Really, Florence!"—until finally, rather flattered by his insistence, she consented.

"For a while, then," she said. "But I shall have to get a wrap, or something. And listen, children"—she cocked an eye at them brightly—"if we're going to have a fire, why not coffee?"

So they brought along coffee and a coffee pot, and tried their best to boil it over a fire. But though it turned out badly, because of drafts and a general inability to get the pot close enough to the flames—"We'll have to work out something better," said Richard, and that was the starting-point of his plan for an open-air fireplace—and although Florence did go off finally to bed soon after, the little interlude, perhaps simply the mere fact that she had been there, was a quieting influence.

She remained, so to speak, as a sort of absentee chaperone—or it may have been simply that by that time the chill, and the night, and the darkness began inevitably to make them all drowsy. (There were stars, but no moon; the moon had set, and beyond the little circle of firelight the darkness seemed almost savage in its immensity, with only the faint lappings of the waves and an occasional white glint of foam to mark the line where the sea began and the land ended.)

It seemed, for one thing, to bring the two girls closer, as if allied, rather restlessly, against the two men. They sat side by side, with a sisterliness that was unusual in them, and sang songs together; and it pleased Richard, a little, to see Crosby, who apparently had had other plans, growing more and more baffled by the turn things were taking.

Once—the two girls had gone off down the beach together, ostensibly to get more firewood—he seemed to try to broach the subject to Richard. At any rate, it was a curious conversation. Crosby had been lying on his back near the fire; he hadn't had a drink for some time and he seemed a little somnolent.

"Baurie," he said suddenly. "We're not getting anywhere. Have you thought about that?"

Richard, frankly, was startled. "Not getting anywhere?" he repeated.

"That's right," Crosby said. He was still on his back, talking, so to speak, to the sky. "They're a couple of swell kids, the two of them, aren't they?" he said a moment later.

"You mean Louisa and Elinor?" asked Richard. "Yes, I think so."

"Always ready for fun or frolic," said Crosby, obscurely, then he turned over on his stomach and propping his chin on his hands stared owlishly at Richard. "You related?" he demanded suddenly.

"Related?"

"Sure. Related. I mean, are you a member of the family? A cousin, or something?"

Richard waited for a moment, as if considering the question. Then he laughed a little. "I could answer that either way, really," he said.

"Well, go ahead then," said Crosby equably. "Either way."

Richard glanced at him. "What I mean is, in a way I suppose I *am* a member of the family, since I live with them, eat with them, play with them. But I'm not related. I'm no cousin, or anything like that."

"O.K.," Crosby said. "I was just trying to figure out the set-up. Well—"

Richard leaned forward slightly to interrupt him. He was getting just a bit tired of all this obvious prying. "There's no mystery. I am just what I seem to be, really. Just a friend who happens to be here. A poet."

"Oh. A poet."

"Do you doubt that?" asked Richard softly.

"Doubt it? Hell, no. Why should I?" said Crosby, but he was apparently losing interest in the conversation. "You don't let any grass grow under your feet, anyway, do you, Baurie?"

"Grass?" said Richard.

Crosby, though, had climbed up on his hands and knees and was reaching gingerly around the fire for the bottle, which had been parked on the other side. The two girls were coming down the beach. "Never mind. It means nothing," he said. "Here they are now, anyway. How's about you and me having a quick little drink?"

"Thank you, no. I'd be glad, though," said Richard stiffly, "if you'd help yourself."

"I don't like this Crosby," said Richard. They weren't all always together, that evening, and soon after the girls had come back, Elinor—it was almost as if she had sensed a disturbance between the two men, on returning—had seized on Richard to help her bring back a log for the fire that she'd discovered, down the beach.

"Oh, it's the *loveliest* big log!" she had cried while they were still near the fire, in that rather gushing, girlish way she some-times had when she was with others, and that Richard was already beginning to recognize, and cherish, as a symbol of her own shyness.

It was an affectation, he knew, but he loved it, if only because he himself had gotten inside it; when with him, she was more natural, and so the affectation became a sort of secret they both shared, a sort of barrier between them and the rest of the world.

And sure enough, once they were out of earshot of the others, she dropped the mannerism completely.

"Oh," she said. "I'm tired. Don't you think we all ought to go to bed soon?" And then, a moment later: "It was a lovely party, though, Richard. Really lovely." And when he didn't respond to that, either, she paced along beside him quite quietly, like a wife walking docilely with her husband. But when he spoke she answered immediately.

"I don't either, much," she said. She was wearing a light yellow dress which now, in the vagueness, looked gray, and her face and bare arms and shoulders looked gray too, but paler and more silvery. Once they had gotten out of range of the firelight the night, so to speak, had surrounded them; everything was enclosed in it, and the sea, the beach, the occasional big boulders and outcroppings of rock spaced here and there along it, all revealed themselves, not as things exactly, but as planes or as bulks, their shapes and substance measurable only by their varying degrees of blackness.

"But *you* know . . . Louisa," she went on. "She does have the strangest friends. I sometimes wonder what she sees in some of them."

"I know," Richard said.

"He's sort of, well, drunk, too, isn't he?"

"I'll say."

"And I know, one mustn't mind that, at a party. After all, people do. But still . . . It was funny, though, this afternoon," she went on, and when he glanced at her inquiringly: "You know, when they were both gone so long, before dinner? I was wondering what they were doing. I went back, you know. I started up to the house, and then I went back to look for my towel, and when I got down to the beach again they were gone, or they weren't where we'd been sitting any more. They were down here by that rock," and she pointed to a boulder just beyond where they were at the moment. "And you know, just when I caught sight of them, they ducked down behind it. Do you suppose they were hiding, or something?"

Richard took her hand. There were times when her innocence surprised him. " 'Something,' probably," he said, teasingly.

"Something, what?"

"Oh, making love, I suppose," said Richard. "You know, kissing, necking."

"Do you think so? Really? But I suppose I shouldn't be surprised. . . . I thought maybe they were hunting for something." They were just about abreast of the rock by then, and she gave his hand a little tug. "Let's go over and look," she said.

The rock was large and smooth-topped and rather low-lying, and when they got close to it Richard could see that its blackness was broken by a multitude of tiny sparkles, faint as frost, as the granite reflected the little light that came from the sky. They prowled around it rather aimlessly for a while, still holding hands; both of them had been past it many times in the daytime, but now, in the darkness, it looked different; and when they got behind it, so that its black bulk lay between them and the firelight back up the beach, Richard somehow, in spite of himself, felt his breath coming faster.

There was something secret and menacing about the mass of rock on the lonely beach. There was a quality of the primeval about it; it was like one long wall of an ancient temple if the rest of the structure had been battered and destroyed by the waves, and when Elinor dropped down on the sand in its shadow it was as if she had dropped back in time, too, into the primitive; for a second he could only stand and stare at her.

But she was sitting there quite unconcernedly, looking up at him. "See?" she said, and he couldn't help noticing that an odd little note of imperiousness had crept into her voice. "They *could* hide here; it's a wonderful place to hide. Come on, Richard, let's us hide too.

"Isn't it nice, though?" she demanded, when he had squatted down rather awkwardly beside her; and then abruptly, with an almost animal swiftness of motion, she twisted up to her knees to peer over the rock. She looked back at him and laughed. "I just thought, what if they had been following *us*," she said. "But they weren't. They're still back there by the fire. Want to look?"

"No," said Richard.

"You can see them quite plainly. And the fire looks so pretty, too." Again, there was that peremptory note in her voice. "Really, Richard, come up here and see."

The fire did look pretty, as she had said. There were no flames visible, at that distance, but only a changing mound of orange and yellow brightness, with a kind of broken circle of light around it that picked, here and there, objects and parts of objects out of the darkness: the slanting plane of the cliff, an edge of boulder, a figure leaning over the fire in the act perhaps of putting some wood on it. He identified the figure as Rick, and a moment later Richard made out Louisa, lying back against the boulder, on the fringe of the circle of illumination. When Rick finished whatever he had been doing to the fire, he went back and sat down beside her.

"See them, hmmm?" Elinor demanded, turning her face to look up at him.

"Mm-hm. Yes," said Richard. He felt clumsy and a little apprehensive. Things were getting out of hand, somehow, and he didn't know quite what to do about it, and when Elinor said, "Let's sit down then, shall we? Let's hide," he let himself be dragged awkwardly down on the sand beside her.

Mostly, though, he was conscious, intensely conscious, of the simple fact of her body. She was alive, unpredictable, capable of sudden movements; and even when she was still, as she was still now, she was breathing, giving off warmth, aliveness. She was a person, existing beside him, and no longer docile; and at the thought of that, resentment began rising inside him, and a thousand suspicions. Had the two girls planned to split up their two men like this? And why? Or had it all been Louisa's doing? But no, that couldn't be, for then, of course, Elinor would have had no reason to imagine that Louisa and Rick might have followed them.

Or was that just a part of the stratagem too? Florence flashed through his mind—Florence, calmly taking herself off to bed and leaving her two daughters alone with two men on the lonely beach, and not caring, just not caring. . . . Elinor now was chattering, simply chattering, in a sort of bright, making-conversation way that she had sometimes, and he sat there and looked at her. "With anyone else but me, my girl," he thought, so clearly that for an instant he wasn't quite sure that he hadn't spoken aloud, "you might be getting into something you wouldn't want to."

But then he knew that he couldn't have spoken, for she paid no attention. "It's sort of chilly, though, too," she said, going on with whatever she had been saying before. "Or it would be if I were alone. But that's sort of a silly thing to say, though, isn't it?" she went on a moment later. "Of course, you're always lonesome when you're alone."

"I'm not."

"Aren't you?" she said. It was then that he tried to kiss her.

He did it blunderingly. He felt guilty and angry and a little frightened; it was only because he thought the situation demanded it of him that he tried it, and when he met her resistance as his arms went around her he felt, more than anything else, a sort of gratitude.

That was right, he felt. It was right for him to try, but it was equally right for her to resist, and it crossed his mind that he needn't have worried; he might have known that he could trust Elinor, he could always trust her. Yet in a queer way, too, the very force of her resistance made him persevere. It aroused a kind of combativeness that he hadn't known till then he had in him, and for a while there was an awkward little tussle between them, as he tried to make her mouth meet his.

"No. No. Richard, no. Can't you understand?" she kept saying. "No. No. I mean it, really. No." He kissed her cheek, and he felt its softness, but when he tried to reach her lips she strained away. He couldn't reach them, and then—just as he was about to release her—unbelievably, he felt her body almost melt as it softened against his.

"Richard. Richard," she said, in a tone that still protested. But her head seemed to turn to his almost helplessly as his own pressed forward; for an instant, her lips met his in a kiss so full and wide and voluptuous that it bewildered him, it was as if suddenly she had been drained of all resistance. Then, as suddenly, she stiffened, and he felt her hands pushing so hard against his chest that he would have had to crush her if he hadn't let go. He let go. She put her hand to her hair and then straightened her skirt a little.

"No," she said. "We mustn't really be silly. But put your arm around me, though, why don't you? It *is* cold, and we *can* do that. And if you're really *very* nice … Well, I won't promise…"

He realized that she was promising him a kiss, and as he put his arm around her he made a slight attempt to turn her face toward his. She held him away.

"But you mustn't be so sudden, Richard!" she said, and in a dim way it seemed it was Louisa's voice she was using. "And anyway, we *do* want to talk."

6

Summer is a queer time, though; it's a chancey time, a time when anything can happen. (Who has ever known a summer when everything turned out just as he wanted, and he managed to get everything he wanted to do done?) There are times when the summer drags out, there are times when it gets mixed up and confusing. There are times when a simple summer cottage, a mere lonely pinprick on the dunes, can become a center of quite unrelated and quite unexpected activity: as if, even in that quiet, unpopulous country, little lines of attraction radiated out, gradually forming a network that bound the Hacketts, and with them Richard, to a hundred places and people that none of them had ever heard of before they came to the cottage.

Again, chiefly, it was Louisa who was to blame, or she, anyway, and her friends. Crosby wasn't the last of the sleek-looking, amiable, adaptable, knowledgeable young men whom Louisa brought down with her on the week-ends; there seemed to be dozens of them. Some were lean, some were tall, some were stocky, and there was one—"Chub" Bassett, his name was, short, blonde, and sort of twinkling; he worked in advertising, and he came down with Louisa one week-end early in August—for whom Richard conceived quite an affection.

But apart from their physical particularities they had a number of things in common. They all worked in radio or in advertising. They all had cars, and the cars were invariably convertibles. ("My God! What would be the use of having them around if they didn't get me out of that awful train ride!" Louisa said once in a moment of frankness. Chub Bassett, for instance, had a Chrysler.) They were all, in their separate ways, good-looking, and they knew a great deal more about everything than Richard could ever possibly know.

They had been to all the latest plays and knew the inside stories about them; they knew the night clubs and the popular bars and the people who went to them. They had a certain ease in all situations that Richard at once hated, admired, and envied. They knew the newest jokes; and the jokes, Richard noticed, were admirably scaled to fit all circumstances—mild ones for the getting-acquainted part of the evening, slightly riskier ones that were told when Florence was still present, and the really outspoken ones that, sometimes, came later.

Even their arrivals followed a certain pattern, although that was as much Louisa's doing as it was theirs. Wisteria Cottage had no telephone. There was a boy who rode out on a bicycle from Port Jefferson to deliver telegrams, but his behavior was erratic, as far as promptness was concerned, and the Hacketts soon learned not to depend on him. As a result, there was no way of knowing when or with whom Louisa was likely to arrive on Friday evenings; as Florence once remarked, about all you could depend on was that she would be undependable.

"I may have to take the train down this time, God help me!" she might say, on leaving, Sunday evening, and in fact there were a good many times when she did come down alone; she wasn't always so surrounded with boy-friends as Richard imagined. Or she'd say, "I'll be down early this time. If I don't I'll try to send you a telegram Thursday." Always, though, things would turn out differently.

Invariably, she would get down later than they had expected, and though they had learned at last not to wait meals for her there would always be a certain restlessness before her arrival. Florence, Richard, and Elinor would have finished dinner. (Richard always came down in the afternoon.) They would be sitting on the screened porch in the dreaming evening. (If you listened hard you might hear the sea, like the very faint rustling of some incredibly satiny cloth, on the beach below; apart from that, once the sun had set and insects had quieted, the silence that came over the dunes was as massive and deep and seemingly as illimitable as the sky itself, slowly darkening. The mere creaking of a rocking chair, or the striking of a match, in that silence, was a noticeable disturbance.)

They would sit there and smoke, and occasionally talk a little; Florence, maybe, would have her knitting. And the dishes would have been done, the kitchen put in order; if the day had been any other than Friday, with Louisa coming, the evening, too, would have stretched away before them as gentle and endless and all-embracing as the silence. Now, however, they waited, and the waiting was faintly restless: as with people floating down a peaceful river, but with the knowledge that somewhere ahead lay rapids, even the present quietness seemed, not menacing perhaps, except to Richard, but a little uneasy.

And then suddenly—at nine, nine-thirty, even later—from behind the farthest contour of the dunes would come a glow, and then headlights, pointing down their road. "Here she comes!" someone would cry—and then Florence would start worrying about the guest room.

And the headlights would dip and rise again, and grow larger; a horn would sound, perhaps, as a kind of signal (and Richard would imagine Louisa, in the dimly-lit intimate car-interior, reaching over to press the horn-button, while the man at the wheel grinned across at her briefly, then addressed himself to the tricky, rutty little road again). On the porch they would begin to hear the motor-sound, loud against the silence behind it, as the car shoved along in low, or in second, up the last little grade. "Take the flashlight, Richard, why don't you? So the young man can see where to park."

And so Richard, feeling suddenly, painfully, the anomalousness of his position in the household, would be sent out to bear the brunt of the arrival.

Almost always, it would turn out that Louisa and whoever the young man with her was—Chub Bassett, Frank Massie, maybe some new one—were too tired and bored with the journey to put the car away at the moment.

"Kenny, this is Richard, Richard Baurie, he's a friend of the family, staying with us. And this is Kenneth Eaton, you can both get acquainted later. God! We're shot!" Louisa would already be sliding out of the car, and from the way she deployed her long, city-silken legs it would be clear that she, and probably he as well, were a little high.

"What traffic!" she would say. "But I mean really, what traffic! And all the way out, too."

"If you want to pull over to the left there," Richard would say, leaning past her to look at the newcomer, still sitting at the wheel. "There's a place, I don't know if your headlights will show it; but if you want, I can stand with the flashlight. I can show it to you. . . ."

But already Louisa would be interrupting. "Richard, listen! We're tired! And who the hell's going to come up this road, anyway? We can put the car over there tomorrow." And then the bags, and the trunk compartment that had to be opened, and the suitcases . . .

The young man would have brought a bottle of liquor ("Oh, you shouldn't! As if we didn't have enough around here already!"), and a box of candy for Florence. He would be very attentive to her and to Elinor through that evening, and would more or less forget about both of them afterward; it was obvious, always, that the young men were completely Louisa's property, and no one else's.

And it would develop, each time, that the reason why they were late—well, there were a variety of reasons: too much traffic, so that they got bored with the crush of it, and stopped off to wait for easier traveling; or a sort of little eating place that they'd heard of, and had difficulty in finding. Or just fun: they had stopped at this queer place, with a waitress who was cross-eyed or a waiter who spilled things, or something, but it had this juke-box, and Denny, or Kenny, or whoever it was, had insisted on feeding it nickels. . . .

They were reasons, Richard noticed, but they were never excuses. Louisa told why they were late, but she never apologized. And meantime they would sit there, drinking coffee

(Florence always had coffee ready for them), and a highball or two afterward, and the young man would sit quietly, cautiously sizing up the situation—and occasionally glancing at Richard unobtrusively. (It was as if, on the long drive out, Louisa had told him something; and he was trying to relate what he saw now, here before him, to whatever she had told him.)

Next morning Dicky, Danny, whoever he was, would appear in white flannels and a white pull-over (rarely, they wore shorts), and then later in the flower-printed Hawaiian swimming trunks that were something of a rage that summer. They swam well, always, and they were usually beautifully tanned.

And if there was a picnic lunch they would help, with alacrity, to serve it, showing special little courtesies to Florence in the process. And meantime, any time, there was the car there, ready to take them all anywhere they wanted to go. . . .

In more ways than one it was the young men—and Louisa—who spoiled the lovely isolation of the cottage. There was a bar in Port Jefferson, or "Port Jeff," as they all called the town by now—a little port-side place called Leary's, that they would probably never have heard of if Louisa, with her instinct for gregariousness, hadn't discovered it one day when she had gone in to do the shopping. And now always, even on the quietest evenings, there was the knowledge, like a thread connecting them with the outer world—and along which they could hear the world's vibrations—that Leary's was *there,* where the sky lighted up a little to the south of them, where the port and the town of Port Jefferson lay. And with a car, of course, one could easily run over. One by one, other threads were spun.

There were some people, the Simmonses, who had a cottage only a half-mile or so down the beach from the Hacketts'—a half-mile, that is, across the dunes; by the road, it was rather farther—and Louisa had known Leila Simmons in town; and so naturally, when they found they had places so close, the two families had to get together. Richard didn't like them much.

They were Greenwich Villagers, the first Richard had ever met, and for that reason he distrusted them. They lived down on West Ninth Street, and he worked in a publishing house and she was a program-director, or something, in radio. She was short and black-haired and black-eyed, nervous, brisk, and energetic; Richard, looking at her, was always conscious of two things, her breasts, which were too large for the rest of her figure, and her hands and arms, which were thin to the point of scrawniness. Larry Simmons, her husband, was tall, blonde, and easygoing, thin-nosed and long-faced; they had two children—a girl, about nine, who screamed rather than talked and who was treated, so Richard thought, far too indulgently; and a boy of fifteen or so, called Roger, or "Rog," whom Richard rather liked.

He was tall, like his father, and blond; he was big enough to be a man, despite his youth, and there was a sort of shy, tentative awkwardness about his very overgrownness—the big, placid form, the long, juvenile legs, and still with it all the childish voice and manner—that was somehow appealing.

And besides the Simmonses, there were others. There were the Cases, the Wurteles (who had a sailboat and lived over near Patchogue, the other side of the island), the Bradleys . . . Richard, really, couldn't understand why they bothered with all of them.

There they were, he and Florence and all of them, a family; they had the beach and the porch and the cottage, if they had only known it; they had the sea and sun and complete peacefulness, if they only wanted it. But on Saturdays, now, almost always, there would be a kind of restlessness. "They're quite nice, the Cases. He's with B. B. D. and O., but as I always say, you can't hold that against him; he's a darling, really. Let's bring Kenny over to meet them."

Or if nothing else offered itself, Louisa might say, "Let's run over to Leary's and feed that juke-box a few nickels."

Almost always Richard went along, though it was mostly because he had found that if he didn't go, and stayed home, he could hardly bear the feeling of abandonment and helpless rage that would often come over him afterward, alone there in the empty cottage, without a thing in the world to do except try to imagine what the others were doing; he hated it.

But he hated going almost equally. The one compensation was that usually, on the way to and fro, he and Elinor would ride together, in the rumble seat if there was one, or in the narrow rear part of the convertible if the car was arranged that way; and the intimacy there, and the slight excitement of it, almost made up for everything else.

Otherwise, he hated the trips, and not only because all the visiting here and there, and the return visits which came later, were an interruption of the peacefulness of their cottage life as he had foreseen it. They showed him, too, a part of the Hacketts' life that he realized he could hardly hope ever to share.

In a way, they brought home his homelessness to him. The Hacketts *knew* these people, in a like-to-like instantaneous way that he could never equal. In spite of Elinor's little playful gestures of possessiveness, which she always displayed at such times and which he loved as a sign of their solidarity ("Where's my compact, Richard? Didn't I give it to you?" she would say; or, "Richard, hand me my glass, will you, darling?")—in spite of these, and the host's and the hostess's forced false hospitality, he always found himself slowly, subtly, being driven into the role of the outsider, the queer one, the one whom everyone else had difficulty talking to and whom they stared at covertly; and he hated it. It was largely because of this, and the feeling of randomness that was creeping into things, that he took to extending his own week-ends, coming down Thursdays instead of Fridays, or staying over till Monday, in a desperate effort to hold his place in the family.

The long week-ends, in turn, led to really serious trouble with Jennie Carmody, at the bookshop; and even before that came about he had begun little depredations on the bookshop till—nothing much; he was careful; only five or six dollars a week, at the most—to finance the extra expense he was under.

But he had no concern about that. There was one thing he flattered himself, that he saw the main thing first; and the main thing now was to hold the Hacketts—not so much for his own sake, really, as for theirs. He saw more and more that they were a family split by a thousand impulses, a few good, many bad; weakened too by the weakness that except for his mother he had always recognized to be inherent in women, and that somehow was heightened progressively when you got two women living together instead of one, and still more when there were three instead of two.

Then not only were they weak themselves but they weakened each other, and there were times when the weight of his responsibility, and the mixedness of it, seemed almost more than he could bear. He was father at times—didn't he have to be, with that lax, lazy, careless Florence?—and he was husband and brother to Elinor; and there were times, like that time on the beach, in a way, when all three of his functions ran together and confused him.

Or the time when they were driving back, late, from Leary's.

It had been a dull evening there. There had been about eight or ten other couples at the place, besides the usual number of locals drinking beers at the bar—the women mostly in slacks or light summer dresses (Leary wouldn't let you in in shorts), and the men wearing soiled ducks or dungarees; sandals and espadrilles were the commonest footwear.

And they had played the juke-box, and danced. They had sat at a corner table, and danced—less and less, however, as the evening wore on; as the evening wore on a kind of boredness took hold of them, so that in the end they just gave up dancing, and drank beers, and watched, too bored, really, to do anything about their boredom—and a woman in a tight black sweater and black slacks got into an argument with another woman in a tight gray sweater and blue skirt. And that livened things up for a moment, but in a way that Richard resented.

There was a tension in the air, and he kept wondering why Florence, at least, didn't have sense enough, or responsibility enough, or something, to take them out of it, and he was just about to say something himself when, at last, she did.

"Listen, children," she said.

"I know. Sure," said Louisa. "It must be all of one o'clock. Well, enough of low life; I can see Richard's horrified by it already. Come on, Howie." Howie was the young man's name. "We'll have a fine, healthy day on the beach tomorrow to make up for it."

Outside they gulped the clear cool air as if it had been water, and climbed into the car; the streets were empty and the houses dark as they went through the town. It was closer to two than it was to one o'clock, Richard noticed. There had been tensions before, in the bar, but when they got out in the moonlit, quiet countryside—he and Elinor alone together in the rumble seat, shut away from the others by the dun-colored roadster top and drawn along through the night by the steady drive of the car— Richard relaxed a little.

"That Leary's!" he said. It was the kind of remark that usually brought them together, in a sort of common mood of tolerant disapproval of the others' doings; riding home in the rumble seat, there was always a husband-and-wifely air about their conversations, like a couple talking things over on the way home after a party. (Riding in convertibles, where they were all jammed in together, there was another mood that presented itself; there, usually, Richard would fling an arm around Elinor's shoulders, brotherly-loverly fashion, and laugh and gossip; then, with Florence and Louisa in front of him, he would feel really like the lord of the family, overlooking, overseeing everything.) But this time, it was different.

"Yes. That Leary's," Elinor repeated.

But there was a kind of mimicking tone in her voice. And you can tell; when you've been around a person long enough, you can tell what their moods are. Richard had yawned and stretched his arms as he spoke, and in the ordinary way of things he might have let one arm, as it fell, fall around her shoulders in his brotherly-loverly gesture; they might have talked that way. But now, even as he started to do so, something in her manner stopped him. "I don't like it, you know," he said. "I don't see why we go there."

"I could see that, all right," she said.

For the moment, what he felt was mainly amusement. "You could?" he asked, with what he meant to be a teasing tone.

"Yes, I could. I could see that you didn't like Howie, either."

At this, Richard had to laugh. "But, my dear," he cried. "Not like—what's his name? Howie? Why shouldn't I?"

She didn't say anything. She had moved carefully away from him, but in the narrow space of the rumble seat it was impossible to be too distant, and her knee was still pressing against his.

"I like you," he said, after a moment.

Elinor just glanced at him. "Oh, Richard!" she said, but she said it impatiently. "I mean, don't just be silly!"

"What's so silly about that!" he demanded. He couldn't understand her, really, and as usual suspicions began to fly through his mind. Was she trying to tantalize him? Was she trying to make him jealous—and then laugh at him? He had a feeling that he was being drawn into a position that he never could tolerate, where a woman could lead him on, tantalize him, and then reject him—or what was worse, and what had happened before in his life, make fun of him.

Yet he still felt, obscurely, that he had to force the issue, and when she didn't speak he repeated the question. "I said, what's so silly about that?"

She had turned away to look at the fields at the side of the road. "About what?" she asked.

"About my liking you," Richard said, making every word sharp and clear, like a challenge.

This time, anyway, she looked at him, but what she said was so wildly unexpected that it startled him. "Richard, really," she said. "Don't you ever think of anything but yourself?"

"Well!" said Richard. He was so surprised that for a while he could only sputter, and she took advantage of that to turn conversational.

"My, it's misty, isn't it?" she said.

"Yes?" said Richard. They were nearing the turn-off onto the dune road that led down to the cottage by now. The ride was nearly at an end.

"Yes," she said. "Or hadn't you noticed? I suppose it's the moon, though, or something. Isn't the moon supposed to do things like that—make things misty, or something?"

He was looking at her, hardly listening, and he could feel anger and frustration rising inside him. She was taunting him, he knew, maliciously and unfairly; she was acting like Louisa instead of herself, and yet he still had to force the issue. "Look," he said. "I should still like to know what it is that's so silly about my liking you."

And of course, it was just what she'd wanted. "Nothing, darling," she said. The smile she turned on him was taunting, too. "Only it doesn't seem to get us anywhere much, does it? Or does it?"

They needed holding together, the Hacketts; that was the truth of it. Richard saw it most clearly when he was alone, riding back into town on the night train from Port Jefferson, or at night in his studio, or—most clearly of all—one long tangled evening when he had stayed home at the cottage, and the others had gone off to visit the Cases, or maybe it had been the Simmonses.

That, indeed, was a fearful night. Richard had had his ups and downs, as the doctors, a long time before—or what seemed to be a long time now—had told him he would. He had had an up period back there in the spring, when he had found the cottage, and a down in the rooming house soon after, and then an up that, in spite of incidents, had lasted thus far through the summer.

He had begun to have a feeling that at last he had mastered himself, or that rather—since such things were always confused—the world around him had at last come under his mastery, and he guided it and controlled it; and his confidence had risen in consequence.

Jennie Carmody herself, for instance, one day in the bookshop (and he, feeling the three folded dollar bills from the till nestling safe in his pocket, even as she spoke)—Jennie Carmody had said one day, in that brisk, burred, half matter-of-fact, half affectionate way she had, "Y'know, Richard, ye're really a rascal, and I could put all the conscience you've got under the nail of my little finger, and not feel it.

"But by Golly, it does become you. Here you come strolling in, of a Tuesday, mind you, and with not even a word of excuse or regret for it, and yet you looking as contented as the cat that swallowed the canary. And mind you, too, I'm not going to put up with it forever, either, but right now it interests me. Are ye engaged to be married to the girl, and is she an heiress, or some such?"

"Ah, no, Jennie," he'd said. He'd been standing at the window, watching the hurrying, oblivious passers-by, passing alternately between the bright strips of sun and the long morning shadows and fingering the three folded dollars, and thinking. "What's this talk about girls?" he had said. He wasn't stealing the money, really. He would pay it all back later, of course. But this way of taking it somehow added to the gaiety and adventurousness of things. And the whole world, just now, seemed to be brimming with gaiety and adventure. "Don't you know you're the girl I mean to marry?"

"You?" she'd cried. "Marry you? It's a wonder I don't fire you. It's a real wonder. Now get back there and unpack that parcel from Doubleday. Now you're here I mean to see at least if I can't get some work out of you."

But she hadn't said it angrily, and he had bowed with a mock air of obsequiousness. "Yes, Miss Carmody. At your service," he had said, and made a great show of scurrying back to the stockroom. And (fingering the three folded bills) he had been thinking: if there was anything wrong in the way things were going for him, he just didn't know it. It was as if everything in the world partook of him, and he of it; every detail flowed through him and was controlled by him; everything.

But that was one mood, and there were others. And the doctors had told him, and it was the one thing they'd told him that he could never be quite prepared for, that the change could come suddenly; he could never be ready for the suddenness of the change.

Like that night at the cottage, for instance, when he had waved them all off on their way quite urbanely; how could he have been prepared then for what was to follow? Until then, it had been a really rather gay evening.

There was a young man named Massie up, Frank Massie, a radio actor and a really quite decent fellow. When Louisa had suggested running over to Leary's after dinner—"to show him what Port Jeff's water-front life is like"—he had shaken his head and turned to the others with a look of mock resignation that was really comic.

"Oh-oh, here it comes again," he had said. "I told Louisa about a couple of sailors' bars I used to go to down on South Street. And ever since then she thinks that's just about my main interest in life—hanging around water-front dives and talking to the characters. I don't say it's not fun, though. Where is this place?"

They had all laughed at that; they all laughed a good deal more than usual, that evening, and Richard himself had had a kind of little triumph of his own, at dinner. It wasn't anything he'd said, though it was, in a way—on the porch, in the pale, lovely summer twilight, with the darkness slowly settling over the dunes and the whites everywhere (of the tablecloth, and the napkins, the picket fence and the circular sidewalls on Massie's convertible's tires, parked outside on the road: the whites every-where) standing out in a last vague, valiant insistence, against the imperturbable nightfall—it wasn't anything he had said, except as it was mixed up with what everyone else had said, and with the general atmosphere: the way the knives and forks rose and fell, and the heads turned, this way and that, and the voices, as if in rhythm. And yes, it was something he had said.

He had said, it was in answer to something Florence had said, and then Massie, and then Louisa; they were still talking about Leary's. "It's a dive, all right," he had said. "And when you dive in there, you go deep."

They had all laughed, and he had had a moment of uncer-tainty, looking at the four laughing faces turned suddenly toward him. What had he said? Were they laughing at him? Then, as his pun caught up with him, and he realized they were laughing at that, not at him, he had a moment of real elation. But he decided to pass it off carelessly.

"I mean—well, really. Well, I mean, you'll see. Bring your diving suit along," he said to Massie; and then they'd gone on to speculate what it would look like, and what would happen, if somebody did come tramping in to Leary's some night, in a diver's outfit.

"He couldn't dance very well," Louisa said, and Richard, in a burst of friendliness and frankness, replied, "Well, *I* can't, even in ordinary clothes," and they all laughed again, even more, at that.

And then the talk, and the laughter, passed on to embrace other subjects; the knives cut, and the forks rose, still in rhythm.

"I don't know what we'll *do* if we have to give up the apartment," Florence said. Beyond the screened porch the dunes and their interweaving, wavering outlines, were becoming hazier, darker; inside and outside, the whites were becoming gray. Richard still felt, in an odd way, triumphant, when a half or three-quarters of an hour later, he waved them good-bye from the porch. "I really have to work," he had said.

He did the dishes (because Florence had told him not to; it was the last thing she had called from the car, and so, naturally), and he put out the lights in the cottage—first, the lights in the kitchen (blotting out the stacked, drying dishes on the drain board he had built beside the sink), and then in the hall (where a tan canvas-covered tennis racket belonging to someone, resting improbably against the lowest stair); then the living room (where the chairs, where they all had sat, when they'd had their drinks after swimming, and on a curved-legged, rickety walnut table that he'd always been intending to fix, a still-lipstick-stained highball glass, where perhaps Elinor—or had it been Louisa?)

From the porch, as he came out, with the dark house behind him, the dunes stretched away, dim, increasingly dim, one gray cut-out in front of a darker one, and a still darker one behind that—and so on to the last sharp line that formed the horizon. (And beyond that horizon the sea, still not seen, but heard, always heard: the sounding gulf between the dunes' edge (near) and the sky's rim (far), and the sea's sinkly swelling welling up, filling it.)

He had a feeling of immensity, standing there, and of the loneliness of immensity. As he watched, the scene compacted, as if the night were a ring that grew nearer and nearer around him. The farthest dunes disappeared, swallowed up in the darkness of the sky, and then the next, and the next. And it grew quieter, darker, lonelier. . . . Night was closing in. The car had long ago muttered away.

"The sea's wave and the wind's wave, meeting."

(It was a poem he had worked on before, and now of all nights tonight seemed to be the night to work on it again.)

"And the clouds waving gulls' wings, greeting.
And the point that drives down, and down.
Shall we drive the stake here? Or there? In the country, or in the town?

"Shall we drive it, or shall we forsake it?
Let the wind and the wild wave take it?
But the wood, and the blood on the wood,
The bloody wood—"

He was sitting at his desk in his studio, working, and at this point he ran into difficulties. And as usual—it was the reason he could never finish his poems—it was because he had too many images crowding in his mind at once. What he wanted to convey was a feeling of wind and waves, and old, salt-caked, wave-washed pilings that the water had lashed at and gnawed at till the grain showed, spiraling down to the mud beneath the waves: the stake standing in spite of the waves and their action—and yet blood that had stained the wood, and, despite the sea's washing, still reddened the sea. The stake standing in mud, wet-bloodstained, and still reaching for the clouds.

"The bloody wood, and the red-stained waves . . ."

But no rhyme appeared. *Would, should, hood,* he thought: *The bloody wood, and its cloud-hood something* . . . Maybe. If he changed things around a little.

But that didn't quite get in everything, either: the red blood on the waves, for instance, and the way the redness ran out everywhere, raveling through the greenness. And there was birth in it, too, or dawn, the quality of beginning. He was sitting at the plain little kitchen table that he used as a desk in his studio, with the lights full on about him. He was really a poet, and the poem he was writing was one he had started some weeks before, after walking on the beach with Louisa—they'd been gathering mussels for a chowder, he remembered, and for some reason Elinor hadn't gone along—and Louisa, for once, had been so pleasant, so friendly, so uplifting, sort of, that he had started the poem soon after.

But he had written seven lines and then stopped, and it had changed as he'd gone along. And now again he was stopped, and the trouble was, again, that he saw too clearly what he wanted: the salt-tasting waves, and the thin strings of blood (like the strings that they weave around a Maypole, he thought suddenly, or still more like a woman's hair: *The woman's hair, and the something, the blood . . . ?*) and the strong stake rising, piercing, from the mud to the awakening clouds. . . .

And the words just weren't there!

"Ah, poetry!" he said suddenly, aloud, and he got up and walked swiftly from the desk to the door and back again. When he got back he didn't sit down immediately. He stood leaning against his chair, looking down at the pad he had been writing on, smiling, musing. Outside, it was very still.

"Ah, poetry!" he said again, this time trying to say it with love and respect and tenderness, and at the same time with amused self-pity for having so hard a mistress—as some day he might want to say it to Massie, or Chub Bassett, or someone—and then, just as he was easing himself down into the chair again, "And then they all go off to Leary's," he added.

He got up from the chair again instantly. It was almost as if he had been commanded to rise, as if the very harshness of the accusation demanded it. For it *was* harsh. He saw that clearly now, though until the moment of speaking he had been thinking of them tenderly, too, and of their action in leaving him as merely a foible. But it was harsh, harsh, *harsh*—and the worst thing was, it was true.

"Florence! Florence!" he said, but not tenderly now, but accusingly, and for an instant a picture of them all in the car, driving off into the night, glimmered in his mind, with Florence queening and preening herself in the seat beside the driver. For it was Florence he blamed, and after her, Louisa—but he was by now a prey to too many conflicting emotions to sort any of them out perfectly. The present one was not the only accusation; it was as if things had been piling, piling up inside him for weeks and weeks without his noticing it, and *now*, now that the dam had burst, thoughts shot through his mind in a mixed-up rush, incoherently, like logs hurtling and crashing destructively down a speed-swollen, foam-fat spillway.

What a fool! What a fool! he thought, thinking bitterly of himself and his innocence. *At the Simmonses, all those people. Always staring and whispering.* He was standing, still holding his pencil and looking down at the scattered papers lying on the table before him; the papers seemed to float and flutter in the violence of his emotion.

"They won't stare much longer," he said, and with a sudden gesture he broke the pencil in two and flung the pieces down on the table. *And laughing—even on the beach,* he thought, his mind glinting simultaneously on the moment a few minutes ago at dinner and another a week ago, almost identical, when he had said something and they had laughed, and he hadn't been sure— and now he wasn't sure about either time—whether they had been laughing with him or at him.

"You won't be laughing much longer," he said, this time to Louisa, and this time not caring where the thought might lead to, for the *snap* of the breaking pencil was still lingering excitingly, lightingly in his mind, and for the moment he *didn't* care, really, he was ready for anything.

But it led nowhere, really, for at the instant of thinking that, he had another thought too, *I'm alone, anyway*—thought gratefully; like a drunkard, foreseeing a solitary carouse, he knew by now that he'd need the safety of solitude that night; he'd need time, and silence—and then instantly other thoughts came crowding, so fast that they overlapped each other, as if thought-leaf were laid on thought-leaf, and he could look through the one to the other and beyond that, but glancingly (like through trees, and the leaves on the branches closing and parting), getting glimpses of other moments and other incidents, of the evils, the hurts, the mockeries. . . . *To what end?* he thought.

"Bitchy, witchy Louisa!" he said.

But it wasn't the hurts he minded so much as the humiliation, and not that either so much as the evil behind it. For that, it was Florence he blamed, at bottom, and only after her Louisa; Florence sitting, smiling complaisantly, on the beach, in the car, in the bar, but always on that fat, soft bottom, while Louisa, grinning, sinning . . .

And poor Elinor! It was a chain they made, with Elinor at the end of it, dangling helplessly. . . . "No!" he said. "No! No! No!

No!" They could not degrade poor, pure Elinor; they must not. That was the one thing he would not permit. "I draw this line, and beyond it ye shall not pass," he said, and (he had been striding about the room) he stopped in a dramatic, defiant gesture.

"I forbid!" And yet could he forbid? When they were working, always, against him? "Oh! Impossible! Impossible!" And then the helplessness of it all, and the pity of it, too, came over him. There was one way, yes . . .

"Yet they meant no harm," he said slowly, sadly. He was getting over his own hurts now; he was becoming more godlike, more selfless, and hence, inevitably, more just. A whole tragedy had been enacted in the moment that he had stood there, and he let his pose melt into one of sorrowing wisdom. And sweet Elinor, innocent Elinor . . .

"They were themselves, as we are *our*selves," he added solemnly. A dozen tragedies, really. A car had overturned; a wave had swept in, and swept out again. In a dozen ways they were dead now, Florence and Louisa, and it was oddly easing to think of them so. "And the fate that was meted out to them . . ."

And yet, somehow, he recoiled. ("Trees," he said, with a sudden vast longing for something—trees, greenery, peacefulness and shade, restfulness; a hiding place. He had been thinking of trees somewhere sometime before, but time and place were getting mixed, a little. But if there were trees you could hide behind the trunks, and watch. He was still worried, a little.) He had been outside momentarily, staring at the lightless cottage, and now he was back in the studio again, looking down at the table. (And he was tired; and there were two bits of broken pencil. Were they a symbol?) And the table had become the world, with all its sins and its evils spread upon it, and he tall and straight and just, above it. . . .

He must think about death. "There's no evil in the world that cannot be cured," he said, and the words came slowly and ponderously, dropping heavily upon the scene below as if his voice had been a voice from heaven, pronouncing judgment. Suddenly he laughed, and gave the chair a wrench as he turned away that sent it spinning across the floor.

He watched it. There were another chair, a table, a commode, some pictures, a cot with its bedclothes, made carefully. "I could wreck you," he said, speaking softly and distinctly, viciously. And then suddenly, "Blame? Blame? Who's to blame?" There had been a time when his thoughts had been wandering, but they had centered now. He was thinking clearly and cleverly now. (And he still had to think about death.)

"Blame?" he cried. He was speaking to the door now, and loudly, and the door—open; who had opened it?—looked as if it might devour him. "Blame makes blame, don't you know that? You went off and left me, didn't you?

"So if something should happen tonight, if I do anything, darlings, *anything*—you're to blame."

But he didn't. He kept control. But it was a fierce night, really; there were times when the lights seemed to go on and off, or his mind did, and the dunes would be lit and then dark, and his body would move without his knowing it; he would be on the porch, and then back in the studio, and then in the cottage, without his knowing, or caring, how he had gotten there. And death . . . For the most part he moved silently. But there was once when he yelled, but that was once when he thought that someone might be watching: "Hi-yoo!" he yelled, "HI-YOO! ANYBODY!" But the fact was that there was nobody; only silence. . . .

The fact was that he *was* silence. He was standing on the cottage porch at the time, and the long table at which they ate was beside him, and there were a couple of glasses still on it. . . . And like a scream (and he screamed: and) like silence: before he knew it he had picked up a glass and smashed it on the floor.

There were times when it was almost like drunkenness: the way the world seemed to move around him, and not he: he, immovable. . . . The way, the way the porch engulfed him, and then shunted him, blunted-eyed, into the (brown-walled, the) living room, and then on into the long-lost, the dark-smelling dining room beyond, that no one used except Florence, who used it (perhaps?) as a study.

"Lights!" he called, and the lights went on. And then, "Florence! Florence!"

But there was no Florence; and of course it was all make-believe. Or was she upstairs, waiting, watching? Instead, he found himself in the kitchen, where the one thing that caught his eye was the mounded-up pile of dishes that he had washed, and they glittering in the light like a nest of diamonds.

He smashed a plate, experimentally, and it flashed and settled like a school of flying fish in the aquarium of the sink; coming back (he was giggling), he snatched up a pencil from the hall-stand and drew a long, strong line along the hall-wall, the height of his hips. "Here passed Richard Baurie," he said.

But he kept control. But it was a fierce night, really. Toward the end it became oddly fragmentary, so that he had difficulty (really tiring difficulty) holding it together, and afterward there were large gaps in what he could remember.

. . . He was pacing up and down the road outside the cottage (and he must, must, must keep control; this wasn't Kansas City). "You'll cry, will you?" he demanded suddenly, of the open-mouthed, staring picket fence. "Then cry!" And he snatched up a stick and beat it, beat it, beat the white-toothed wood of the fence till it moaned and groaned, like a woman.

He was sitting on the bed, in his room in the shed, in his moody old studio, in the darkness, and suddenly there came before his eyes a vision of a bottle, with the legend "Rectified Spirits" printed somewhere on it. It was like a vision, there was such precision; and he got up and, fumbling, stumbling, mumbling (did he go back into the cottage? to the kitchen? to the upstairs bathroom? And, stumbling (and not really mumbling; it was just that it rhymed) and) anyway, he couldn't find it. . . .

He was walking down the steps of the porch, one step, two steps, three steps, four—and at the fourth step, there was the earth, the dune-sand, gritty, shifty, but receptive. He reached down and patted it; it was there, where he wanted it. . . .

"We must start with the earth," he said solemnly. "The great rectifier. . . ."

He was standing in the door of the wed-bed the shed (and so tired, so tired) when he saw the first glimpse of the glow of the headlights of the car, coming over the dunes. And the lights of his room were lighted! He put them out, and then ran to the door again to look over at the cottage.

There was a light on there somewhere too, and—the car's lights were coming nearer now—in a sort of panic he ran over and up the steps and, the screen door banging loudly, loud as a shot in the silence, and then down through the hall: it was a light that was the light that was in Florence's study that was on. He put that out and ran out, and back, and looked back to make sure, and made sure, sure, sure: things were dark now, every-where, and it was only just in time: the car's lights were shining plainly now, he could hear the motor-mutter. . . .

He was crouching in the darkness of his room beside the window when the car pulled up in front of the cottage. Flor-ence got out first, and then Elinor and Louisa, and then finally Massie, and they apparently had seen something.

"It was probably a lighthouse, Mother," Louisa was saying. "God! Why am I so tired?"

Richard had peeked once, and then he hadn't dared look again. He had heard the car door shut, but no sound of footsteps afterward. They were apparently still standing there, looking things over.

"But, my dear, what lighthouse? The only lighthouse I know is away over there, by Port Jefferson," Florence demanded, a little peevishly. "You, darling, you only come down here week-ends, or when the spirit moves you. But I'm here all the time, and I flatter myself that by now I can tell the lights of a light-house from my own cottage."

"Oh." Louisa was being peaceable. "Well, then, I don't know. About all I can think of is bed, right now. Or maybe it was the lights on the Connecticut shore; you know how bright they look sometimes. Anyway, the house is dark now."

"But I *tell* you . . ."

"But, Mother, I can't believe . . ."

"Richard! *Richard!*" It was Mrs. Hackett, and her voice came so loud and compellingly that in spite of himself Richard was startled. But he made no move.

"Listen, Mother! Now, really! Are you getting the jitters or

something? Suppose Richard's asleep!" Louisa cried, and then
Massie's heavier voice cut in suddenly.

"Or you know, the thing I was thinking," he said. "You know,
sometimes, the way a car's headlights will catch on a window,
and reflect from it? I was wondering if that mightn't be what had
happened here. Because, really, you know, Mrs. Hackett—"

And then Florence: "I know." And more graciously, now that
a man was involved. "I suppose, after all, you may be right. I
suppose I was just being womanish, really."

"Oh, no, no, not that. I know how upsetting these things can
be, and one can't be too careful about them, either. If you want
me to go in first and look around—"

"Oh, that won't be necessary, really. Please don't make me
seem sillier than I am."

And then the scramble of footsteps going up the path to the
porch and the screen door banging.... Richard waited, and
watched, and waited, while the lights went on, downstairs first
and then upstairs, and then off downstairs and off upstairs, and
(at last) the cottage was dark against the paler darkness of the
dunes and he could sleep.

7

There was something like consternation among the Hacketts
the following morning, particularly on the part of Florence, and
the situation was made a little more difficult because of the presence of a guest. It was some time, though, before the full extent
of what had happened was discovered.

Florence came down first, as she usually did; like most elderly
people, she slept less than she had in her earlier years, and she
had built up an elaborate little self-indulgent ritual about it. Like
all really good things, she used to say, morning coffee was best
enjoyed alone, and that long, lazy, comfortable half-hour or so
she spent over it was, according to her, the best part of the day.

"I come down, and I brew my coffee. And I'm in my coziest,
oldest bathrobe and I speak to no one, not God himself or even
the King of England, if he should happen to turn up unexpect-

edly," she would say. "And it's wonderful! For that first half-hour or so I'm like the immortal Greta. 'I vant to be alo-o-one.'" And the too-early-rising guest or visitor, finding her reading and sipping, curled up in her armchair, with her face only partly made up and her bathrobe tucked around her, was likely to be made to feel, for an awkward moment or two, that he was definitely *not* the King of England—before she unbent and, so to speak, admitted him into her company.

"Please just wander about and help yourself," she might say, on such occasions, "and forgive me if I'm not much assistance. I haven't really waked up yet, you know. You'll find coffee in the pot, freshly made, and eggs and bacon in the icebox. And—oh, yes—bread already sliced, all ready for the toaster, on the kitchen table." She would smile a bright smile. "Do you think you can manage?" she'd say—and then, like as not, after the young man had stumbled out to the kitchen, properly chastened, she would come bustling out there to help him a few minutes later.

"I could tell you're the helpless type, just from the way things sounded, out here," she would say. "You are, aren't you? But then, I suppose all men are, really. Eggs? Bacon?"

And then, if the young man protested—"Yes, I know," she would say, as determinedly hospitable as she had been unwelcoming at the start. "But at the seashore you really need a hearty breakfast. Not to mention the fact that it'll probably be hours before we get around to having lunch."

She would fry him the eggs and bacon, and make toast, and arrange the whole thing on a tray. "I suggest we bring it all out on the porch, don't you think? It's so pleasant there in the morning. I'll join you, and I promise you I'll be cheerfuller from now on."

This time, though, it was Richard who first appeared. He found Florence in the kitchen, just pouring her first cup of coffee, and since it was only he she didn't bother to pull her bathrobe over the **V** of nightgown that was showing at her neck. She merely waved one hand toward the broken china in the sink.

"Richard, darling," she said faintly. She always spoke in a slightly exhausted tone in the morning. "When you *do* wash the dishes . . ."

Richard stared at the sink. He was a little in the mood of a man who has been drunk the night before and feels likely to be blamed for anything; at the moment he had no clear recollection of having broken the plate. "Did I do that?" he said.

"Who else could have?" demanded Florence impatiently, and having filled her cup she walked out to the porch. Richard stayed behind for a while, looking silently at the racked dishes on the drain board and the debris of the broken one, and then around at the rest of the kitchen.

Things were coming back to him now; darkness, lights, and the feeling, rather than the sound, of shouting, and in the kitchen (he *had* been in the kitchen) a sort of sudden, twinkling shower like an explosion of diamonds. Had that been the plate, breaking?

He was like a drunkard, expecting to be blamed for everything, but he was different, too, for he had none of the drunkard's feeling of guilt. He felt really that he was *not* to blame; it was the others who were, and in that sense the night before had been almost a revelation. It had been, and it was likely again to be so: even as he stood there, uncertainties and suspicions, even hates, that had been flaming in his mind then— and had died since—now were coming to life again, twinkling like the smashed plate, glittering, ready to grow. But he had to go carefully. . . .

He poured his own cup of coffee and followed Florence, a few moments later, out to the porch—to find her standing motionless, still with her cup in her hand, looking down at the spatter of smashed glass by the table. When he came out she glanced at him a little strangely, and his heart gave a leap of mingled excitement, defiance, and apprehension. He did remember breaking that one (hadn't it been in a moment of challenge, of something?) and he stood simply looking at her, waiting for what was to come.

(And he was ready, ready. . . .)

But she only nodded him closer to her, conspiratorially, and then went over to the porch settee and sat down. He followed. She leaned tensely toward him.

"Richard, tell me," she said. "Did you see anyone around here last night? I mean, while we were gone—do you think anyone could have been in the cottage?"

But he was a great deal saner and sharper mentally than a drunkard would have been, too. Richard, later, was to remember with satisfaction how quickly and clearly his thinking went in the few seconds that followed; it showed him, really, that he could handle anything.

"Did I *see* anyone?" he repeated, as if puzzled. But—and staring almost stupidly at her—all the while he was thinking rapidly. Suppose he said that he had, would that frighten her? Would it change her feeling about the cottage, or upset something in their relationship? Or suppose he said that he hadn't, and it turned out that someone else had noticed something, the lights on, or him moving about, or yelling . . . someone passing on the beach below, perhaps, or on the dunes a long way away; someone he hadn't seen, even, but who might have seen him. What would happen then?

"You mean while you were away?" he said.

"Yes, of course. You'd have noticed if the lights had been on, wouldn't you? Or if there had been anybody about?"

Richard pondered for a moment. "Well, I was working, of course. And you know how I am when I'm working." He had decided the best thing to do was to confuse things as much as possible. "But I can't help feeling . . ." Then he looked at her suddenly, frankly and innocently. "But why, Florence? Why are you asking?"

"Because, this—" And she broke off to point dramatically at the broken glass. "You didn't do that too, did you?"

It was only then that he permitted himself to look at it. "Why, of course not, Florence!" he cried roundly. "I couldn't have! All I did was wash the dishes in the kitchen. And then, well, I went straight to the studio and started working, working on a poem. And then later I took a walk, and sort of idled around for a while, and—but this! Are you sure one of you didn't do it? I mean later, after you came in last night? Or do you think the wind could have blown it?"

"We didn't. We went straight up to bed. But there was a strange thing, Richard." And then the whole story came out, about the mystery of the lights being on in the cottage when they were driving down the lane (for she was sure now they had been on, though the others had tried to convince her they hadn't), and the way they went off just as they came nearer, leaving the cottage all dark (now, it seemed, suspiciously so) when they got there. "You would certainly have heard, wouldn't you, Richard? If there'd been anyone here?"

He affected to be judicial. "Well, I certainly think I would. But I did turn in early, and you know how I am when I sleep. Even so, though, I can't believe there was anyone—except possibly some kids, and even then ... Don't you think it might have been the wind, or something? That broke this glass, I mean? Or we might even have dropped it last night, when we were clearing off the table. Only then we'd have noticed it, wouldn't we?"

Richard looked at her blankly, as if to say, Well, here we are, and it seems to be a dead end, doesn't it? Then he got up and patted her shoulder.

"Don't worry, anyway, Florence," he said.

"Don't worry!" she repeated bitterly. "When all I have to do is to leave the house to have I don't know who-all running through it?"

It was a strange, troubled, upset day all round, and Richard realized in the course of it that Florence was far more worried and frightened by the occurrence than he had ever expected, though because of the presence of a guest she did her best to minimize it.

Frank Massie came down while they were still talking about it. He was in shorts and bathing sandals, with a striped jersey pull-over, and Florence made him wait on the threshold—"I'm *so* afraid you might get cut, you know"—while she sent Richard to the kitchen for the dustbrush and pan. Then, while Richard swept up the debris at their feet—like a servant, he couldn't help pointing out to himself—she told Massie about their discoveries.

Massie was amazed. "But it's incredible!" he kept exclaiming. "Away out here, just where you'd think you'd be safe from that sort of thing. And with Mr. Baurie, ah, Richard, here all the time, too. You didn't hear anything at all?" he demanded of Richard suddenly.

Richard shook his head silently. He wasn't going to be cross-examined, and by a stranger, too. Florence laughed. "Richard, Mr. Massie," she said, and her tone was a little acid, "has one of those things people call the artistic temperament. I'm quite sure, when the mood is on him, the house might fall literally about his ears, and he'd not hear it."

Richard grinned at her thinly, while Massie gave her a dutiful smile. "Oh," he said, and then: "Well. It is odd, though. I don't understand it." By that time the two girls had come down, and they all stood in a little cluster, staring at the spot where the broken glass had been, while they drank their coffee. "Did they do any other damage?" Massie asked.

"I don't know," Florence said. "I haven't looked—except, of course, where I've passed, on the way downstairs, and in the kitchen, and so on."

"Don't you think we ought to look?"

"I suppose so," Florence said. She had gotten up to walk about nervously and now she went over to the porch swing again and sat down. "I don't like to think about it. I keep thinking, suppose they'd still been here, whoever they were, when we got home last night."

"Mother, really!" Louisa protested. "If you're going to worry about that! When it was probably just some drunk who wandered in and out again. Or as Richard says, some kids."

"I suppose so," said Florence, uncomfortably. "I suppose I'm just being silly and womanish"—and she smiled briefly at Massie—"but I can't help it." Then, as if to prove she could still show gallantry under stress, she sat up a little straighter and looked brightly about at all of them.

"Well, we mustn't let all this spoil Mr. Massie's week-end with us, at any rate," she said. "Children, how would it be if I made some more coffee? Mr. Massie?"

"I think that would be fine," said Massie. "But don't you want to look?"

"Afterward," Florence said. She was being gracious now, and womanly, and when she had reached the doorway she stopped and looked back at him. "And I'd planned such a nice breakfast for you, too," she said ruefully. "Pancakes. Maple syrup. And now—well, will you forgive me?"

"Forgive you! Of course," cried Massie gallantly. "And all the easier because I probably couldn't have eaten all that, anyway. I'm one of those light-breakfast guys myself." When she had gone he turned to the others. "I still think we ought to look around," he said.

"Oh, we will," said Louisa. "I'm a little bit worried about the thing, too, though I wouldn't want Mother to know it." They were still talking about it when Florence returned.

"It's so odd, you know. You'd think, if it was kids, for example, they'd have made a racket," Massie was saying, and he turned to Richard. "Yet you didn't hear anything?" he said.

Richard looked at him. "You have asked me that question already, Mr. Massie," he said evenly.

"Yes, I know, but—"

"Do you doubt me?"

"No, of course not," said Massie hastily. "Why should I?" He glanced at Richard in some surprise. "It's just that—well, the whole thing is so funny, sort of. For one thing, you'd have thought they'd have seen your lights, if you had them on, and that would have scared them."

Richard took a deep breath and stared at him. ('Brassy Massie,' he'd decided he'd call him, for his interferingness.) "I can only assure you," he said, "that I saw and heard absolutely nothing."

It was later on in the day that Florence, going into her study, discovered the chairs up-ended. There were three of them that had been disturbed—a small, old-fashioned armchair that Florence had adopted, to use when sitting at her desk or when reading, and two straight-backed ones—and they had been placed in a rough sort of circle in the center of the room, so that, upside down as they were, they looked like three animals, awkwardly nuzzling each other in a ring.

It was something that Richard had no recollection of whatever, and though he knew in a way that he must have been responsible for it he was free of the feeling of direct, conscious guilt he had had on the porch and in the kitchen. He could look on the whole thing as an outsider would, and his first reaction was one of simple merriment.

"Oh, how funny!" he cried. "With their bottoms showing!" And he was seized with a queer fit of giggling that made the others look strangely at him for a moment.

Florence, though, was horrified by the occurrence.

"This—" she said, and it was funny to see how, under the shock, all the fullness drained out of her face, leaving it wrinkled and sagging and pasty-colored, with all the loose little dewlaps showing. "This—" she said, and at her almost breathless way of speaking Richard felt an odd surge of malice; I'd like to see you really frightened sometime, he was thinking. "This shows, really—it really *does* show that someone *must* have been here. Richard, *really*, didn't you notice anything, any lights, any sounds at all? Because, really, you know, people don't do things like this, just wantonly, without making some sort of noise; why, they must have been drunk, or crazy. I can't see how you failed to hear them."

"Florence, darling, I told you," said Richard tiredly, and then he stopped abruptly. "Now, wait, though," he interrupted himself. "There was one time there, around—oh, I guess it must have been ten o'clock—" And he stopped again, as if to make sure. It had struck him that this business of the chairs up-turned was *proof* that someone had been in the cottage, and if he insisted too definitely that no outsiders had been around—well, then, mightn't he find himself eventually with no one left to blame for it but himself?

It was a time to be very careful, and so he affected to consider. "What I was going to say," he went on, "there was once around ten o'clock, when I thought I heard something like someone going along the road outside. It was like kids, sort of running and giggling, and the first thing I thought was that it was a bunch of them, taking some short cut across the dunes."

"But didn't you look?" Florence demanded.

"No, I didn't, honestly, Florence. You see—it's hard to explain." He looked over at Elinor for understanding, but she merely gazed back at him. "I was working, you see, and I heard this noise—very slight, too, it was—and at first it seemed natural to me, for some kids to be passing that way. And then a few seconds later, it *did* seem a little odd. But then when I listened I didn't hear anything, and I thought probably I must have imagined it.

"I *did* look, a few minutes later," he added. "But of course, then, I didn't see anything."

Florence stared at him for a full second, then she took a deep breath. "You see?" she said. Then she turned to Richard. "Oh, you poets, writers, artists!" she cried, and underneath her air of raillery there was a considerable edge of annoyance. "I suppose if the cottage burned down you might look, too—a few minutes later."

"Florence, Florence," Richard said mildly. "You're not being fair, you know. And I still think it was a bunch of kids, if it was anybody. Doesn't this look like kids' work, really?" He waved a hand toward the up-ended chairs. "You didn't lose anything, did you?" he asked.

"No. I looked. But now I mean to look again, I can tell you." She stopped a moment and looked at Richard uncertainly. "I'm sorry if I've been bad-tempered with you about this, Richard," she continued. "But you *were* here all the time, after all, and—well, never mind. It's just that it's so upsetting to me, somehow, to think that someone could have been in here while I was gone, making free with my things. . . . I don't know if you can understand how I feel about it. It upsets me." And, surprisingly, she put out her hand and touched his, in a gesture almost of supplication.

Richard gave her hand a little comforting squeeze in return. "I know, Florence. I know," he said.

So, in the end, the whole thing blew over. Louisa, earlier in the day, had discovered the long pencil-streak, drawn along the wall in the hall. But that was one thing they couldn't be sure of; it seemed so senseless, really—so insane, almost—to believe that any marauder would have troubled to do just that, that they decided finally that some one of them must have done it, carelessly, one day, and forgotten it.

They couldn't even be sure that it was pencil; and one explanation (they had several, all equally acceptable) was that maybe, away back when they were moving into the cottage, some piece of furniture had rubbed against the wall and had somehow discolored it. Or perhaps some utensil, of pewter, or something; because pewter did make streaks that looked just like pencil-streaks—or didn't it? They didn't know for sure, and so, in the end, the whole thing blew over.

But it didn't quite disappear entirely. Like a cloud that had once hung overhead and then drifted away down the summer sky without ever discharging its thunders, it still remained on the horizon of their minds—only a slight shadow now, and far away, but still there, a darkness—and for some time thereafter they would recur to it.

"I still wonder who those kids could have been," one would say, and they might be just coming back from a shopping trip, or returning from the beach, and getting the first glimpse of the cottage; and the sight of it, and the fact that they were returning to it after an absence, would remind them.

"If it was kids, of course."

"Oh, Florence! It must have been!" Richard rarely entered into these discussions, and when he did it was with a slight air of annoyance, as if the whole thing should have been forgotten long ago. "Who else could it have been, after all?"

"Richard's right. It was probably just a gang of those young roughnecks you see around Port Jeff, out hell-raising."

"Yes, I know. But still—"

"And they might just as easily have picked on some other cottage instead of ours, you know. It's really nothing to worry about, Florence."

"They're probably scared to death right now, over what they've done."

"I suppose. But you know, I still wonder about it. You know yourselves, no one ever comes down this road—"

"Which is just why they did come, probably, silly Florence."

They discussed it in puzzlement at first, and then resignedly ("Oh, well, anyway," one might say, "there's one good thing. There wasn't anything stolen")—and then at last (and the cloud was far down on the horizon now) it became merely a landmark in time, a date-identifier. "That was the same week the cottage was broken into," someone might say, or the week-end before, or the Thursday after. And by that time, or very soon afterward, the Hacketts had other things to worry about.

Meantime, it was Elinor who came closest to the real solution, but she met with such disbelief that she immediately disavowed it. She was sitting with Florence one evening on the porch a day or two after the incident, and both Louisa and Richard had gone in to the city; the two women were alone and Florence, though she tried to conceal it, was still a little nervous.

"Did it ever occur to you that Richard might have done it?" Elinor said suddenly, and then when she saw the surprise on her mother's face she added hastily, "I mean just as a joke, of course, a sort of trick to scare us. You know, he was alone here, and so on," she went on. "And he may have been annoyed, a little, because we went off and left him. . . . And then, well, when he found out how frightened you really were, he was probably afraid to admit it."

It was such a new idea to Florence that she had difficulty in grasping it. "I, frightened?" she said first. "I should like to know who wouldn't be. Except I wasn't so much frightened as—"

In the midst of her sentence, the meaning of what she had heard caught up with her, and she narrowed her brows and stared at her daughter almost angrily. "Richard? Richard?" she exclaimed. "Are you trying to tell me you think Richard might have done it?"

"As a joke, Mother, only as a joke," said Elinor, but she could see already that there was no use insisting. "Anyway, it was just an idea I had."

"A fine joke that would be!" cried Florence. "And whatever would be the point of it? What made you think of such a thing, anyway?"

As a matter of fact, Elinor would have had difficulty putting into words just why she thought as she did, and yet she was sure, in a way, that she was right. But there was no use insisting now. "I don't know. I just thought," she said. "I can't see that it would be so bad, if he'd done it as a joke."

"Well, I can, even if you can't, my dear. And I'm quite sure that Richard could, too," said Florence; and she added, a little irrelevantly, "Don't you know he's the only protection we've got?"

"I know, Mother, I know," Elinor said. "It was just an idea I had."

But Florence merely stared at her, silently disapproving. ("My Lord, she thinks she owns him," Elinor was thinking.) "I thought you *liked* Richard," Florence said finally.

"Jennie, tell me," said Richard, one morning a day or two later in the bookshop. "What sort of a bottle would you find 'Rectified Spirits' on?"

He had found himself sitting up, stark awake, in his room in the rooming house the night before; it had been three, three-thirty in the morning, and the dream he had been dreaming was still so much in possession of his mind that it was at least a minute—a long, puzzling, disturbing minute, too, in the hot, crowding, heaving darkness—before he could pull himself out of the dream and back to reality.

For it had been a bad dream, a dream that troubled him. He had been walking outside on the dunes in the darkness, late at night, watching the sleeping cottage, and then abruptly it had been sleeping no longer; it was blazing with light from every window, and there was something so strange, so ominous even, about this burst of nocturnal illumination that he had run to the door and looked in.

He had run quietly, for there was a suggestion of evil in the atmosphere, and there was evil inside the house, too, although the scene that he came upon was one that he had often seen in reality, that summer—just the three women sitting together in Florence's study, Florence sewing on something and Louisa and Elinor reading. But it was wrong for them to be sitting like that so late at night, and the whole thing had an air of artificiality about it, as if they had merely posed themselves there in that fashion to conceal some other, secret purpose; and sure enough, as he looked, Louisa reached out and touched Elinor's hand while Florence touched the other, and as if that had been a signal the three of them got up and, smiling strangely, began a sort of slow, weaving dance.

"Elinor!" he had cried, and stamped his foot. "Elinor!" And from then on the dream became fragmentary: a confused chase in and out of rooms that were and were not the rooms of the cottage, with the figures of the women always twinkling before him—and then the house had vanished and the women with it, and he was out on the dunes again, still running, but this time running *from* something and not toward it, and yet with a vast feeling of triumph. . . . The dream had ended inconclusively, and it hadn't been until morning, when he was walking up to the bookshop, that he remembered the bottle and the label on it, and then (Richard always had more difficulty than most in dissociating his dreams from reality) he could no longer be sure if he had seen it in the dream, or elsewhere—in the kitchen, maybe, that night when he had been alone at the cottage? All he knew was that it was somehow important.

Jennie's voice brought him back to his surroundings. "You mean 'in,' don't you, Richard?" she was saying.

"In what?"

Jennie glanced at him. She was checking off some lending-library returns against their cards while Richard was restacking the books on their shelves. "In the bottle, of course. You were asking—"

"Oh, yes. No, I mean 'on.' You know, on the label, like a little line of fine type, saying 'Rectified Spirits.' Could it be something you'd see in a kitchen, perhaps, like spirits of ammonia, or something? All I know is, I've seen it somewhere."

Jennie looked at him again and laughed. "You *are* an innocent, aren't you, Richard?" she said. "But you'd never find spirits of ammonia in a kitchen, I can tell you that much, my lad. Don't you know what it is? It's a sort of aromatic solution the ladies would use, the old-fashioned ones, to revive them if they felt a bit faint, you know. It's in the bathroom you'd find that, or on the dressing table, if you were to find it anywhere at all nowadays."

"Oh," said Richard. Had he been in the bathroom that night, or in Florence's or Louisa's bedroom? Or Elinor's? Or had the bottle, after all, been just something connected with his dream. "Anyway, would it have 'Rectified Spirits' on it?"

"That I don't know, darling," said Jennie. "Did you want to know specially?"

"Oh, no. Not especially," Richard said quickly. "It was just something I wondered about." He took a book from Jennie's desk and slipped it into its place on the nonfiction shelf. "It's a funny name, anyway, isn't it, Jennie—'Rectified Spirits'?" he said, and then he added carefully, "Wouldn't it be wonderful if there was a bottle or something you could rectify human spirits with? Cure their evil, and make them—well, right, rectified, again?"

Jennie laughed. "I'm afraid the bottle is the last thing that'd be good for that, my lad."

"Oh, it wasn't just drinking that I was thinking of," Richard said vaguely. "It was just human weakness, and—well, I don't know. Tell me, Jennie, do you think evil *can* be cured?"

8

But the summer is a time of impermanence; nothing lasts, in the summer; all the rest of the year is the summer's destroyer. You make tracks in the sand, in summer; you may deepen by an inch or two the path from the house through the dunes, and from the dunes down to the beach. But when the summer is over the tracks disappear, smoothed away by the fall winds and rains and the snows of winter. All that's left in the spring, next year, is the ghost of a path, ill-defined and wavering, with the sands here and there drifted over it, and with, already, the new dune grasses taking root again and spreading to obliterate it entirely.

You do this and do that, in the summer. You mend the rusted parts of the screens on the porch with new porch screening. You paint the kitchen—because, after all, the kitchen is one place that should be neat and sanitary, especially in a rented cottage— and the job turns out to be a delightful one, with you and Elinor working together all through one evening in the cramped little room, she in an old woolen bathing suit that seems almost embarrassingly revealing in the harsh, white, hard-shadowed light of the single electric bulb, and the two of you working so close together that half the time you are touching, and yet with a nice sort of brother-and-sisterly feeling about it all: you two painting long after the others have gone to bed, with the moths banging hard against the screened windows in the stillness and the smell of the paint itself becoming a sort of intoxication, so that you laugh and act silly together, and when Florence drifts in rather casually in a dressing gown just as you've finished, you look dizzily, drunkenly at her and at each other. . . .

It had been an evening that Richard always remembered. But now, barely two months later, there was a tinge of sadness about it; in a way, it was already vanishing.

You do all sorts of things, in the summer. You put up clothes-line for Florence, stringing it out from a spike in the siding beside the kitchen door to an old pine post set precariously into the sand in the back yard beyond. You build a fireplace on the beach, and bring a flat slab of rock to set beside it for a table. You cut steps in the place where the path is steepest, leading down to it. You buy whitewash and touch up the walls of your study; and then, having some whitewash left over, you whitewash the pine post the clothes line is fastened to and the section of picket fence that borders the road. You put up hooks and hangers in the closets.

But the very spike to which you tie the new clothesline has a dangle of rotted and raveled line hanging from it, left there by the previous tenants, and you know that even as they did, so you will do; when summer's end comes you will pack up and leave just as they did; you will go away, and the clothesline will serve, parsimoniously, to tie up a few of the bundles.

A summer cottage is a fair-weather craft, and the abandon-ship order comes easily, when the first storms and gales of September begin their heavy pounding. There were times, that August, when Richard looked at the cottage and saw it already desolate, as he had seen it at first and as next year's comers would see it in their turn, the screens rusted and the paths over-grown, the whitewash cracked and streaked and scaling, and no sign, no sign anywhere, that he or anyone else had been there;

no permanence. And yet it had been his place, *his;* he had found it, he had discovered it. . . .

Richard did a number of odd things during that mid-August period. He began to prowl. "I used to watch over them," he said later. "They never knew how much I watched over them." And though he meant that his watchfulness was general—"I used to sit there sometimes, at table," he said again, "and they'd be talking and I'd be talking. And yet all the while I'd be studying them"—the main form that it actually took was a kind of nocturnal surveillance.

As if the dream he had had had been a guide—or as if it had been, of itself, a sort of crystallization of all the fears and suspicions that he had harbored almost unknowingly—he found himself setting up the kind of night watch the dream had suggested; and the women were hardly in bed, the lights out, the cottage quieted, before he would be up again, and out, prowling around on the silent dunes—crouching here, moving there and again crouching, and then moving on again, in a slow, furtive, doglike circuit of the cottage, staring up at the lightless, lifeless windows—dark at some times against the grayer darkness of the walls, gray themselves at others, and again as if shimmering with all the moon-and-cloud changes the sky itself held—staring, studying, waiting. . . . He would keep it up sometimes till almost dawn.

He began it as a kind of game, as a way of projecting his dream into reality—and, incidentally, to see what truths, in reality, the projection of the dream might uncover—but once begun he discovered that it satisfied deep, long-hidden, but extremely powerful impulses in his own nature.

Richard had always felt himself to be the locked-out one, the outsider, in his relations with the Hacketts. He was a member of the family and yet he wasn't one; he was a son and a brother and at the same time he was neither, and still less was he the "man of the house" that Florence sometimes, in her cajolery, called him. The way the women acted toward him only showed the carelessness in which they held him.

He saw them stripped on the beach, or almost stripped, in

their flimsy bathing suits—"in their nakedness," as he put it later—he saw them running, half-dressed, to the shower and back again, after the swim, or coming down, sleep-swollen, wrapped in bed warmth as in their bathrobes, to breakfast. Like a proctor or preceptor at a girls' camp or school, he was privy to all their intimacies, and yet, as with the proctor, the net result was to push him still further into anonymity. They made free with him because to their minds he wasn't there; he was a no-one, a nobody, and with Louisa at least, and to a certain extent Florence (Elinor, he excepted), he would not have been surprised if either of them had walked naked past him in the house, unconcernedly, as Louisa at least had done, on the few times when they had gone swimming without clothes, at night, on the beach.

The thing was, though, that they didn't, and the fact that they didn't only served to increase the feeling of being left out of something, something secret and suspicious, that he was beginning to have.

And yet, what could he do about it?

He was good, he was goodness himself, he knew that; he was an influence for good, or he could be if his goodness were to be accepted. But he knew too that when good meets evil it is frequently rejected, and he was beginning to feel now that there was a whole side of Florence's and Louisa's and even of Elinor's life that he was not admitted to: a life that went on amongst them when he wasn't there and that he only caught glimpses of occasionally, when he came upon them talking in a room in the cottage or on the beach and (it seemed to him now, suspiciously) stopping when he appeared; or—perhaps most of all—when the good-nights had been said and the downstairs lights put out, and he had gone back to his own studio, to watch in silence and darkness, alone, eager and fearful, while the lights in the bedrooms went on and then the light in the bathroom, and then the bathroom light and then the other lights would go off; and the cottage would be dark and (but what inner whisperings?) silent, and he, Richard, would still be kneeling by his window there, watching, waiting, studying. . . .

"Evil, evil," he said. "I knew all the time that there was evil there somewhere. I knew they needed me." It was then that he would go out and prowl.

"I knew I had to watch them. I knew there was some way they could be saved."

But the summer is a jerky time, too; it's uneven, uneasy—especially if, like Richard, you can spend only two or three days of the week in the sun, on the beach, in the ocean that you love—really *in* the summer, and enjoying it—and the rest of the time are condemned, like a prisoner to his cell, to a small, dusty, ugly, noisy, uncomfortable room on Third Avenue, with the El trains racketing past the window, and the heat coiling softly and silently, sluggish and persistent, inert; and instead of the space and freedom and airiness of the dunes, the sense that everywhere there are people, people listening, peering, prying. . . . There were times when he felt that the trials and tribulations that were being visited upon him were more even than saints should be asked to bear.

He accepted all that, however; it was part of the life Fate had chosen for him. He was being tried and tested for something, he knew; he knew too that in time, in God's own good time, the purpose of the test would be revealed . . . when he had at last achieved full identification, perhaps . . . when the goodness inside him had burned through to the surface everywhere, and become so goldenly manifest that all must perceive it; when his mere touch might burn, but would also cure, would purely rectify. Meantime, too, he knew, secrecy was imperative; silence; the unchanging, unyielding smile.

But it was hard, nevertheless, at times. "I would throw myself on the bed there sometimes, that hard, hot, aching bed, hard and friendless as any bed a saint ever lay on . . ." There were times, many times, indeed, when he almost welcomed the El: when the harsh, heavy roar of it, knifelike at first and then rising and swelling, was in itself a kind of surcease—a sound that voiced his own anguish and pain so truly, surely, purely, that he couldn't help mingling his own voice with it; it was as if sound was drawn from him, and as the train rushed up, roared past, vociferating, he would scream like the wheel-scream, hammer the furniture.... Afterward, when the sound had died, he would cock his eye toward the wall where he knew that, even now, old Mr. Whittaker had an ear pressed, listening. "Did you hear anything, old Mr. Nosy?" he would whisper. (The smile, still; secrecy.) "Did you learn something, maybe? Something of value?"

He had a near-row with Jennie, at about that time. He was getting more and more annoyed with the looseness and laxness he saw everywhere around him; he ran into it constantly—in the streets, in the subways, even in the lunchroom where he ate his breakfast—and though usually he merely smiled and passed on, invulnerable, there were times when more active measures were indicated. If that forced him sometimes to be "difficult," even "troublesome," as the other people might put it, he knew that was his right and his privilege, even his duty. ("Don't go making trouble here, now," the lunchroom counterman had said. "Take it easy." In the subway, they had merely stared.)

It was his duty to be strong, and to maintain his strength against the attacks of others; though he smiled now and then, and passed on, he knew how subtle and devious the attacks were, and how often, and with what devilish obliqueness, they were directed against him. "I knew what the score was, all the time," he said later. "But it wasn't easy to go against them. Not against all of them...."

The row with Jennie was really a minor matter, however, though it showed how subtle the attacks could be, and from what unexpected quarters they might come. Jennie wasn't a profane person, far from it; it was one of the reasons why he liked her. And yet he'd noticed that lately, and almost as if to taunt him deliberately, she had begun working more and more profane references into her talk. "Oh, my God!" she would say, or "God help us!" "God save us!" she'd say, if she happened to drop some papers or the phone rang suddenly, and though she never went beyond that into real obscenity it still irked him a little, and he knew too, vaguely, or he thought he knew, that it wasn't her fault; there was something else stirring, somewhere;

something deep, something aimed at him. All he knew was that it was something he would have to stamp out.

And so, one day, he turned on her.

"Oh, God *damn* it!" she'd said—about something, the heat, or the mess that the books, or her cards, or her files were in, or something—and there was something about her manner that told him now was the time for action.

"Who told you to say that?" he demanded.

But it was wonderful how quickly she, they, everyone, could cover up, when they wanted to. She glanced up at him as innocently as a child. "Say what, Richard?" she asked.

"That. That! Saying 'God' all the time. Do you think I don't notice it?" he said impatiently. And then when he saw the look of surprise on her face his heart almost failed him. If she was mocking him, really, and could still hold that expression on her face, then she was deeper than he'd thought she was, deeper than *he* was, really. And if there was someone or something behind her, then that someone was pretty deep too. It was a time to go carefully. "I'm not God, you know," he said gently.

"You? God?" she repeated, as if bewildered. "But, of course, Richard—"

"No. Not 'of course,' either," he interrupted her, but still gently. "Look, Jennie, if you want to be logical about it, if you want to be reasonable ... I've been around about as much as you, you know, maybe more. I know what the score is. . . ."

And then the sheer impossibility of communicating with her in the face of her stubbornness made him lose his temper. "But if it's me, if it's me that you're aiming at," he almost shouted. "Or if it isn't you that's doing it, but the others that tell you . . ." And he advanced on her, one step, two steps, three.

She retreated—one step, he noticed—and then stood stock-still, staring at him. "Richard! Richard!" she cried, as if desperately. "Whatever's got into you? Is it the heat, or something?" (It had been the heat she'd been speaking of first, he now remembered. "Oh, God *damn* it! This heat!" she had said.)

The main thing he remembered afterward was her face, filled less with fear than with a sort of anxious concern. (*I could frighten you, though, if I wanted to; I could really scare you,* he remembered thinking.) After that, it had degenerated into something close to an open quarrel—"All I'll ask you is not to say 'God' so much in my presence." "And this to me, in my own shop! Heat or no heat—" "Exactly, it isn't the weather we're talking about." "I know it's not. And I know I've stood about enough from you." "And I from you!"—it was that sort of thing; he could hardly keep from laughing about it afterward. In the end, of course, he had stamped out of the shop; indirectly, it was because of the quarrel that he happened to call on Chub Bassett.

He had stamped out of the shop; it was near his lunch hour, anyway. And he had lunched at a place that he knew on Lexington Avenue, and had chatted amiably with the waiter; the place itself was Italian, and the waiter, short, broad-faced, swarthy, obviously a Sicilian, had a kind of grumpy cheerfulness that he liked.

"Did you ever feel like shooting somebody?" Richard asked him once.

"Huh?" the waiter said, startled.

"You know—bang, bang. Shoot somebody."

"Nah," the waiter said, and then seeing Richard's smile, he grinned a little. "Only, sometimes, myself."

"That's the way I feel too, sometimes," said Richard, though he didn't feel that way at all. But it was fun, for the moment, to be agreeing with somebody.

Afterward, instead of going back to the shop, he walked. Summer, somehow, was always his walking time; it was as if the heat itself was an imperative, and the hotter the day the more furious the activity he was impelled to. "My God! Why do you *do* it, Richard?" Jennie would say to him sometimes, when he would come into the shop dripping, after some errand. "There are buses, you know. There's the subway."

But this summer, perhaps because of the sense of crisis rising within him, he seemed to walk more than ever—nights as well as days, and dull days as well as bright ones—and so, almost automatically, when he left the restaurant, and as much because of the pull of the streets as because of the argument, he turned up Lexington and away from the bookshop instead of down; he had gone only a block or two before all thought of Jennie and her problems passed out of his mind.

More than that, he was losing himself, losing that intense concentration on life and his position in it—and the fears and suspicions that went with it—which had been making him so nervous, so irritable and unpredictable of late. He knew that, knew his troublesomeness and the angers that flared in him. But he couldn't help it, and anyway it was the people around him who caused it; even the solidest rock must tremble a little, when the waves batter it.

Now, however, he was becoming calmer. It was as if every corner he turned broke a thread, and every street that he crossed broke another (and the cars and the buck-trucks streaming out, glass and steel and enamel all glittering, shieldlike; the cars, when the lights changed, crossing behind him, barring pursuit—and the people on the sidewalk, scissoring)—until at last every tie had been severed, and he was wandering totally anonymous, cut off from everything, even himself, in the constantly shifting, anonymous crowd.

He felt aloof and yet jaunty, firm and yet flexible; he was a *flâneur,* a young collegian, a big-game hunter; he was a scion of the idle rich, suave, contemptuous, strolling over to visit his bootmaker, he was a wealthy young rancher, flown in from Wyoming in his private plane to see the city, and dryly amused, in his Western fashion, by what he saw. He was anything he wanted to be, and he turned west on Fifty-first Street, passing an antique shop and then a tailor's, and then an old-fashioned tenement stoop where three children were gravely chalking diagrams on the worn brownstone steps; he was a soldier of fortune, famous in international circles, but unknown here— though even here his assured stride and steely fearless glance should have betrayed him. . . .

Going down the street, past another small shop with an array of costume jewelry carefully displayed in the window, Richard suddenly burst out laughing. "Dock God!" he cried cheerfully, and then, "Oh, Jennie!"—to the surprise of a white-haired old man in a spotlessly laundered seersucker suit who happened to be passing.

He had remembered an incident in their quarrel—at the close of it, really, just as he was about to slam the door—and the whole thing was far enough away now so that he could laugh about it quite frankly, like a joke on two other people. He had been going out the door, in a rage (but a rage that was still shrewdly held in check; only he knew how fiercer, how fuller, how thoroughly devastating his real rage could be), and there Jennie had been, standing staring at him, thwarted, frustrated, fuming.

"I'll dock you!" she'd cried, when she saw that he was going.

And he, beautifully, boldly, oh, beautifully ironically: "Dock God!"

And then slamming the door ... He still remembered the strange look, of fear, startlement, anger, and incomprehension, all blended, that she gave him as he went out the door.

Jennie was sweet, though, he thought; she was sweet. He wasn't worried about Jennie, even though this had been their most violent quarrel to date. Least of all was he worried about taking the afternoon off; in a way, in a way that he understood without really even thinking about it, that was the wisest thing he could do. For if he went back now, they would fight again, and with her temper up this time it might be a real one. While if he waited till morning ... in the morning she would be cold, hurt, querulous—and, finally, forgiving. ...

He wasn't worried about Jennie, and on the instant of thinking of her a vision of her face as it had looked when he had gone out the door came before his mind. Anger, startlement, and yes, just a trace of fear; there had been fear in the shine of her eyes and their wideness, and the way her cheeks stiffened, tightening her mouth at the corners.

Jennie had been scared, in addition to everything, and at the thought of it he felt again the queer, powerful, lifting buoyancy of his anger. Sweet anger, compelling and all-engulfing ... *I could scare you a lot worse than that,* he thought, and he may actually have spoken it, for he saw people look at him—or was it at the young big-game hunter? He was walking up Park Avenue at the time. *I could really scare you, sweet Jennie.*

Perhaps fright is the real purifier, he thought.

He never knew everywhere that he went that afternoon—but then wasn't that always the way when he walked? There were times when anyone might become bemused. Once he found himself in Grand Central Station, Heaven knew why, except that possibly he had felt the need of crowds. Or perhaps it was the sense of departure that he needed; anyway, he remembered the clotted clusters around the train entrances, and the feeling of their lowliness, sweaty, harried, hurried, worried, scurried, blurried, furried, hunched around their ranked suitcases, under the high, airy, beckoning ceiling. "A Grand Vacation Awaits You in the Empire State," a sign said at one side of an advertising display, high up on the Lexington Avenue side, and beside it a series of stereopticon pictures on a screen showed sailboats on a lake, and then canoeists, and then a group of hikers walking along a trail in the mountains. Any one of the places would be interesting to go to, he thought.

... Or again, he was on Fifth Avenue, looking in at the window of a travel agency, with a model airplane cut open to show the seating arrangement, and a map of Canada with a red streak across it to show the route: Quebec, Montreal, Ottawa, Winnipeg, and then Vancouver. Did he want to get away? Was that what he was after? And was that the solution? If so, it could easily be arranged; he had moved on before, and under worse circumstances than these were, and right now he had the feeling he could handle anything. . . .

Did he go in? Did he talk to the clerk in the travel agency? He didn't know, but he had a remembrance of a clerkish-looking fellow in a narrow black tie and a neatly pressed gabardine jacket, standing stiffly behind a glass-topped counter and looking strangely at him. . . . The word "Banff"—did that mean anything?

Central Park was a long, sunny, cheerful smile, with the women's legs lined up like teeth along the benches. . . . He was a painter there; young but already famous; immensely successful; strolling up one path and down another in search of material for a picture—and, if anyone asked, he had some old envelopes in his pockets that he used for sketch paper, to prove it.

... And then later; it was getting later; he could tell by the way people moved on the streets that it was getting close to five o'clock; the lovely afternoon was drawing to its close—perhaps, maybe, it may have been, it was a mistake to call on Chub Bassett; in fact, he knew it was as soon as he entered the office.

But he had been walking down Fifth Avenue and nearing Radio City, and suddenly a mood of depression had taken hold of him, so profound and so all-embracing that even in the clash and shimmer of the crowded sunlight it seemed to plunge him momentarily into actual darkness.

Florence, Elinor, he had thought; *Louisa*—he had forgotten about them, somehow, and now suddenly remembrance rushed in, and the full weight of his anguish and apprehension came with it.

And then guilt ...

And then melancholy ...

... Then a wave of overwhelming sadness; sadness that seemed to rise up and engulf the whole summer, and then suck it away again, down, down, down—as a wave might, slowly, powerfully, terribly—into a darkness that was as deep and complete as his own.

Had there ever been anyone, anywhere, who had been cheated so badly as he had been, all through that summer? He had planned so hard for it, and so innocently; he had wanted the summer to be so free, so friendly, so splendid. He had found the house, found the real-estate dealer, engineered the rental; he had gotten them all out there, and with no single thought but of goodness and friendliness in his mind. He had wanted to make a family. ...

But he was no nearer that than when he had started. He was further away from it, really, because the very fact of trying had put the thing in issue; the one great penalty of making an attempt is that then you must either succeed or fail, and there was no question now but that he had failed. Somehow, evil had crept in, and instead of growing closer together into the goodness of a true family relationship they were drifting steadily apart, into suspicion, disappointment, evil.

He was passing a men's-wear shop at the time, with a series

of ramrod-stiff torsos, wearing men's jackets, in the windows; they were all fall jackets, he noticed. *And then after that the winter,* he thought, *the winter. Where would they all be in the winter?* For a moment the streak of the air-line route, thin and sharp and red as the line of a knife stroke, cut across his vision, and vanished. Suddenly he felt lost and lonely—loster, lonelier than he had ever felt anywhere else before in his life.

It was in this mood that he went up to call on Chub Bassett, though his mood changed as soon as he got into the office. Of all Louisa's young men who had been out to the cottage that summer, Richard had liked Chub the best. He had been out there only twice, both times early in the season. But each time he had really been friendly—and what was more he had made the whole atmosphere of the cottage seem friendlier, too. Even Louisa, though she kidded him a good deal, seemed simpler and easier when Chub was there, while with Richard he had had a kind of man-to-man attitude that hinted at real understanding.

"Look me up in town sometime," he had said, apropos of something, one day when they were all lying on the beach, and though Louisa had looked at them both a little quizzically, or perhaps because of it, he had gone on, it seemed a little defiantly. "No, I mean it. Or call me at the office."

And he had given the name—Fox and Folkestone, Advertising Consultants—and the address, 594 Fifth Avenue. Richard had remembered.

So, now, with his gift for finding strange meanings in simple happenings, Richard found it little short of miraculous that he should notice the building directly abreast of him at the moment of his deepest melancholy. The firm's offices, it turned out, were on the eighteenth floor—but by then he was too excited to register consecutive impressions.

He remembered a neat, squarish reception room, with green leather chairs and gray-paneled walls, and a girl at a desk who took his name and smiled at him considerately while she phoned it in. Then a walk—with the girl, nurselike, leading the way—down a corridor like a hospital corridor, except that the doors on either side had glass panels in them and gave, when they were open, on men sitting at desks or talking to other men, instead of on beds and hospital furniture. And then a door and the girl saying, "This is Mr. Bassett's office, sir," and—

"Why, Richard!" Chub was saying. He wore reading glasses when he worked, Richard noticed—big, heavy-rimmed tortoiseshell ones that made his round, rather small-featured face look curiously youthful and studious—but he whipped them off as he stood up behind his desk, and there was something so odd in his tone that for a moment Richard's suspicions began rising. The girl had gone.

"Were you expecting me?" Richard countered.

"Well, not really," said Bassett. "I mean—well, if I sounded surprised, the truth is I was expecting somebody else. A guy named Richard Lowry, and when the girl gave your name— well, hell, never mind." He made a funny little wave of his hands and grinned. "He's just a fellow I know, works for Brandt and Russell, and he was supposed to drop in sometime today or tomorrow. Sit down, anyway, Richard. Sit down. What's been doing?"

He was subtly different in his office from what he had been at the cottage, Richard noticed—brisker, less relaxed, a little nervous, and he grew more nervous as Richard stayed on; did Chub too have his worries, his problems, Richard wondered. Otherwise, though, he was the same as before, friendly, easy to talk to, sympathetic—the one true friend he had, Richard thought—and he made up his mind to confide in him frankly, though at the moment he didn't know what.

They had, as it turned out, a rather long conversation, though not all of it was at Chub's office. At a certain point—he had been shuffling papers on his desk in his nervous fashion for some time before—Chub glanced at his watch and suggested going out—"for a drink," as he said. "It's time I got out of this place anyway"—and though Richard explained that he rarely drank much he went along. They went down to a place called Cherio's. "I thought maybe you might know it," Chub said. "It's a great publisher's and magazine people's hang-out."

Richard had to laugh at that. "If you think just because I work for a book shop—" he began, but Chub interrupted.

"No, I mean, what I thought was, your poetry," he said.

"Oh, my poetry," Richard said, and fell silent for a moment. Cherio's was an odd, crowded, slightly hazy place—like a speak-easy in a movie, Richard thought—with a small, very busy bar in one corner, booths, all crowded, along one wall and tables along another, and a general air of everyone knowing everyone else, or at least of being thoroughly at home in the place itself. All the booths had been taken and the bar had been jammed, so they had sat at one of the tables. " 'I may be wrong, and I could be,' I said to them," a woman in a brown linen dress and a tiny, rose-sprinkled straw hat was saying to the man opposite her at the next table. " 'But my bet is that that book will do fifty thousand copies or over.' " She leaned back and looked fixedly at her companion. She was a large woman, with intense blue eyes and a sharp jaw. "Three weeks later it hit both the best-seller lists."

"My poetry," Richard said, and he could feel a sob rising in his throat as he spoke. Just then a small, baldish, worried-looking waiter paused before their table to take their order. Richard glanced at Chub Bassett helplessly. "I don't know, I don't drink much. I'll take whatever you take," he said, and it seemed to him that for a moment Chub looked almost annoyed.

Then Chub turned to the waiter. "Two Scotches and soda, Harry," he said. "And the next thing I knew, those damned sequins were all over the place," the woman at the next table was saying. Richard felt a wave of real honesty—the kind of honesty that lies, usually hid, within ordinary honesty—swelling within him. The time had come to tell something, anything really, that would bring them together; it was a moment too precious to lose.

"You're good, Chub, you know. Really *good*," he said earnestly.

"Good?" said Chub. He had been watching a thin-armed, thin-legged, tanned, shock-haired blond woman at the bar, with three men, each identically holding a cocktail glass, clustered around her; and he looked almost scared as he turned around.

"Yes, good. Didn't you hear me?" said Richard. He had meant it as a joke, but his voice came out louder than he had antici-pated, and his excitement was such that as he leaned forward on the table his elbow slipped a little. Glancingly, he was conscious that the woman in the brown dress had looked over at him and then said something to her companion; then the two of them passed out of his mind entirely. Words, the words that he had been waiting for and that would explain everything, had begun coming.

He did, though, make the concession of lowering his voice a little. "And it's just because you're good, Chub, you know—or maybe you don't know; but I do; I've been thinking about it. It's—it's the good people, really good people, like you—" ("who don't know their own goodness," he had meant to add, but it seemed now it could go unsaid. He rushed on; he had a feeling he was losing Chub's attention.) "And it's the same thing with evil," he said. A drink, somehow, had appeared before him, and he picked it up and put it down and then slid it back and forth restlessly on the table.

"Listen, Chub, it's a thing I've just learned—" And since he had lowered his voice—why, he didn't remember—he had to lean still farther across the table and whisper it. *"They don't know they're evil, either!"*

In a way, it was a sort of triumph. Chub was listening; so were the two at the next table; if he were to raise his voice, everybody would be listening. . . .

But he didn't. This was something for Chub alone. "I've seen plenty of it, you know, these last few weeks. I've had a chance to study it," he went on. He was talking about the Hacketts, of course, and equally of course, Chub knew it; there was no use mentioning names. "And the thing is, they just don't know it. And if they don't know it—" The whole thing had suddenly come brilliantly clear in his mind; it was the solution, really, but it was hard to put it into words. What he meant was that evil, in a person who didn't even know it was evil (like Florence, for example; or Louisa) was no worse than goodness; even, if you thought about it, no different, really. But there was no point in underlining every word; Chub would understand what he was getting at. "Florence," he said slowly, spacing his words carefully. "Louisa. They can be cured. That's the thing that I've learned. I've learned that."

He had learned tolerance, that was it, and he had learned

it through Chub. "But it's hard, just the same, sometimes," he went on. Chub was sipping his drink and studying him; all around them hands were raising and lowering glasses, and with an idea of fitting his actions to the rest Richard picked up his; when he set it down it was empty.

"Kid, listen," said Chub. Richard interrupted him.

"No, no, no," he said gently, shaking his head and smiling. "Don't deny it. Because if I wanted to—" He was talking about the other's intrinsic goodness, and Chub knew it, but he was talking about a hundred other things besides. "If I wanted to, I could prove it. Like that time when you mentioned my poetry, for example—and don't think that I didn't appreciate it. . . ." The other couple had gone back to their talking—which just went to show—(To show what? that if you kept your voice low enough, no one would bother you?) Having secrecy in mind, Richard leaned again across the table.

"Do you know," he went on, "that's the first time anyone has mentioned my poetry to me for weeks, for sheer really for weeks? And me there all the time, working, working, working—" Chub had glanced at his watch and then signaled the waiter; two fresh glasses appeared before them.

"Or!" said Richard. It came out loudly, unexpectedly, like a command, and he lowered his voice hastily. "Or back there; you know, there—" He meant, there in the office, and this time, surely, he knew that Chub understood him. "You said, 'How are things at the beach?' Or the cottage, or something. And I said 'Fine.' There again, there's your goodness, Chub; you don't *see* things, you're better even than I am. Because I lied. You said, 'How are things?' and I said 'Fine,' and all the time they're not fine, Chub. They're terrible. That's what they are. They're—"

"Look," said Chub, and he had been going to say more, but Richard cut in on him; if one could interrupt, certainly the other could. And besides, there was so much he wanted to tell Chub about—about his sadness, and his disappointment in Florence, and the way she and Louisa were bringing nothing but harm to poor Elinor; and the way things were breaking up at the cottage, like the night that the boys broke in. He wished briefly that he could tell Chub about his mother.

"No, no, Chub. Don't stop me," he said. "This is important."
The woman next him was talking assiduously to her companion. Chub and he were alone, as they were meant to be, and suddenly a feeling of embarrassment came over him: here he was,
sitting drinking—and Scotch, no less—in a place like a scene in
a movie, and Chub's face poised before him. . . . "Do you mind
my calling you Chub?" he said suddenly, timidly.

"What?" cried Chub, and burst out laughing, so loud that
the couple looked around again. Then, out of the real kindness
that was in him, he stifled his laughter. "No. No. God, no," he
said. "I'd feel hurt if you didn't. But I don't think you mean what
you're saying, Richard, about the cottage and so on, I mean."
He gave a quick hinting nod toward the couple next them. "We
won't mention any names."

"That's right, Chub," said Richard. "Don't say anything to
anybody. But I know. I know. . . ." Suddenly, he found himself
telling about the night the boys broke in. He told everything,
about the chairs and the scratches on the wall and the glasses
smashed and everything, and he must have talked for some
time, because now when he looked over at the next table the
woman and man had gone and their place had been taken by
another couple. He was happy to note, too, that Chub took him
seriously.

"Do you mean this, Richard?" he asked once. "Aren't you
exaggerating a little? Because the way Louisa told me there
wasn't anywhere near such damage."

"Oh, Louisa," said Richard, dismissing her. He was already
thinking of other things that had to do with that episode, mainly
of his own humiliation. "They blamed me, you know, Chub;
that's the worst part," he went on. "Me. Me. Right in front of
that Massie, too. After all I've done for them."

"Nonsense, Richard! That's really nonsense. I happen to
know."

"Nonsense?" Richard repeated, then he shook his head sadly.
"But it doesn't matter, really. I'll be moving on soon myself, you
know; somewhere—" As he spoke, he could see the way leading
out before him—Cleveland, Kansas City, Chicago. . . . *Maybe
Canada,* he thought.

But it seemed he was losing his audience. "Will you really?" said Chub, but he seemed less interested now; and when Richard, daringly, signaled the waiter as he had seen Chub do, to order another drink, Chub canceled the order and paid the bill instead. It was only three dollars and something, Richard noticed; he could have paid that himself, and would have, only he had thought it would be more.

But Chub paid, anyway. And it turned out he had to meet some people for dinner, so he had to hurry. At the curb, outside the restaurant, he turned suddenly, solicitously, to Richard. "Are you sure you can make it home all right, fellow?" he said.

"Who? Me?" Richard had to stare at him. "Why, of course I can. Why shouldn't I? That is, if I do go home."

Chub still looked at him. "I'd advise you to, fellow," he said—Richard thought, mysteriously. "Get something to eat, anyway."

Then a vacant taxi came past and Chub took it. Richard waved him good-bye, and then watched as the cab slid away down the street, stopped at Park till the lights changed and then turned north. That was the way Chub should go, he thought—in a taxi, leaning back in the cushioned interior, looking out at the sights through the window, as it took him from one engagement to another; for drinks, for dinner; afterward, he supposed, the theater. . . .

Late that night, very late, for there were milk carts and other traffic to be heard in the avenue below and the window was graying, Richard woke in his bed in his room and lay thinking. Good Chub, really good Chub, he thought; if only everyone could be as good as he was. And they could be; he knew that too, or rather he had known it, and known too how they could be made so. . . . He had known it that afternoon, with Chub, or had almost known it. And though now he seemed to have lost it, he wasn't worried. . . . It would come to him later; it would come again. . . .

But he wished he had paid that bill. . . .

9

But the summer is a nervous, testy, unstable, uneven time, too. It's a time when anything can happen. (There was one night when Richard, waking up in his room on Third Avenue—waking staring, and with a sense of overbearing haste and pressure, and in the background of his mind a memory of some sort of argument: was it with Mr. Whittaker, the whimpery Mr. Whittaker? About something to do with the stairs? Passing on the stairs?— there was one night when Richard suddenly demanded of himself, "Am I losing my grip? Am I going . . ." But he didn't want to say the word "crazy." He lay alone, in the battering darkness, while a series of quick recollections, sharp and instantly clear, disconnected, shot like rockets across his mind's vision—the soft sluff-sluff of hospital slippers and the long, waxy-glimmering corridors, the steam smell and the smell of food, the steel screens and the desk like steel too, like a knife, and the endless questioning. And lay twisting and struggling as if already bound: "Am I going back to that?" he asked himself. And: "I won't. I won't.")

It's a wearing, testing time too, the summer. It's a time of inexplicable, sudden changes. There are times when the summer seems to stretch away like a haze into the distance— like the haze on the sea when the sea itself is still, and both the sea and the sky, though the hour is early, are already trembling, trembling, with the packed heat beyond the horizon—and times again when it looms up, close, compact, frightening, like the faces or forms that one sees sometimes in fever dreams, shrinking, looming, receding, approaching, fading, swelling. . . .

It's a time of thunder, the summer, when the weather itself gets beyond control and goes prowling, prowling, prowling around the hazy undulations of the sky line while the heat and the excitement lie closelier and closelier compacted at that spot which is the center of every circle of sky line: a small spot on the dunes, a road's end, a cottage. . . .

Never, never, Richard thought, had Florence been so deliberately disagreeable as she was that next week-end, when he came
down to the cottage.

He was late, but could he help that? It was the train's fault.
And he *had* come down a day earlier than he had expected, on
Thursday instead of Friday. But was that so awful? Hadn't he
done it before, once or twice, without anyone's making such a
to-do about it? And if a man couldn't do that in his own home,
what could he do? If, that is, it was his home—and that was one
thing that troubled him, and he was hardly across the threshold
before he noticed it: she seemed determined to make him feel
that it *wasn't* his home any more, that he was merely a guest
there, and a troublesome guest at that.

It seemed, almost, as if she were trying to fix some blame on
him.

"Darling Richard, you should let us know, you know," she
said, being very gently-reproving. "Not that we're not glad
you've come, and all that. It must have been frightful in the city."

"But I thought—" he began.

"You said Friday, darling," she said, emphasizing the day
a little. "You *could* write, you know. With us here all alone and
everything. . . . We hadn't planned to go shopping till tomorrow."

And then, having driven home her point to the limit, she suddenly relented. "But we'll manage, don't worry. We'll manage.
Elinor!" She was being the *grande dame* again, the chatelaine—
God, how he knew her!—able to take on a dozen extra guests
without blinking. "Elinor, we've got eggs, haven't we? We've got
bacon? Well, then—" and she turned to him, smiling graciously
(and as coolly as she might at any guest, Richard thought). "Are
you hot? I should think you must be, after that awful train ride.
Wouldn't you like to run down for a swim? We'll wait dinner for
you, if you do."

They had scrambled eggs and bacon and a salad, and in the
middle of dinner she turned to him. "Richard, tell me," she said,
and he noticed that Elinor stopped eating for a moment, and
was watching. "Did you notice—when you were down here
last week-end, I mean—did you notice anything wrong in the
kitchen? When was it, Elinor, Monday morning?"

"That's right," Elinor said.

Florence turned to look at Richard again, and he glanced away. He was remembering something, and it troubled him. It was getting darker now, and the dunes were losing their color, grass and sand growing grayer together, and all fading softly and gracefully into the folding, enfolding darkness. He wished suddenly that he was out there instead of here, where they queried and questioned you. He didn't belong here at all.

Florence was staring at him earnestly. "Did you notice, particularly, if those bottles on the shelf above the sink had been moved around in an odd way?"

He looked back at her, coldly, calmly, directly. He had remembered, and he didn't care what happened now. He felt remote, detached from everything. "Yes," he said, very clearly.

"You did?"

"Yes. I did."

"You did what, Richard? Don't get excited. It's nothing, really. Only, after that last time . . ."

He was almost shouting now. "*I* moved the bottles. Don't I have the right—can't I do anything at all around here? I was looking for rectified spirits."

"Of ammonia?" Florence stared for a moment and then, to his vast amazement, she burst out laughing. "But whatever in the world moved you to look for it there? I don't even know if we have any at all—had you seen some around here, or something?—but if we had it'd be in the medicine chest upstairs. And what happened—were you feeling faint, or something?"

"No, of *course* not!" said Richard, but he couldn't help feeling relieved. "I was just wondering, and I wanted to find out—is that really what it is, Florence? Rectified spirits of ammonia?"

She nodded at him brightly, still enjoying herself. "So it is, child, and before your time—and mine too, I'm happy to say— ladies used to carry it in their reticules. And they'd sniff at it, delicately, whenever they felt a fit of the vapors, or whatever, coming on." Her smile grew warmer—almost like the old Florence's, really—and she reached out and laid her hand on his. "Oh, Richard, really, you don't know how glad I am it was you! I was worried, you know, really worried. Because, coming right after that other time, I was afraid someone really was bothering us."

She gave his hand a little pat and smiled at him. "Though why on earth you should go hunting for spirits of ammonia in the middle of the night, apparently—"

"I told you, didn't I?" said Richard. "I was wondering." And for a moment, though he smiled, he let his anger rise—but not dangerously—a little nearer the surface. "Do I have to be queried and questioned about everything?"

There were no questions, no queryings on the dunes, only loneliness, peace, darkness, and silent acceptingness. Richard now knew the dunes as he knew few other places. He knew the sly, gritty slide of the sand underfoot; the quick insinuations of the wind, ghostly soft, as it blew through the grass and the gorse on the level places. (And the skir-r-r of blown sand, hardly audible unless you stopped and listened closely, that almost always underlay it. He had stopped, himself, and listened, many times.)

He knew the ups and downs of the dunes, their topography; he knew the places where you were hid and well hid, where you skulked, and where you had to walk openly. He knew the hollows, and the way the sea's beat resounded there; he knew the heat that lay there, too, even late at night.

(He knew one hollow, a little to the west of the cottage, where some bricks and other rubble, lying around, hinted that there had once been a cottage or some sort of building there: *They all vanish in the end,* he thought.) He knew the way the coolness cut you—and the sense that you might be seen, too; the sense of nakedness—when you climbed from a depth to a summit. He knew the cottage from every angle.

He knew the cottage and he knew the dunes, and till now the two had been related; it was the dunes that contained the cottage, and if he could make himself part of the dunes—if he could *be* them—then he too would contain and control the cottage. Tonight, though, he didn't care. He came out when the lights had gone off, downstairs, upstairs, bathroom, bedroom, and for a while he wandered.

But he did it more openly now than he had before. Now he didn't care whether anyone saw him or not, and he paced back and forth on the beach path for a while and then walked down to the edge of the cliff overlooking the beach and lit a cigarette and stood there, conscious that he was silhouetted, that if anyone were to look from the cottage windows now they would see him, dark, lonely, mysterious—and not caring.

Let them look, let them wonder, he thought, thinking of all the times he had looked and wondered.

He had his back turned to the cottage now; he didn't care. *Loneliness,* he thought; *vanity; desolation*—the words coming separately into his mind, each more as sound than meaning, but with an atmosphere of sadness enveloping them all. Looking down, he could see the huddle of rocks which was his fireplace on the beach below, and the steps he had carved in the cliff-path to make it easier to get down to it. "Desolation," he said, and for a moment he saw the broken rubble in the hollow, only now it was the cottage itself, smashed and broken by some disaster, wrecked, ruined, abandoned; it was so clear that he glanced back quickly to make sure.

But the cottage was still there, all right, dark and quiet, gray-walled, blank-windowed, waiting for its destruction, with a row of white rectangles—towels, probably—hanging from the clothesline at the rear, and he turned back to the sea again and forgot it. The sea was dark, and so still that only occasionally would he see the white line that marked a swell form along the shoals and move, straight and crayon-clear, slowly, inflexibly, in to the beach. *Sus-his-s-s-sh,* it would say when it got there, and then start lazily clawing the pebbles. There was no wind, only now and then a patient stirring as the day's temperatures re-adjusted themselves, coolness eddying in from the sea and the heat from the land rising dustlike up through it. The sky was gray as the sand itself.

He stood there for some time, but he often did things without knowing it, and he must have moved around, for he found himself farther up the cliff than he had remembered being, and he must have lain down; he was lying on his back looking up at the sky and it was somehow confused with Jennie—or was it what-was-her-name, the tea-room woman he had worked for in Rochester?

But that was all right, too; such lapses never bothered him, and anyway it was a drifting thing he had recalled. "How high *is* the sky, Jennie?" he had said. (For it had been Jennie; he remembered her bright, snappy, Scottish look as she spoke, though he didn't remember her answer.) And she had laughed and said something, the ice melting in her eyes as her anger vanished....

I can always get round them, he thought, and he chuckled. *I know what the score is,* and for a while he was all shrewdness and stratagems, staring up at the smooth, approving sky. *I can fit them all in, the Hacketts, Chub, Jennie, all those gloomy roomers; you make a loop and you cast it, and then pulling them all together... Or if you can only get high enough*... He may have slept, though he didn't think so, because sleep was a different kind of disconnectedness. "Then—to travel," he said, not quite knowing what the travel came after—and felt a touch on his cheek and rolled over.... Elinor was kneeling beside him.

For a second or two he could only stare at her, as unthinkingly as he had been staring at the sky, only this was a face, close, close; it was Elinor's face, and she was speaking. "It *is* you, isn't it, Richard?" she was saying. "Did I wake you? Were you sleeping?"

"No," he said. He had heard, but he hadn't heard. He felt trapped, like an animal, and his first move had been to twist over on his hands and knees and look back at the cottage; all he could see, from here, was the roof and a section of the upper story. But even seeing that somehow calmed him a little, it placed him, and he sat back and looked at her. "How'd you get here?" he said.

"I just walked." She had on shorts and a pull-over jersey and her hair looked tousled. She was sitting back too, as she knelt, so that her thighs looked broader and whiter than usual—solider, too, somehow—in the night's grayness; for the moment, he didn't know why she was there or what he would do with her. But he was growing calmer. "You don't seem very, shall we say, pleased to see me," she commented.

"Perhaps I'd better go back," she said a moment later.

"No," he said. "It's just—you know, you startled me. I was thinking."

"I know," Elinor said. . . . But there still were lapses. She had been kneeling beside him, facing him; and now they were sitting side by side, looking out toward the sea, and it seemed she had asked him why he was out there. "I saw you out here one night last week-end, too," she had said.

—To guard the cottage, he had said. There were times (he was so busy looking at her) when he wasn't sure if he spoke or only thought he did. But she always answered him.

She had looked at him, smiling a little. "You don't mean that, do you really?" she asked.

—But if Florence is worried.

She smiled at him. "*You're* not worried, though, are you, Richard?" And then, when he looked at her, "I thought *you* did it. Tell me the truth now, didn't you, Richard? I mean all that business about the chairs, and the glass, and so on. I bet you *did,* you know.

"I bet you did it as a joke," she said.

"And then, maybe, you were too scared to say so."

He watched her, and listened. "Did you tell anyone else about this?" he asked.

"I did, once. I told Mother, after you and Louisa had gone down to the city. I said, 'I bet Richard was the one who did it, just as a joke.' But she got so *mad*—" She shook her head in amazement at the recollection. "Mother loves to dramatize things, you know, and I thought, Why not let her have her fun? You *did,* though, didn't you, Richard?"

"Yes," he said. A sudden feeling of utter kinship with her had swept over him. There she sat—Elinor, a *person*—alone, beside him, and yet almost childishly self-possessed. (There had been something delightfully childlike in the way she had shaken her head a moment earlier, as there was too in her simple directness; no one else would have dared, he thought.) And yet such sweetness, such understanding . . . "You know, I wouldn't have told it to anyone but you," he said.

"I know," she said. "You know, sometimes, I feel—" She shot him a quick glance and then looked away almost shyly.

. . . They were sitting at the edge of the cliff, and his hand had somehow found a place on hers. *Sus-his-s-s-s-sh,* went a wave on the beach below, and then rattle-rattle-rattle as it clawed back among the pebbles. For a moment, he had the feeling that she knew everything—knew him better than he knew himself. "It's been a funny sort of summer, hasn't it, Richard?" she asked dreamily.

(Knew him, yes, and still willingly accepted him.)

"It must have been even stranger for you, though, sometimes."

"Why?" he said.

"Well, I mean, with us all here, and so on. We're such a funny family, really. Mother trying to keep young, and me trying to convince them I'm old enough not to be treated like a child any more. And Louisa—well, sort of popping in and out, the way she always does.

"And now it's almost over," she said.

. . . But there still were lapses. There were times when he felt only stillness and calm; the night, the silence; coolness, darkness. There were times when he hardly saw her, herself.

She had on black shorts and a light-colored pull-over, white or gray—"Is that gray?" he asked once. She said, "No, it's yellow, really. But it looks gray now, doesn't it?" and she pulled it out a little at the front to examine it—"I just put anything on, to come out," she said, and he had a sudden shivery feeling, that was in part his own sharing of her perceptions ("I'm cold," she had said once), that she had nothing on under the jersey at all. . . .

There were times when she was merely a presence: combinations of dark gray, lighter gray, and blackness that together gave a feeling of roundness, of softness. . . . A voice, an odor; but more than that—a sense of beauty, mystery, understanding. She seemed to lean and withdraw, appear, disappear, reappear. . . .

"You don't like Louisa really, do you?" she was saying.

And there were times when she was Elinor again, a *person;* he had never realized before how terribly *real* she was. . . . She was blood, flesh, bone; little silvery-satiny feelings along the skin where his skin now and then touched hers; life, strength, movement.

And the bare, cold breasts . . . "I don't like many of her boy-friends," he said.

"They? Oh, they're all right. They're just silly, most of them." He had been calm, but now he was growing excited. She seemed content now to talk. (There had been once, in Kansas City, and again once in Albany, and, both times, they had let him touch them: the breasts, the nipples; and, both times, the cool, vulnerable, malleable softness.) She was sitting hunched forward a little, looking down at the beach. "No, I mean Louisa," she was saying. "You don't sort of approve of her, do you? I've noticed."

"I don't think she does you any good!" Richard said, almost explosively. "She or Florence either!" But it was sort of drawn out of him, really. It was something he had wanted to talk to her about for a long time, too; and yet here, on the dunes, suddenly he didn't want to; it was too long, too involved, it would take too much time explaining, and when she said, "Why, Richard? What can poor Mother do to me?" he said. "Lots," noncommittally, and let it go at that.

. . . But she seemed bent on talking. He had reached the point now where he couldn't follow all she had said. (The one in Albany, he remembered, had laughed—and then, putting her bare foot against his belly, had pushed him angrily away. But this was Elinor, his Elinor, a *person*. . . .)

Yet it was as if, all the time, she knew what he was thinking. . . .

"Funny. Usually everybody falls for Louisa," she said. . . .

"She's so clever. But of course, some of that comes from working, instead of staying home all the time. This winter, really, I'm going to get a job. Don't you think I should, Richard? . . .

"I think you learn more, that way. Not just about the job, or whatever. About everything. . . .

"Darling Richard, don't you think you should *say* something once in a while? Here we sit in the moonlight, or at least if there was a moon we would be, and you just sit there and let me do all the talking."

As if he had been a long way off, or as if everything around

him had been far away, Richard spoke: "Does Florence know . . .
I mean, won't she wonder . . . ?" he said.

"About what?"

"About your being out here, I mean."

"Oh, no. Mother—I doubt if anything could wake Mother,
these days. She takes a nembutal every night now; it really worries me. And then, anyway—" she said, and left the sentence
unfinished. She was sitting beside him, and she bent her head
back and slantwise to look up at him, and then reached up and
touched his ear. "You know, Richard, you have the cutest ears,"
she said.

He had frozen, still as a statue, at the touch. "No," he said.

"But you do, though," she said. She was still fondling his ear.
"Even Louisa says so."

"Does she?" he said, and tried to move his head away without
her noticing. But her fingers followed.

"Don't you like me to tickle your ears?" she asked. She was
teasing him now, openly, and he somehow resented it.

"No," he said.

"Shall I pinch them, then?" And then the surge that he, without knowing it, had been waiting for came and picked him up
and threw him on her.

It was the beat of his heart he heard most. "No. *No,* Richard.
Not here," she said. And: "Don't. *Darling!*" And: "Don't!" There
was a time when it was all struggle, arms wrestling and shoulders burrowing. And his head somewhere, thrusting, under her
chin. And then the bare, cold breasts uncovered, the black shorts
like a bandage unwrapped. "No!" she cried, and he heard his
own voice shouting. "Yes," it cried. "Yes. Yes. Yes." He felt sand,
and he felt her body.

Toward the end it was like lightning flashes, with his eyes the
lightnings and his heart thunder; he was the sky itself, pressing
down upon her ("I can cure you! I can make you whole!" he said,
or did he say it?). He saw her only fragmentarily: a grimace, and
a glimpse of tight-shut eyes, and then darkness, and a curve of
bare shoulder against the darkness, an arm lifting, and darkness.

It was not love, it was not beauty, it was not even Elinor. It
was merely possession, and yet even in the midst of it he felt

helpless, so that he could not tell who was possessed the more, she or he. When the end came ("Oh, Elinor!" he heard himself saying), it came with such violence that the reaction was almost physical, thrusting him brusquely away from her. He sprang up.

"Richard!" she cried, and though his impulse had been almost overpoweringly for flight, her voice stopped him. It was she, after all, it was Elinor; as he stood looking down at her, sitting hunched like a castaway, half-naked and lonely-looking on the sand, the first feeling of real tenderness that he had ever had for her welled up in him, and he dropped down beside her.

"Oh, Elinor, I'm sorry," he said.

"Don't," she said. "Don't say anything now." She had her back turned toward him, and he could see, very clear in the gray light, the row of shadowy little protuberances where the line of her backbone showed through the flesh. They made her look somehow frailer, more vulnerable than ever. She was reaching for her shorts, and when she picked them up she inspected them vaguely, like a child looking at a garment she hardly knew how to put on. "You tore my shorts," she said at last.

"I'm sorry, Elinor. Really, I'm sorry."

"It doesn't matter," she said, still vaguely. "But it was so sudden, so—I don't know." And then suddenly, with her knees drawn up and her clothing clutched on her lap, she put her head down on her arms and he realized she was crying. "Oh, Richard! Why did you? Why did you?" she said.

It was so unexpected that it forced a reply from him. "Well, you wanted it, didn't you?" he demanded, and she stared up at him suddenly.

"I? Wanted it? Wanted what?" she cried. "What do you mean?"

"Well, I mean—" he began, and then an idea occurred to him that would explain everything, but most especially *her* behavior, and the difference between the real innocence that he knew was in her and the wanton way she was acting. He leaned closer to her, and—although they were alone there, far away from anyone—almost whispered. "Did they send you?" he asked, and she stared at him, startled, again.

"They? Who?" she said.

But he could see there was no use going on in that line, either.
If it was a trap and she didn't know about it, this was no time to
enlighten her. And if she did know—well, then, it was high time
that he himself was on his guard.

"Never mind," he said. And then suddenly the sadness and
the aloneness that had been waiting and gathering all around
him came flooding in upon him and he turned his head in bitterness away from her. "Oh, Elinor! Elinor!" he cried. "Can't I even
trust you?"

10

That night was bad, but the next day was worse. They didn't
stay much longer on the dunes, after Elinor's fit of weeping and
Richard's outburst, and while they were there she acted more
and more oddly. "Can't I even trust you?" he had said, but instead
of showing any understanding she answered him angrily.

"How can I trust *you?*" she demanded, and then they fell into
a sort of wrangle about that which ended nowhere.

And all the while he wanted her away, and yet he wanted her
there, to talk to. What he wanted, really, was to get back his old
feeling of calm ascendancy over her, and which he now somehow sensed he had lost, or was losing, forever. He had been put
on the defensive, in some way; she had *him* now, instead of him
having her at a disadvantage, though he wasn't quite sure when
the change had happened or if she herself even realized it, for all
the while she kept acting oddly.

"I'm sorry, Elinor. I'm really sorry," he said once. They were
walking back toward the cottage by then, and she had been
walking without even speaking, she was back in her dull mood
again and it had seemed to him a good moment to re-establish
some contact. But all she said was, "Don't keep saying 'I'm sorry.
I'm sorry,'" and then added, "When you don't even mean it."

But when he tried to reassure her about that—he even tried
to put his arms around her—she pushed him away capriciously.
"Don't be silly!" she said sharply, and then suddenly, soon after,
her manner changed again.

It became brash and brittle in the best modern manner and, well, Louisa-ish, he thought, when he thought about it later. Louisa, too, must have had her affairs many times, up or down the beach, week-end nights, with her week-end boy-friends; and got dressed, and arranged herself, and smoked a cigarette afterward; and it occurred to him, later, that Elinor, probably, was trying to act the same way with him.

So she too demanded a cigarette, and when he lighted it for her she looked at him oddly.

"Richard," she said.

"What?"

"Never mind." She stood looking at him silently for a moment. "Don't you even love me?" she said.

"Why, of course I do."

"Well, why don't you say so?" But then when he put his arms around her she just stood there, almost woodenly, and then suddenly she threw her cigarette away. "No, no, *no!*" she said; and, as suddenly, she bent down and retrieved it, still glowing, from where it had fallen in the sand.

"Now I really *must* go," she said, with the same sort of brisk composure that she, or perhaps Louisa, might have used if it had been a cocktail party she was leaving, or some casual appointment. "It must really be frightfully late."

They went back separately, and it was she who took charge of things. "You go first," she said. "And if you see Mother— Well, you won't. But if you do, tell her something. Tell her you were out walking, or something. But don't tell her you saw me." And then she waited, and suddenly he realized what she was waiting for, and he kissed her. When he tried to draw away, it was she who held him.

"No. Like this," she said, and then her mouth came against his, hard and full, and the lips loose and open so that he could feel, almost smotheringly, the soft fleshy wetness of them.

For a second her teeth ground against his, then she pulled her head back to look at him. "You see, Richard? I'll have to teach you how to kiss."

Then they separated, and he walked back to the cottage alone. He saw no signs of Florence, and he had been in the studio for some time, waiting, still dressed, in the darkness, before he heard Elinor's step coming up the road—the road away from the dunes, he noticed; she must have circled the house; perhaps she knew the dunes as well as he did—and peered quietly out the window, and watched.

She walked quickly and a little stiffly, as if conscious of being watched, and she gave not a glance toward the window where he was standing. She walked past, and he saw her turn in at the gate in the little picket fence. Then she passed out of sight.

He heard the screen door close, not too loud, not too gently, and her footfalls, crossing the porch. After that, he heard nothing. The cottage stayed dark.

It was then that the doubts began. He had no idea at all what time it was when he got to sleep. He undressed, and lay down, and shut his eyes, first against the darkness and then later against the first paling of the night into morning dimness, but there was no sleep for him. No thoughts either, really; as that last time, in Kansas City, voices came to him—*Well, you did it,* they said. *You're as bad as the rest of them*—only this time it was worse, because that time the girl had only been a girl in the candy factory where he had worked, and he could quit, leave his job, get away from her . . . while this time it was Elinor, and he couldn't leave without—well, without leaving everything.

"Oh, God, why . . . ?" he said aloud ("Why did you? Why did you?" Elinor had said), and for a moment he cast wildly, futilely, about for reasons why he might not have done it at all—if he hadn't gone out on the dunes, for once, or if he hadn't stayed there so long; if he had been stronger, stricter, colder. Or if he hadn't come down to the cottage so early—if he had waited until tomorrow, for example, Louisa would have been there too, and probably with some week-end companions; and in the confusion of so many people this could never have happened, never.

But it did, it did, it did, said the voices.

And then, thinking of Louisa, a sudden vision came to him, of something not seen but often imagined—Louisa, and some lover, far down on the beach together, she bare-legged,

bare-bodied, bare-breasted, and he naked too, and both wet
from the sea; both coiled amorously, and then the hot, heavy
thumping, pumping. . . . She would light a cigarette, afterward,
and lie there, loose and lax and shameless as any wanton—and
then the sly, furtive slidings of hard hands over smooth skin, the
gigglings, the nudgings, would begin again. . . .

"So much evil," he said. "So much evil!"

And now you, said the voice. *And with Elinor.* . . .

"Mother," he said. For now a new thought had come to him,
or rather he could feel it coming. It hadn't risen to the surface
yet, but he could see it rising, like something rising in the midst
of a sea of memories: it was his mother, and she was sitting
where she always sat, in the rocking chair across the table; she
was half-turned to look at him; and her face in the gaslight was
stern and solemn. Drowned, too, for though he saw her he saw
her waveringly, and though he saw her lips move he couldn't
make out what she was saying. . . . His thoughts drifted back to
the present.

Yes, Elinor. . . . *And that kiss,* and that sly, shy smile. "I'll have
to teach you," he remembered suddenly. *Oh, they learn; they learn
young nowadays.* Yes, but where? He could swear, somehow, she
hadn't learned it from another man. Then perhaps from Louisa?
From Florence even? Did the two girls practice together—one
the man, one the woman; and kiss, and fondle, and imitate,
in private, as in public they went openly arm in arm, waists
enlaced, as he himself had seen them? And then, Florence . . . ?

*Oh, they know what they want, and they go after it. They get it
somehow.*

"Yes, but Florence," he said. And then again, his mother. . . .
He could see her plainer now. "There's some girls that'll do
anything to get a man," she was saying, and he could remember
now too, though vaguely: there had been a girl—he saw her
dressed in yellow, and living somewhere down the street, and he
had laughed and tried to argue; Mrs. What-was-her-name, the
girl's mother, was a pleasant-enough woman, he had said.

But his mother, staring sternly at him from across the table,
had been inexorable. "You watch out, Dickie. That's the way
they get you," she had said. "And don't put too much trust in

the mothers, either. I know. I'm a mother, too. But thank God I'm not that kind. There's some mothers that'll let their own daughters do anything, just to get them a man."

. . . He would have to leave, there was too much evil here; that was the truth of it. But then it struck him, he couldn't leave now, he couldn't; there was Elinor to be considered. He couldn't just walk away and leave her. And the cottage. And everything.

The cottage, after all, was his. He had found it. He had brought them there. . . . In Heaven's name, what had ever made him think of leaving it?

And the evil . . .

But if he could get *them* to go, and leave him and Elinor, and the cottage . . . "I have got to do a lot of thinking," he heard himself say.

And then—there must have been a lapse; he had been awake for some time, or had he?—and yet there was Elinor standing, small and precise, in the doorway. Instead of joy at seeing her, he felt only guilt and resentment. "Hello," she said, uncertainly, and then after a moment, "We were wondering about you. May I come in?"

She was in already, for the matter of that, he told himself, and there was something possessive about her manner; she walked right up to the side of the bed where he was lying (and she must have seen that he wore no pajamas), and stood looking down at him. "Do you know what time it is?" she said.

"Time?" he said. She had on a blue-and-white striped dress, very crisp and fresh-looking, and beyond her, through the open doorway, he could see the blaze of sun on the sand and grasses in the yard outside. She did look pretty, and she looked very composed and very sure of herself; he wished suddenly that she would go away. "What time?" he asked, and he managed to make his voice sound drowsy.

"Time for breakfast, of course," she said, her voice determinedly bright and cheery. "And past it, really. It's almost eleven o'clock, if you want to know, and we've all been up for hours. But there's coffee and everything still, if you want to get up and have some. We thought, afterward, we'd bus in to Port Jeff and do some shopping."

"I don't want any breakfast," he said. For an instant he had had a very clear picture of Florence, sitting waiting there on the porch, at the head of the table; Florence, the matriarch, waiting ready to catechize, chide, forgive. Oddly, too, he could see himself, coming up the steps, facing her.

Elinor was staring at him troubledly. "Don't be silly!" she cried. "Of course you want breakfast!" She had just come from Florence, he knew, and so far she had carried something of that atmosphere with her. Now, however, she stepped nearer to him and her manner changed. "Richard, listen," she said, and (it was almost as if Florence might overhear her otherwise) she lowered her voice conspiratorially. "I think you ought to."

"Ought to what?"

She gave a little jerk of her body, almost as if she were stamping her foot impatiently. "Have breakfast, silly! Don't you know it will look strange if you don't." She hesitated a moment. "Mother didn't see you last night, did she?"

Richard shook his head. "No."

She stood looking at him, almost smiling. "Well, then," she said.

"Well, what?"

"Well—oh, Richard!" And her face seemed to crumple up suddenly. "Are you trying deliberately to hurt me, or what? You know what as well as I do. Are you coming to breakfast or not?"

"I don't want any breakfast, I told you."

"But that's silly! And besides, didn't I tell you it will look strange?"

"There are a lot of things strange around here."

"Meaning what?"

"Meaning everything, darling," he said. He was suddenly beginning to enjoy himself, and he lay back and pulled the covers up around him and grinned at her. (And Florence, wilting, waiting, alone at her place at the head of the table. . . .)

And then there must have been more, but there also were lapses, and in one of them Elinor was gone; there was only the battering brilliance of close-to-midday sun outside the doorway, and his own restless silence within. They were both gone—to Port Jeff, probably—when he got up and went over to the cottage. He had breakfast in the kitchen, eyeing the bottles above the sink, and then, on an impulse—or it was really a kind of direction: *Better look, better look, better look, they'll all fool you if they can,* the voices said—he went upstairs to the bathroom and looked into the medicine cabinet there.

Coming back, he glanced in at Elinor's room as he passed. It had two windows, one looking out toward the sea and the other facing east, and the white curtains drawn back with red ribbons were ones he remembered they'd found there, and laundered, earlier in the summer. There were a couple of framed reproductions on the walls, both left-overs from previous occupants, and the dresser top was littered with the kind of things girls use and leave on dressers—a brush and comb, both with green sort of iridescent backs, lipsticks, handkerchiefs, cold cream and powder jars and a box of Kleenex—all of them Elinor's.

They looked so used, so casual, so purely personal and so innocently a part of her that they brought all his tenderness back again. Elinor must be saved, he thought; careless, casual, innocent as she was, she must somehow be saved. . . . Otherwise, her room was just like the others', an iron bedstead and a bedside table, matchboard walls, brown-stained, a cane-bottomed chair and a rocker—all of them things that other people than they had used last summer, and others, and still others before them.

He went on downstairs, and for some reason washed all the breakfast dishes, theirs and his, and dried them carefully. When they came back he was down on the beach, and he listened quite amiably to their account of the trip to Port Jeff. It seemed they had seen a man with a goat in a cart, or some such nonsense.

So the day passed, one way or another. He got through it somehow, though there were lapses—or rather, for part of the time, it was as if a mist enveloped him. He could see them outside, looking in at him, and uneasily too, and sometimes he could see himself as well, moving purposefully and somberly, full of unsuspected meanings.

But there seemed to be no communication. They had lunch on the beach, at Elinor's suggestion, but he remembered none of it, and there was some sort of talk with Florence afterward. But he laughed that off.

And then evening, and Louisa was there, alone, this time, and by evening the mist had lifted a little; he found himself talking quite gaily at dinner—quite like his old self, in fact, so that they watched him and seemed to hang on his words—about, oh, about everything: about Jennie, and the bookshop, and how, with decent management . . . And yet, after all, who cared about making money? Thinking, thoughts: thoughts were the main thing. And travel . . .

"I guess I talk too much," he said once, with that generous, willing-to-give-way-to-another feeling of one who has governed the conversation long enough, and he was a little surprised when Louisa more or less took him up on it.

"You do, Richard. You do," she said. She had gotten up from the table and was sitting on the porch railing, smoking a cigarette. The dunes were dark, outside; the little, lighted rectangle of porch and floor and table was all there was to the world, or all there was to be seen of it. He glanced at her, all his senses instantly alert.

"I do, do I?" he said. "Well, there are others—"

"Not in the same way, darling," she said, and then she swung herself off the railing. "How's for cleaning up the dishes?" she said.

It was not till next day that she explained what she had meant. They were on the beach at the time, and as it happened he and Louisa were alone. Florence was practicing her breast stroke just off the shore and then Elinor walked off somewhere; as soon as she had gone Louisa approached him directly.

"Look, Richard," she said, without preamble. "Don't you think it's going a little too far when you talk to a stranger about the people you're living with? And tell lies, too," she went on, as he stared at her. "I don't care about myself. But, my God, when you talk that way about Mother . . . What's she done to you, anyway? Were you drunk, or something?"

"Drunk?" he said.

"Chub said you were. But, God damn it, drunk or sober—" Suddenly she dropped down beside him. "Look, Richard, I haven't said anything about this to Mother. And of course Chub won't, either. So don't worry about that end of it—"

"Chub?" said Richard. He was still thinking about Elinor. *Let her go if she wants to,* he had been thinking.

"Yes, Chub!" Louisa said impatiently. "Do you think he didn't tell me about that day when you busted in on him at his office? What's got into you lately, anyway, Richard?"

"What's got into me? What's got into you?" cried Richard. He had caught up with her at last. He was face to face with her now. He was ready for anything. Down the beach, Florence had landed, and was walking back, squeezing out the water from the skirt of her bathing suit as she walked. "Besides prying and spying on me," he went on. "Did you tell him about yourself?"

"I can't see that I come into it, darling," said Louisa. "And I didn't tell him. *He* told *me.* Remember? But let's skip that for the moment; it isn't important. What I'm worried about really is you. You've been acting so oddly lately, and I've been wondering about it. We've all been wondering. And then kiting around drunk like that, and spinning these frightful lies." She smiled suddenly. "It isn't like you, kid. Is anything the matter?"

Richard hardly heard her. " 'Drunk,' " he said. " 'Drunk' again. Not that I think Chub ever said that, either. He wouldn't. And of course you didn't tell him anything—of course not. Just enough to try to break up our friendship, that's all. Oh, I know you!" He was almost shaking at the wickedness of it. "But did you tell him *you're* drunk half the time you're out here? More than half, if it comes to that, and the rest of the time chasing this one and that one, f—ing, f—ing, f—ing, up the beach, down the beach—"

"*Richard!*" cried Florence. He saw her, all right, now that she had spoken. She was standing over them, her thin, scrawny, old woman's legs so close that he could have reached out and slapped them. But he wasn't concerned about her. He was watching Louisa, and Louisa had drawn back a little, her face white, her lips tight. She was staring at him. "You know the word, don't you?" Richard went on. ("Where is Elinor?" he was wondering.) "Do you think I don't know it too? Are you afraid now to hear somebody say it?"

Louisa looked from him up to her mother. "You see, Mother? It's just as I told you," she said. "All I did was just try to *talk* to him. And you see what happens? I don't know what to make of it."

But Florence was being very outraged and virtuous. "I know one thing," she said. "I know that no man can speak in that way to a daughter of mine, and remain in the same house with us, without an apology and an explanation."

So that was that, and Richard laughed about it afterward. Laughed, but he still kept his wits about him too; and as soon as he was dressed, before they could do anything to circumvent him, he walked up the road and took the bus in to Port Jefferson.

He bought a padlock and a hasp—a good, solid-looking one too—at the hardware store there ("There's been a lot of prying and spying going on around where I live. A man's got to protect himself," he told the proprietor, and then laughed to show that what he was saying had deeper meanings than the surface ones. "Is that so?" the man said, cautiously.)

When he got back (and he could see himself, plodding, intent, portentous, up and down the little dips and rises of the dune road), only Elinor was visible, and a great surge of delight rose in him to think that she, and she alone, had been waiting for him. As soon as he saw her he hurried toward her. "Where is everyone?" he said.

She looked at him uneasily. "You mean Mother and Louisa? They've walked over to the Simmonses," she said. "Richard, what's happened to you?"

"What's happened to me, how?" he demanded. He had come to her with love and tenderness, and now again he felt resentment rising.

"About Mother and Louisa, of course. They're so angry, especially Mother—"

He cut in on her. "*They're* so angry? And what about me? My place, my cottage—and they talked about putting me out of it. . . . Who're you siding with, anyway, me or them?" he demanded suddenly. "I've got a right to know, you know, *under*" (and he emphasized it) *"the circumstances."*

But she didn't get the drift; she just looked confused. "I'm not siding with anyone," she said. "Only, Richard," and she hesitated. "*Is* anything the matter, really? I mean, besides all the row, and so on. Was it because of last night?"

"Was what?"

"Was—? Well . . ." She looked down at the little bronze thing, the key, the extra key to the lock that the hardware-store man had given him, and that, without thinking about it (perhaps because, all the way out on the bus he had been thinking about it), he had pressed into her hand. "What's this?" she said.

"It's the key." Richard said, and just seeing it, and remembering it, made his spirits rise a little. Coming out on the bus it had struck him that if anyone was to have the extra key, it should be Elinor; this, he thought, was the thing that would prove his love more completely than anything else in the world.

She still stared at it puzzledly. "But for what?" she said.

"For the lock on my studio." He was impatient now.

"But you haven't *got* a lock," she said.

"I know, darling. I know. But with so much prying and spying going on, I just thought I ought to have one. Look," he said, and he tore open the hardware-store man's package and showed her the hasp, and the hinge, and the screws that went with it. Then he raised his eyes suddenly and looked at her. "You knew, too," he said.

"I knew what? Richard, *dear*—"

"Knew I didn't have a lock," he said. . . . But then tenderness triumphed. There was sun all around. They were alone. She had waited for him. "You know, darling," he said, and he wagged a finger at her playfully. "That might sound suspicious, what you just said, if I wanted to look at it that way. And after all the sneaking and peeking . . . But let's not talk about that," he went on. (He could see himself, tolerant, cheerful, relenting.) He smiled at her. "I know it wasn't you," he said. "And it never *was* you. I know who did the prying."

He was urbane, suave, relentless and yet relenting—and then suddenly she threw the key on the floor. "I don't want it!" she cried. "I don't *want* it!" And rushed into the house.

And surprise, and dismay, chagrin, anger, bewilderment . . . tumult, really; for a moment, there, he lost sight of himself. But the main thing that came to him, then as afterward, was the realization that she had been weeping. I can make her cry, too, he thought.

But then what? said the voices; it was about then that the voices began to say, *Death, death, death.*

He put the hasp and the lock in place, using nails because he hadn't a screw driver, and at the moment he didn't want to go over to the cottage and borrow one. But it was solid enough, nevertheless, and he tested it ostentatiously—*they* were back from the Simmonses by that time—and then went in and spent some time putting his desk in order.

And he had brought some sandwiches and a bottle of milk from Port Jefferson, too. That night he ate alone in the studio, and enjoyed it—no nuisance, no nonsense, no fuss about formality or playing up to *la* Florence; he just ate in the camping-out way he'd been used to in earlier days, with his papers spread out around him, and in the midst of the meal a new ending came to him for the poem he had been working on—how long had it been ago?

> *But the wood, and the blood on the wood,*
> *The bloody wood,*

it had gone before. But when he looked at it now he saw now that that part was meaningless; he didn't even know what it was supposed to convey himself, except that it had been something about a stake, or something.

No, we'll give it to the sand. It's the dark sand's claim, he wrote, swiftly, and then *maim, same, blame.* . . .

Let it stand where we stood, though we never will be the same.

And that finished it, and he wrote off a fair copy. (He left it on the porch of the cottage, a day or two later, in an envelope addressed to Elinor.) And then afterward he took a walk—this time not toward the dunes, but up toward the main road, and he remembered later stopping in at the little old real-estate agent's house in Mount Sinai (Debby-something, his name was, but Richard couldn't recall it clearly later, though he knew they had a little joke about it at the time). After all, he had as much right as anyone to inquire about buying the cottage. Stranger things than that had happened, and he might as well get his bid in first. And then, afterward—well, then, afterward, he went home and slept.

He awoke, and it seemed the most natural thing in the world to go over to the cottage for breakfast. It was early, apparently; he could tell that, now that he thought about it, by the way the dune-grasses' shadows lay so long and thin and spearlike. But Florence was in the kitchen when he got there, just up, and alone, and as usual, grouchy. She had just finished making coffee, and she looked at him, but she made no comment; she just poured herself a cup and then carried it, in silent grandeur, out toward the porch.

When he followed, she had established herself in her chair at the head of the table. "Sit down, Richard. Sit down," she said, weightily.

(He was already sitting down by then; but he let that pass, he let it pass. He felt gay and light-hearted, and ready for anything.)

But it was funny, the way she started. She sat looking him over for a moment. (He just waited.) Then: "I am glad you came over, Richard," she said. "And I am glad you had the tact to come early. In the circumstances it would have been decidedly awkward if either of the girls had been around at the moment." She stopped and looked at him again for a moment. "I assume you have come with an apology, and an explanation."

Richard made his eyes, oh, so wide. (*Oh, you bitch, you triple bitch, bitch, bitch,* he was thinking.) "An apology for what, darling?" he said.

Florence looked at him again, one of her long, impressive looks. (All around them, outside, the grasses were suddenly splintered with tiny light-crystals, as the sun struck the dew on them, and reflected. It was really early.) Florence took another sip of coffee. "Richard," she said, "I am a woman of, I think, considerable experience. But I must tell you that the things you said to Louisa yesterday, in my hearing, are such things as in my whole long life I have never before heard a civilized gentleman address to a lady before. And furthermore—"

"Lady?" said Richard quietly. (*But I could frighten you. Lord, I could frighten you.*)

"I beg your pardon?"

Richard merely bent his head ironically. "I beg yours," he replied. He was really enjoying this.

Florence stared at him silently for several seconds. "I shall try once more," she said, "because you so obviously at the moment are not yourself. I don't know what it is, Richard, that is troubling you. But whatever it is, it can hardly explain your actions of yesterday, not to mention all those other incidents that Louisa herself was talking to you about—and all this to a family who have gone out of their way to befriend you—who took you in, made a home for you, treated you practically as a son or a brother—"

She was getting excited, and Richard knew (he could always handle Florence; he knew) that the wilder she got the more self-contained he must be. He cut in, but he still spoke quietly. "Made a home for me, Florence?" he said. He picked his cup up and then put it down on the saucer. "Has it occurred to you, darling, that it was me that found this place? Me that brought you here? Me that made all the arrangements?" He picked his cup up again and this time he took a drink from it. "If you stop to think about it, darling, it's as much my place as yours, you know. Maybe more."

"I shan't mention such matters as rent," Florence said, and she smiled. "Ordinarily, it's the one who pays the upkeep of a place who has title to it."

But he had her there, too. "In that case, then, I guess it's Louisa who's the boss around here. She pays the bills," he said.

But she was clever, clever. "Exactly. My daughter. And whom, incidentally, to come back to the business at hand, you insulted most grossly yesterday. I'm still waiting, young man, for your explanation of that."

It was his turn to smile. "Insulted?" said Richard, and again he made his eyes wide and innocent. "My dear Florence, where in the world have you been keeping yourself?" And he paused to let the barb strike home. "I insulted no one. I merely told the truth. And you can't insult someone that way. It may hurt, but it isn't an insult. It's merely the truth."

And so then there was another row; by this time he was getting used to them. Only this one, it seemed, was the final one; he had the feeling, even as he sat there, that this was the moment of crisis.

"Young man, do you mean to sit there and tell me . . . ?" she began.

And then: "Please remember whose roof you are under. . . ." (But he hardly listened. . . .)

"I can only repeat what I said to you yesterday," she was saying, and they were both shouting then; there were movements upstairs, Richard noticed. (Where was Elinor? he asked himself.) "I can only repeat," she was saying, "that no one, no one, can remain in my house who has used the language you did. I suggest to you, Richard—and if necessary I shall do more than suggest it—that you leave this house today."

"But suppose I say no," said Richard. (But already he was saying yes; an idea had occurred to him. Mr. Debevois, that was the name; the real-estate man; he must have a talk with him.) "Suppose I don't go," he said, just to tantalize her.

Florence heaved herself up from her chair. "I'm afraid, then, young man, that would be a matter for the police to take care of. And don't think I would hesitate," she said. "You were our friend once, Richard, but you seem to be one no longer. I shall expect you to be off the premises by nightfall." And she started in to the kitchen to get another cup of coffee.

Richard watched her shrewdly. "It would surprise you, I'll bet, if it turned out I owned this place—if I bought it right over your heads." (He must see the old man at once.)

Florence hardly hesitated. She just paused for a moment in the doorway. "Richard, nothing would surprise me after this," she said dryly. "You will have to come back for your belongings later, I suppose. But I shall expect you to be off the premises by nightfall." And—*bitchy turkey, old-wattley, waddly Florence*—she disappeared into the cottage.

That night Richard vanished, and he was not seen again—by anyone who knew him well, at least—until the following Thursday. Meantime, for a while at least, no one knew what had become of him. This was partly due to their lack of communications at the cottage.

He spent most of that Sunday afternoon burning papers in the yard behind the studio and, presumably, packing; toward nightfall he set his suitcase and haversack ostentatiously outside the studio door. No one saw him leave, for the family went down for a swim soon after, but when they came back his luggage was gone, and Louisa, reconnoitering, discovered that the studio was locked and empty.

They assumed that he had gone in to Port Jefferson to get dinner and then take the early night train to New York; and Louisa, who waited till the last train to avoid him, went in to the city herself on that assumption. Actually, he had done nothing of the sort. He had left the house, but once out of sight he had doubled back around it. He spent most of the next four days camping out on the dunes.

But it wasn't till Wednesday morning, when his poem was found in its envelope on the cottage porch, that Florence and Elinor were sure of it, and not till later that Louisa, in the city, knew anything about it at all.

II

Camping out is fun, if you know how to do it, but one thing you have to allow for is that everything takes more time than it does ordinarily. Richard had had the foresight to pack a couple of blankets in his suitcase, in addition to a change of underwear, his flashlight, some socks and a few other odds and ends, including an ancient metal-framed shaving mirror, with hinged side panels, that he had found in the studio at the beginning of the summer and to which he had become oddly attached. In his haversack he had put handkerchiefs, a jersey, his swimming trunks and his more important papers, as well as a box of kitchen matches, a knife and fork and a cup and saucer that, unknown to the Hacketts, he had taken from the kitchen of the cottage just before leaving.

He had also put in the two sandwiches that had remained

from the ones he had bought in Port Jefferson, and an apple from the same source. He was well equipped, then, for camping; he had left the cottage at about 5:00 P.M., and—moving, of course, circuitously and surreptitiously—he reached the ruins of the older cottage about half an hour later. Even so, it was almost dark before he had completed his arrangements for the night, and after eating the sandwiches (he saved the apple for tomorrow's breakfast) he sat awhile on the cliff's edge, looking down at the skein of little white threadlike ripples in the dimness below, and then, quietly—peace had come to him; here there were no quarrels, no nonsense, no nuisance, no tensions of other people's bodies pressed or not pressed against his own; silence, too, had come, quietly—he crept down into the hollow behind the cliff where the cottage and his blankets were, and got ready for sleep. Before he knew it, sleep came.

Monday. Monday, he woke up a little bewildered. He was sleeping in a cellar somewhere, and the city was in flames around him; it was some time before he realized it was only sunlight and the smashed timbers and other wreckage of his cottage that had created the illusion. "His" cottage.... He thought about that, and he thought about it bitterly, when he remembered that other cottage that was also his, and where now *they* were staying.

But the sun and the warmth of the day soon charmed him away from the trials that had come upon him. He was north of that other cottage now, by a good half-mile or more, and the region in that direction was deserted; it was south of him, and south even of the Hacketts, that the little clusters of cottages began where the Bradleys, the Simmonses lived, among all the others whom he had met or not met, seen or not seen, in the course of the summer.

Here, though, he was away from them all, and he could feel his aloneness, welcomed and welcoming, settling in upon him with the very air that played above the dunes. He munched his apple contentedly, and then, feeling that he had the whole day before him, he decided to go in for a swim.

First, of course—just for safety's sake—he had to post lookouts, and after packing away his blankets and luggage in a hide-away he had found in the foundations, he put four stout pieces of timber upright in the sand, like sentinels, at the four corners of his new property. (They would serve too, it struck him, to mark off its limits, in case anyone else tried to claim it.)

Then he climbed down to the beach. He swam naked, of course, and for the first time that summer he did it happily. He had gone in with the Hacketts that way a few times in the course of the summer, but with them he had always been uncomfortable. "They tried to pervert me, they did their best to," he said later. "But they couldn't. They couldn't."

It had always seemed wrong, somehow, with them, and now really for the first time in months he enjoyed it; even the faint possibility that someone might come along unexpectedly and be startled only added a proper sort of titillation to his enjoyment. He swam up along the beach a short way and then back, and as he passed the cliff he noticed the ragged little stitching of spilled sand that showed where he had scrambled down it.

"I could build some steps there," he told himself. (There was no reason for not talking aloud now all the time, and he did so.) And then suddenly it burst on him: "I could build the whole place up. I could live here! Why not?" he said. "Why not? Why not?" And he swam swiftly to the shore to look things over.

Looking things over took time, and—he didn't know why—was not particularly encouraging. Perhaps because it was so very bitter, comparing these ruins, this wreckage, with the neat, tidy place (and his bed, his desk, his papers: he supposed *they* were prying and spying among them now) that he had built up before and now had been ousted from.

Or maybe it was just lassitude. He felt strangely tired, after all the bickerings and tensions, and he knew he needed rest to get over it. He needed rest, too, for a deeper reason, that he could put into words but not yet into meaning.

"I must gird myself," he kept saying. "My test is still to come." He didn't yet know what the test would be, but he knew that when it came he must not be found wanting.

"A man can't run away from his fate," he said. He was picking over the timbers of the cottage at the time, and he raised his head suddenly and looked long and intently in the direction of the other cottage, where *they* were. He knew their habits; it was a little past ten o'clock now, and they would have finished breakfast, they would probably be getting ready to go in to Port Jeff for the Monday morning shopping. Elinor would be down in the kitchen, finishing the breakfast dishes, and Florence upstairs in her bedroom, dressing and getting ready.

"So much evil!" he said. "So much evil!" In a way, being away off here gave him a sort of perspective on the cottage and on its life that he had never had before. As if it were a doll's house, with all its sides removable, he could look in and around in ways that he had never dared before; he could see *her* before the mirror—he was thinking of Florence—primping, powdering, painting, dressing up that old, sagging, scurrilous figure, and then smoothing the dress down over it, preening obscenely. . . . And downstairs, no-longer-innocent Elinor . . .

There was a boat, white-sailed, far out in the twinkling Sound abreast of him, and he addressed himself to it. "There are things that should be avoided," he said solemnly. "Unless it's absolutely necessary." And then he put the two women out of his mind altogether.

It was an interlude. He was tired. He was hungry, too, and on the spur of the moment he decided that he would not eat that day. He had money in his pocket, nine dollars and more, and he had no need to stint. But in one way that made the penance more enticing; it would make it even better for him. Knights had done it, on the eve of their knighthood, and had benefited by it. Saints did it, and had their saintliness refined and made more manifest by the experience.

"—And wolves, too," he added darkly. Wolves went hungry, too, and had their hunger sharpened to a needle point. Suddenly he put his head back and laughed up at the sky. "The lone wolf!" he cried delightedly; and then, not bothering for the moment who might or might not hear him, he bayed and bayed at the empty dunes around him. . . .

Around noon, he spied a solitary couple, in bathing suits,

walking along the beach, and luckily he saw them before they spotted him. He dropped down in the grass and watched them. They were a man and a woman, the man tall, dark-haired, and very tanned, and the woman blond and considerably shorter. She had on a shiny green bathing suit, very tight, and he wore only blue trunks. But nothing happened. They walked on a little way past his vantage point and then, stopping occasionally to look out to sea, they turned and walked back again. He watched them out of sight.

So time passed, and in spite of himself it still hinged on what *they* were doing, back at the cottage. It was one o'clock, and *they* would be coming back from Port Jefferson. Lunch would be late; it was past two o'clock when they sat down to it, and even then it was usually what Florence always called an "icebox meal"—warmed-up soup, perhaps, sandwiches, a salad, and of course ("They drank coffee like water") the eternal coffee. He saw them sitting at the table on the porch, two women in their mystery, and of course, being women alone, they gave up all the primness and pretense that they adopted when men were present.

Skirts rode up, legs were shown, and bosoms: for a moment he had a quick, scattered vision of even wilder things than that— things that he could imagine but couldn't quite visualize, so the pictures in his mind came inconsecutively, legs, arms entangled, white buttocks showing. . . . And then both of them laughing, laughing. Were they laughing about him?

"Sluts!" he said. "Sluts, all of them!" For he had changed his mind about Elinor, all right, or he had been changing it since that morning. "You can't go against the things that you see," he told himself, and the pictures he had seen were too clear, too vivid, too lifelike to be anything but true. And still, Elinor . . . She was young, of course, so perhaps there was hope for her. (That was something, he remembered suddenly, he had promised himself to think about. But she was so close, so close, too close to Louisa. And closer still, of course, to Florence. . . . Had she really told Florence everything?

"And my key!" he cried, in sudden anguish. "I tried to give her my key!" Lord! They must have laughed merrily over that!

So time passed. It was three o'clock, and Florence probably would be napping; Elinor would be sitting as she had sat so often in the summer, feet up on the porch railing, in the rocker, reading a detective story. "Like a whorehouse," he said. "Like a whorehouse when the men aren't around."

And if a man, any man, were to come along . . . For a while, Richard had to admit, he was tempted to be that man. But he put that aside. That would be degradation, and he busied himself going over his papers, and unpacking and repacking his baggage instead. He knew somehow that safety, the only safety for him, lay in staying out on the dunes.

Tuesday. Tuesday passed somehow—in contemplation? Vegetation? Relaxation? Incantation? Transmigration . . . ? His mind ran on and on. (In the night, that night, Tuesday, he heard a voice saying, *You. You. You. You. You* . . . and woke instantly, knowing that he had been chosen.)

Wednesday. Wednesday, he woke wary and apprehensive. (*Death. Death,* the voice was saying.) But that died out as he awakened. Again it was early, and he had a feeling that he had been somewhere, though he couldn't tell where. (It was Wednesday morning that the Hacketts found the poem to Elinor lying on the porch of the cottage.) But the four sentries still stood, strong and upright, in the sand; the dunes were empty; the only sounds were the wide, wide rush of air through the grasses and the solemn, omnipotent hammer—louder now than it had been yesterday—of the waves on the beach below.

There had been a wind in the night, then, or possibly a storm. (And that, perhaps, was why he felt so tired.) But apparently he had slept right through it—and now awakened only in its aftermath. He lay listening and looking about him for a while: at the stakes, standing upright against the brilliant sky, and the carvings of sand that all the winds of the years had made around the rubble and rubbish of the old foundations; at the rectangles he had marked out yesterday by dragging his feet in the sand, to show where the rooms of *his* cottage would be. (He was lying in the bedroom now, and the living room was just beyond.)

"A man could live here forever," he told himself. And then the thought came: Could he? Or could *he,* anyway? Everything was the way he had left it, last night when he had gone to sleep, and yet it was all subtly changed somehow. He was at peace, but he was not at peace. He was alone, but he was beginning to feel lonely. He was hungry, too, and when he got up a few minutes later he walked over to a diner that he remembered seeing, at a crossroads a little way beyond Mount Sinai, and had his breakfast there.

He had fried eggs and bacon with a side order of fried potatoes, and tomato juice and toast and coffee—all very good—and while he ate he chatted amiably with the man behind the counter. "Do you get much business here?" he asked him.

"Oh, so-so," the man said. "We do O.K."

"I ask because I'm thinking of settling down here," said Richard easily.

"That so?"

"I have business in New York. But I'm thinking of buying a little place out here, or else building. Along the beach, you know. I wouldn't want it to be too crowded."

"Well," the man said, and he sniggered a little, "you can find places out here to be quiet in, all right."

"What're you laughing at?" Richard demanded suddenly, and the man looked up at him in surprise.

"Why," he said. "Like I said, if you want to find places to be alone around here you can find 'em. Maybe that's what you need, mister," he added, after a moment's pause.

"Maybe that's what *you* need," Richard replied. But the man's feelings were hurt, apparently, and he went down to the other end of the counter where the icebox was, and started stacking and restacking the food on the trays inside it. He had a small, round face, so red that it looked like a ripe tomato, Richard thought, and he may have said so.

There was a store at the crossroads, too, run by a rather thin, elderly woman, and he bought bread and sliced meat for

sandwiches, and some fruit and a bottle of milk there. "Walkin'
trip?" said the woman cheerily, as she watched him stow his pur-
chases into his haversack.

"No, I'm staying in the vicinity at present, thank you," Richard answered politely. He was not in the mood for talking now,
and he fitted the straps of the haversack over his shoulders and
went his way back to his encampment.

So time passed. But he still felt restless. He took a swim, and
then made himself some sandwiches and sat in the sun in his
dining room and ate them; he would put a big picture window
on the sunset side, he decided.

But he still felt restless, and he walked about the dunes a good
deal that morning, sometimes crouching and prowling like an
Indian or a hunter, and sometimes scorning all concealment.
(It was that morning that Elinor saw him, or thought she saw
him, from an upstairs window of the cottage, walking along
the cliff's edge farther up and gesticulating ("But the world
needs me too!" he was saying protestingly. "I can't bother about
individuals"), and then as soon as she'd noticed him he dropped
suddenly, almost as if magically, out of sight. It was so sudden
that for a long time she was sure that he—whoever he was;
Richard or some other man—must have fallen over the cliff as
she watched, and later on, after lunch, she forced her mother to
walk up the beach a way to investigate. They saw nothing, and
they had no knowledge that Richard was watching them as they
walked.)

He watched them then, and he watched them later, when
they went down to the beach for their afternoon swim. Earlier
in the day he had put the Hacketts out of his mind—or rather,
since he had now reached the point where he let his mind govern
itself as it willed, they had simply dropped out of it, leaving only
emptiness and a vast melancholy.

He felt sad, he felt abysmally sad. He felt lonely and as if he
had no purpose in life, and it wasn't till later, when he happened
to notice *them* walking up the beach, that remembrance of *them*
really returned to him. Though it brought back all his tensions
and worries, it still made him feel better, somehow.

It gave him confidence, it gave him excitement, and he hurried quickly down along the cliff—but remembering, of course, to keep cover—to the spot where he judged they would be. Then he peered very cautiously over the edge.

He had guessed fairly accurately, he discovered. *They* were a little beyond him, and nearer the cottage, and for some reason they kept glancing up at the cliff top, so he had to be careful. He drew back, and it wasn't till they passed directly beneath him that he could hear their voices; even then they were lost sometimes in the ring and wash of the waves.

But it seemed that Elinor wanted to go on and Florence wanted to go back, and there was some talk of somebody jumping. "But I tell you I *saw* it!" he heard Elinor cry impatiently, and then Florence replied rather pettishly, "But where? First you said it was farther back, and now you think it was farther on; I must *say*, Elinor—" and then a wave came in and drowned out their voices.

Richard inched himself forward a little again. He was wildly excited by now, but he went cautiously, and it was well that he did so, for when he reached the edge of the cliff he found that they were staring up at it, almost at the spot where he was hiding. They didn't see him, although they were so close to him now that if he'd thrown a rock it would have hit them; they just stood there, scanning the face of the cliff as if they were looking for something. They inspected it carefully for a while, and then Florence turned to Elinor.

"Well?" she seemed to say (again, there was too much wave sound for him to hear their voices), and then Elinor said something, and then Florence looked at her and laughed. It was after they had turned back toward the cottage that Richard threw the stone.

It was only a small stone, and it landed some feet behind them. (After all, he hadn't really tried to hit them.) But its impact, apparently, was enough to startle them—Elinor, he was somehow surprised to notice, as much as Florence—and it was like a joke, really, to see them both turn and look back up the beach and then at each other, and then (carefully not hurrying exactly, but still moving faster than usual) walk on down the beach.

Watching them while they swam, later on, was not so exciting. He knew their habits, but when he got there at around three
o'clock, their usual time for a swim, they were late, and when
they came it was not from the cottage but along the beach, from
the direction of the Simmonses; they had been visiting again,
probably, he decided.

He watched them sit on the beach for a while, Florence
reading and looking up occasionally as Elinor talked to her;
and then, Elinor first and Florence later, they went in the water.
Richard watched, but he didn't feel cheerful now, or ironic, or
excited. He felt mournful and melancholy—aloof, too: as aloof
as a god, sitting there on the cliff-top, looking down at them and
at the evil they represented.

To be sure, there was little evil to be seen there now. Elinor,
when she came out of the water, undid the brassière top of
her bathing suit and lay bare to the waist in the sun; Richard,
when he saw the round brown breasts exposed, with their little
brown-button nipples, felt his heart beat a trifle faster in antici-
pation. But nothing happened; she just lay there, scooping sand
in her fingers for a while and then reaching in the beach bag for
cigarettes and, having lit one, lying back again; Florence, owlish-
looking in her reading glasses, turned to glance at her once or
twice, that was all.

He sat staring at them, brooding, not thinking, as a god
might sit brooding, not thinking, but merely embracing his
knowledge, itself all-embracing: evil, all the world's evil.

He shut his eyes for a moment and sat there, waiting. He felt
close to something real now, something fundamental, and there
was no point in trying to hurry it; when he opened his eyes,
nothing had changed.

There they were before him: two women on a beach, apparently harmless, apparently innocent. (If he cried out to the
world about them, the world would deny him.) And yet there
they were, the embodiment of everything that had gone wrong
with him; they were the instigators, or at least Florence was, and
as he sat there the whole summer seemed to revolve around him
like a maelstrom, black-centered (and they were the center), like
a funnel, like a target (*Death*).

"That's the way some girls get their men," his mother had said.

Elinor, lying spraddle-legged, spread out, shamelessly bare to the sun, turned her head toward her mother, and apparently she said something, for again Florence focused her owlish stare at her; then she shook her head slowly and let her eyes drift back to the book again.

And the sun beat down. And the waves curled in. There they were, the embodiment of everything, of the scorn, of the mockery that had been heaped on him, the debasement. And he had come to them so happy, so eager, so willing to be friendly with everyone.... "I just sat there and thought, and if I'd listened, you know" (*Death,* the voice said, *Death*), "I might have known then; I might have gone down and finished them. But I still hadn't settled about Elinor.

"But I was too confused. I had done a good deal of thinking, those days on the dunes. But I still wasn't clear in my mind. I hadn't thought things out yet, really; all I could think of was that if I went near them then I'd just get into an argument, and I didn't want that. I had too much respect for them. I was too confused."

So he sat there and watched, and all the while the tight core of his anger was growing harder and tighter. *If they would just go away,* he thought. (But he knew even then that they wouldn't do that.) *Or if they would disappear. If they would just simply vanish. If a wave would smite them.* (He shut his eyes again, and—counting really on magic, this time; on God, maybe; on Fate—he kept them closed long enough for the slowliest forming wave to form, far away out on the Sound, and grow slowly, and swell, and break.... He could almost hear the crash of it, breaking, and he opened his eyes.

They were there, of course. They were still there. Elinor had turned sidewise a little, as if to brown some as yet unbrowned part of her nakedness, so the next man would find it more appetizing; Florence was still deep in her book. Down the beach, at the rocks where they sometimes had gone to get mussels, a flight of gulls was circling.

And if they had disappeared, of course, that still wouldn't have solved the problem of Elinor; that was something he still had to think about. Could she, *could* she be saved? And if so, how? So—"I had to do *something*"—in the end, he went away himself. "I have business elsewhere," he said, and then a phrase that he had used earlier in the day came back to him.

"I have business in New York," he said, and as so often it seemed to happen with him at that time, he had no sooner said the words than a reason came, like a revelation, to explain them and justify them. Of course! Jennie, he thought; Jennie Carmody and the bookshop! He had business there, he had money there too; if he counted this week he had a whole week's wages due him. It would only be plain common sense to go down and collect that.

And there was his room that he had to look into. And Chub Bassett, maybe, he was sure there was something he had wanted to ask Chub. "Why, I've got a lot of things to attend to, first," he told himself.

So he went to New York, though he had no sooner got there than he decided that the trip had been a mistake. It did one thing, though; it made it clear to him what he had to do.

Otherwise, it was simply a waste of time. The bookshop, of course, was closed by the time he got there, so he could collect no cash from Jennie, and from now on he was forced to watch his money. He had had six dollars and sixty-odd cents when he arrived at Long Island Station, and after going past the bookshop and finding it closed he had dinner at the Automat on Lexington Avenue, up above Grand Central; that left him with five dollars and ninety cents, even.

And there was something about the tumult and movement of the city that confused him. It was somehow not *his* place; his purpose lay elsewhere. He belonged on the dunes, at the cottage. He had a mission there, a problem, and he had to solve it; here he was merely wasting his time, and because of his nervousness and confusion he did something he rarely did—he went into a bar and had a drink.

It was a pleasant place, quiet, agreeably dark. He talked to no one, because there seemed to be no reason to, and besides he was busy with his own thoughts. But he enjoyed being there, and when he had finished his glass and the bartender happened to be passing he ordered another one. Once before, and no farther away than that afternoon, when he had been sitting on the cliff looking down at the two women, he had felt that he was approaching clarity, that the real solution was almost within his grasp. Somehow, then, he had lost it.

And now, again, in the carefully dimmed, yellow-paneled room, he had something of the same feeling. He was approaching it again, and this time he was determined not to lose it.

They were *there,* to begin with, that was the way he was thinking. And *they* were evil. And being evil, *they* must be stopped. Suddenly it burst on him, brilliantly—"like a vision"—the real solution: *to be stopped, they must be done away with!*

It was as simple as that, and it was also inevitable. It was the only way out for all of them. They must simply be stopped. Stopped, like that. Done away with. "It was just like a vision," he said later. "I was standing in that bar, far away from everyone, and it came to me. If I was ever to be anything, *do* anything, that was it. Things got cloudy later, but right then it was the clearest path I had ever seen, leading straight before me."

He had his second drink by now, and he drank it, and when the bartender paused in front of him again he pushed out a dollar to pay for it. He was outside, on Madison Avenue, before he realized the rate at which he had been spending. The drinks there had been fifty-five cents apiece, or a dollar ten together. And the fare to Port Jeff was one seventy-three, and the bus twenty cents on top of that. And at the moment—he stopped dead on the sidewalk while he counted—he had four dollars and eighty-six cents exactly.

Four dollars and eighty-odd cents, he thought; that was drawing things fine with a vengeance! Here he was, in New York, far away from the cottage, and far away even from the train that would take him there, and if he kept on like this . . .

The thing to do was to make sure of his ticket at once. He saw a downtown bus coming, and ran for it; he wasn't truly at ease again until he had reached Thirty-fourth Street, and walked cross-town to Long Island Station, and reached the ticket office, and bought a ticket back to Port Jefferson.

"I want it for tomorrow," he said to the man behind the window. "I can't go down there tonight. I have things to do here. Are you sure this will be good for tomorrow?"

The man was bald and sallow, in a tan alpaca jacket. He thrust a finger toward the ticket which still lay on the counter between them. "Good for thirty days," he said. "All train tickets are. You can read it there."

Richard looked at him. "Good for thirty days," he repeated. "Then it will certainly be good tomorrow."

"It will certainly be good tomorrow," the man said wearily, and when Richard passed two one-dollar bills through the window he made change with brisk precision. Richard hesitated.

"I've got to get back there," he told the man, earnestly.

The man had picked up a pencil and was making notations on a pad. He didn't raise his head. "You'll get back there all right, friend," he said. "On that ticket."

And it was somehow just getting the ticket, and having it, and holding it, that solved everything. He felt sure now, sure and at peace. He had been lost, before, and now, miraculously, he had found the way again. He was safe, and he could afford to look largely, calmly, even tolerantly on the world and its people as he made his way back along Thirty-fourth Street to Third Avenue and up it; he could afford to go back to his room now, and sleep.

He slept late, and awoke feeling calm, poised, and confident. Coming out, he met the landlady on the stairs and had some words with her, but his feeling about such matters—about everything not connected with his mission, in fact—was so detached that, once out on the street, he couldn't clearly remember what it was they had talked about; he had given her some money or had promised her some, or something; that was the gist of it. He had forgotten about Jennie, and he didn't go near the shop; he had forgotten about everything but his largeness and his definiteness, and the largeness and definiteness of his purpose.

To be sure, there were moments, queer, shaky, indecisive moments, when it seemed as if a tremor had passed through his brain, blurring everything, and he wanted to draw back and at the same time to hurry forward. But though these were to increase later on, they still came infrequently, and that morning they hardly bothered him. For the most part his purpose and himself were one, and it was a wonderful feeling. There was even, now, plenty of time, and on his way to the station he stopped in at a lunchroom, and had some ham and eggs and some toast and some coffee. "I was in a bad way a while ago," he told the man when he brought him his order.

"So?" said the counterman.

"Yes. A fire. Burned my cottage. Just a wreck it is, now, all that's left of it. I couldn't see straight, either. You know how it is, sometimes. Women trouble, too." He took a drink of his coffee and smiled at the man. "I'm on my way now to straighten things out," he said.

And then the long start-and-stop, start-and-stop, start-and-stop, start-and-stop of the train, where the thing to hang onto was the feeling that now you were winding up the threads instead of unraveling them. At Port Jefferson, he stopped in a hardware store and bought a length of clothesline and, as an afterthought, an ice pick and a hatchet. Coming out on the train, he had got to thinking of Elinor. "Poor Elinor, she's all tied up," he had thought, and that was why he had bought the clothesline; he was still so uncertain about Elinor.

He bought the ice pick and the hatchet because he hadn't figured things out yet, completely, and he wanted to be prepared. As he paid, the salesman said something cheerful to him—about "stocking up," or something; he couldn't remember. But he was in one of his brooding moods at the moment, and he didn't answer.

He was brooding still when he took the bus—brooding and resentful: "All the trouble they're putting me to," he was thinking—and he nearly went past his stop in consequence. But he got off in time, and when he reached his camp it was a pleasure to find that nothing had changed.

Everything was the same as before, his luggage still hidden beneath the boards he had placed to cover it, the lines marking his rooms still there, the stakes still on guard—everything. There was even a half loaf of bread still left where he had stored it, and though he hadn't so much as a piece of butter to go with it he sat down on the cliff's edge and munched a couple of slices quite cheerfully.

Now the only thing to wait for was the night.

12

Thursday, Louisa had a dinner date with Chub Bassett. They were to meet at the Madison for cocktails at about six, but before that she had a telephone call from her mother which changed things a little.

The call came through at eleven-thirty, to the apartment, and Florence was properly apologetic for calling so early. "I hope I didn't wake you up," she said, and Louisa carefully assured her that she had been up for hours; Louisa's irregular hours had always been a point of contest with Florence, who made a virtue of early rising.

"What's up, Mother? Where are you calling from?" she asked. It was unusual for Florence to call from the country.

"I'm in Port Jefferson. We came in," Florence said, and she hesitated. "I don't want to worry you."

"Worry me?"

"Yes. It may all just be something quite unimportant. But I thought, since I had the chance to phone." She hesitated again. "It's about Richard," she said. And then, as if, in her phone booth in the drugstore at Port Jefferson, she sensed Louisa's puzzlement and impatience at the other end of the line, she poured out the whole story—about the poem, undeniably Richard's, found on the porch; and the strange, gesticulating figure that Elinor had seen; and, above all, the feeling they both had, of fear. "But I don't want to trouble you," she said. "I just thought, since I was here, I'd call."

"I know," Louisa said. As a matter of fact, she had just gotten up, and she was sipping her first cup of coffee as she spoke. She knew too, already, what was expected of her. She was supposed, if possible, to get down there as soon as she could and straighten out matters.

"The thing is, Mother," she went on, and she was speaking honestly, "I just can't believe it. After all, he left Sunday, didn't he? Didn't we see him go, with his suitcase and everything? And the poem, or whatever it is—well, I mean, couldn't he have left it then, some time on Sunday, and you just have discovered it?"

"We thought of that. In fact, at first, it's what we *did* think. But then when Elinor saw him—"

"But you said yourself she wasn't sure."

"I know. Well—" said Florence.

"And after all, you know, Mother, really," Louisa was pushing her advantage, "what can he do? The poor guy, he *is* nutty, really, and I told you so long ago. But my God, he's no maniac. He's harmless. And anyway, if you lock the doors—"

"We've got the Simmons boy coming to spend the night," Florence said, in a voice that had a thin, dispirited sound as it came over the phone. "But—" and then Louisa heard the operator's voice cutting in: "Your three minutes are up," she said. "If you wish to continue will you please deposit forty-five cents for an additional three minutes?"

Somehow, the intrusion had an instant effect on Louisa. It made the distance and the isolation of her mother come real, and she found herself trying almost desperately to keep the call open. "Have you got the change, Mother?" she cried. After all, if they had gone so far as to get in touch with the Simmonses, they must really be worried. "Can I call you back?"

Then—and even at the sound, her moment of panic subsided—she heard the *bong* of a quarter and the higher note, repeated, of two dimes, as Florence deposited them. The thing was to be realistic.

"Look, Mother, what do you want?" she said as the coin-sounds diminished. "Do you want me to come down, or what?"

"Oh, no. Not if it's inconvenient. I just thought—"

"I know, Mother." She knew what her mother had thought. "Listen. I *can* come down, if it's important. But if I do, it means I run out on the Bakewell show this afternoon, and at the last minute, and you know what that means in radio. And tomorrow—well, tomorrow I *could* come down, except that Friday's the day I usually hear from the agency. But I suppose if I had to I could say the hell with that. I could come down tomorrow morning. Or if you want me to, really, I could come down on the late train tonight. The thing is, I don't know if it's that important. Is it, Mother, really?"

"I don't know. I don't really know, Louisa," came the voice, and Louisa found herself faced with the necessity of balancing all that she knew of her mother—her pretensions, her weaknesses; her demandingness and her strange sudden moments of independence—against the sound of it over the phone.

"You don't know! Well, my God, then!" she cried, and then stopped. She was trapped and she knew it, and she might as well accept it. "Look, Mother," she said. "I'll get down when I can. Tonight, maybe, if I can make it, or anyway tomorrow. On the early train, probably, tomorrow." There was no answer, and for an instant she feared the connection had been broken. "Are you still there, Mother?" she said. "Will you be all right tonight, if I don't get down till tomorrow?"

"We'll be all right tonight," said Florence.

Chub, though, unexpectedly, was more impressed with the turn of events than Louisa had been. Louisa was only a few minutes late at the Madison, and while she told him about her mother's phone call he gazed around the gray-walled room, listening without speaking.

"The fellow is pretty crazy, you know," he said when she had finished.

Louisa looked at him. "Oh, Chub!" she said. "I suppose so. But isn't everybody, in one way or another? Don't you go getting steamed up about him too."

Chub smiled. "I'm not, kid. Only—well, they'd be pretty helpless out there if anything happened."

Louisa studied him for a moment. "Do you really think—?" she began, and Chub waved a deprecatory hand to interrupt her.

"I don't know," he said. He picked his glass up and looked at it and then took a sip from it. "No, I suppose not, really," he said. "That kind . . . He was a little on the fairy side, wasn't he?"

"Well, not actively. I don't think so, at any rate. But I know what you mean."

"Yes. Well, what I mean is, that kind don't do anything violent, do they? They shout and scream and make scenes, just as he did. But beyond that . . ." Chub stopped suddenly. He had remembered that they sometimes did turn violent, and the look in his eyes told Louisa what he was thinking.

She smiled at him, a little grimly. "Listen, honey," she said. "You may not know it, but you're being about as optimistic about this as—well, I don't know. But if you're trying to cheer me up!"

Chub reached out and put his hand on hers impulsively. "I'm sorry. I didn't mean to upset you. Let's have another drink and forget about it."

But, as if by common consent, they returned to the subject later. "You're sort of worried still, aren't you, baby?" Chub said. They had their second cocktail before them, and Louisa smiled at him gratefully.

"It's what you said a few minutes ago," she told him. "They *would* be helpless down there, all right, if anything happened. And then too, I was thinking about the way Mother sounded over the phone. I never heard her so sort of—well, submissive, I guess the word is. Anyway, I could tell she was worried. Of course, tonight, they've got that Simmons boy coming over. . . ." She glanced at him suddenly. "Look, honey, would you mind very much if I ran out on you tonight, and went down there? There's a train, I think, around eight o'clock."

"I'd mind like hell if you tried to do it that way. What's the matter with my driving you down?"

Louisa stared at him, honestly astonished. "But, my God, Chub! Don't you have to be at the office tomorrow?"

"I can come back tomorrow morning, if I have to. But most likely there won't be anything important, and I can phone from Port Jefferson and find out. No, I mean—" Chub's face flushed a little, and he signaled to the waiter to cover his embarrassment. "I mean, really, I've been worried a little, too. The guy's nuts, I tell you, and I don't like the idea of them having to handle him alone."

He put some bills on the waiter's salver and started pushing the table aside to make room for them to get out. "Let's get going, shall we? I suppose I ought to get a toothbrush and stuff from the apartment. Do you have to get anything from yours?"

They were getting Chub's car out of the garage; they had been to the Hacketts' apartment and then to his; they had had a quick drink "for the road" at his place; and it was nearing eight o'clock and they were edging out from the garage into the traffic of Fifty-fourth Street when she turned to him. "Oh, Chub, honey, you're really a lamb to be doing this," she said. And Chub grinned at her.

"I hope I get my reward some time."

"Well, my *dear!*" she said. "Haven't you?"

"I don't mean it—that way," Chub said, and Louisa glanced at him demurely.

"Why, darling! You mean—?" she said.

"I mean for real," said Chub, and then the lights changed ahead of them on Second Avenue, and the cars, his among them, began getting under way.

They took the Fifty-ninth Street bridge and then out Northern Boulevard to Grand Central Parkway and Route 25 to Smithtown; it was Thursday, and once beyond the local traffic of the city and suburbs they had little to delay them—except a certain shamefacedness on their own parts about too much worrying and hurrying.

And it was the end of August then, and still balmy. . . . They turned off onto the Parkway at about eight-thirty, and for a while they drove silently, with now and then a car spurting to pass them, now and then passing one themselves, but for the most part with the road fairly clear ahead of them and the fields and occasional houses or groups of houses on either side of them lying golden and quiet in the long autumnal twilight.

"I suppose—" Louisa said. She was lighting a cigarette, and when she'd lit it she used it to light another and then passed the second one to Chub, at the wheel. "I suppose we're being just about as silly as— Well, we'll get out there around ten-thirty, I suppose, won't we? And by that time they'll probably be sitting there peacefully, thinking mostly of bed. And they'll look at us—"

"Meantime, though, it's fun," Chub said, and she moved a little closer to him.

"Did you think to bring that flask?" she asked.

They had dinner—a drink, a club sandwich, a cup of coffee—at a gaudy and glamorous diner that they had discovered previously, near the end of the Parkway extension, and they ate quickly and rather silently.

"Damn that Richard!" Louisa said once, in the midst of a story Chub was telling her about an old schoolmate he had run into. "I can't see why the devil Mother ever took up with him." Then she looked at Chub penitently. "I'm sorry, honey. I didn't mean to interrupt you. But—you know."

"Sure," Chub said. "I was just filling in time, anyway. Let's get going."

They went through Smithtown at about ten o'clock, past the boys hanging out around the drugstore and the restaurant and the long row of cars parked in front of the movie house, and then out underneath the double line of big elms at the farther end of the town's main street. Chub, by that time, had long ago switched on the lights. By that time, too, they were frankly hurrying a little, though as far as either one was ready to admit it was as much because they were nearing the end of a fairly long journey as for any other reason.

Louisa, ordinarily, was a rather scary passenger, but she didn't complain when Chub whizzed round the intersection at Coram, or at the speed with which he juggled the car around the curves on the side road it led into. They were getting out toward the sea now; roads were ruggeder, narrower, and more winding, but Chub took them at hardly diminished speed and though Louisa winced once or twice she said nothing. When they came to the dune road leading down to the cottage, though, he had to slow down, and as the headlights swept across the dunes and then settled on the rutted little track ahead (it is quite possible that Richard saw them, as he left the cottage, but he thought they were only flashes in the sky), they both found themselves leaning forward a little in their seat.

"We're being fools, of course," said Louisa, and then a moment later, "But they seem to be up, anyway." And indeed, as the cottage came into view—brightly lit, sitting snug and cozy-looking in the surrounding darkness—and dipped out of sight and then rose again like a ship at sea as the car climbed out of the intervening hollow, nearer, clearer, its windows streaming with light, it seemed that everything must be all right within.

But when they stopped in front of the house, something—Chub later thought it was the fact that the front door was standing wide open, and this, coupled with the blaze of light and the silence, seemed ominous—made Chub reach out and check Louisa as she started to get out of the car.

"You stay here. Let me look around first," he said, and without quite knowing why she obeyed him passively.

Chub went in, and seemed at once to be gone a long time and to be back almost immediately; he came down the cottage steps without a word, and as he ran around the front of the car on his way to the driver's side and she saw his face, white, ghastly, frozen, as he passed through the glare of the headlights, Louisa found herself seized with a violent fit of shivering.

13

It was like a wind, like those soft on-shore winds that often spring up on the dunes at night, only this time it was more like a wind that was *in* him instead of outside him, that made him its spear-point, him the force that produced the first flutterings, the first bendings and waving—of the dune-grasses, for example, which remained still and quiet until he had passed, and then fluttered, and bent, and waved.

He was extremely conscious of his surroundings. "I knew it had to be at night. There is a rightness about things like that. And it was something that had to be done. From the minute I bought the ticket—I guess even before that, from the time I was standing in that bar—I knew everything was right; I was sure; I was on the right track.

"But I knew it had to be at night. They would be alone then, that was one thing, and I didn't want any interference. And besides, at night, they would be more themselves."

And besides, there were things he still hadn't figured out. "You'd be surprised, you know, even when you are right up against it, how hard it is to really think about death."

He was extremely conscious of his surroundings. He had come down on the three-o'clock train, having missed the morning one, and had got out to the dunes at about six o'clock, and at that time the sun was still shining. He watched it set, out across the Sound, and the blue line, no broader than a pencil stroke, that was the coast of Connecticut, growing grayer and dimmer against the graying water; watched the night slowly settling over the dunes, darker and still darker, and the wink of the lighthouse at Port Jefferson harbor growing steadily brighter.

He wasn't always calm, and he wasn't always cheerful, waiting. There were times when an almost panic sense of hurry took hold of him, and only the feeling that whatever he did would be the right thing, if he waited for the impulse to guide him, restrained him from going over to the cottage and confronting them instantly. ("But I knew that would only end in an argument. And I didn't want that. I had had enough of arguments.") And these times alternated with others of a churning, resentful despondency, when he could almost have screamed with his rage, his hatred, his bitterness.

But he had to wait. His hatred wasn't strong enough yet, or it still wasn't centered; he hadn't yet reached the point of action, and meanwhile he had to wait till the right moment came. He couldn't think. "I had thought and thought before. But the funny thing was that once I had decided what I had to do I just couldn't seem to think any more. And that troubled me. I had a lot of things still that I wanted to figure out."

Florence had to die; he knew that. But he wasn't so sure about Elinor. He had somehow a picture of her in his mind, naked, naked to the waist anyway, and tied up with ropes and straining at them, like a picture he had seen long ago of someone—Brunhilde; or was it Joan of Arc?—in a history book that his mother had had, and he had looked at it secretly, and felt guilty about it. But it didn't fit in, because as she leaned forward, breasts bared, her arms straining at the ropes, he could see flames licking at her: was it the cottage, burning? Was he fated to burn the cottage—and then rescue her?

He didn't know, and the whole thing was vague, and uncertain, and misty. But it was strong enough still to make him unreel the rope he had bought and wind it carefully, mountaineer-fashion, around his waist.

And Louisa—Good God! Had he forgotten Louisa? He had, of course, because she wouldn't be there; she just wouldn't, until the week-end, and it showed how important it was, or it would have been, to have everything planned out first. Because she, in a way, had been the key to everything—or had she? Or was it Florence?

Anyway, it was too late now. It was too late for planning, or for changing anything. Louisa would have to wait. She would be down for the week-end, certainly, and then he would be waiting for her; he could finish Louisa up then.

The one thing he was sure of, as sure as he could be sure of anything, was that tonight he was right, he was certain, and in the end he decided not to think, to let things take their course, confident that when the right moment came he would know it, he would be told.

In the end, the right moment came.

The right moment came and, unexpectedly, it was just like any other moment before it, except that before it he had been sweating and fretting, he had been jumping up to pace back and forth and then sitting down and jumping up to pace again, he had been as uneasy as a man waiting for the start (and the starting delayed) of a long journey—and in the midst of it he stopped and looked up (Go. *Now,* he had heard), and the next moment was walking slowly, steadily, solemnly across the dunes.

Like a soldier, he thought: "Like those war-time movies—you know? Where you'd see the man standing, nervous and sweating, waiting. And the next minute he'd be walking, with the guns going off all around him. . . ."

It was dark, but he had no difficulty seeing; as with the soldier, there seemed to be flashes of something—his resolution, his impulse, his direction—and if he stumbled a couple of times that was in the dark spots; other times, the whole expanse of the dunes seemed as bright as day. There were no sounds to accompany the gun flashes, but he knew that if he wanted to he could imagine them, and for a moment he did imagine them; he imagined them and they came—the great crash-boom-crash and the roaring symphony of explosion and exploding destruction, the destroying hammering that he knew could be made to grow and grow till it blotted out everything in its own fury.

But as soon as it started, almost, he stilled it. Quiet, now, was what he wanted. There was a fold in the dunes that he knew, and a rise beyond it where the lights of the cottage came into view. Looking down, he could see that all was quiet there too.

There were lights in the living room and lights in the kitchen, but none elsewhere; they were just about finishing the dinner dishes, probably, which was just as he wanted it. They would be together, and he crept down the last slope of dune and up the porch steps and across to the door as quietly, and as somberly, as an Indian.

The door was locked.

The door was locked, but in spite of himself he couldn't help rattling it, and they must have heard it. There were footsteps along the passageway inside, and then a voice—it was Florence's —saying, "Is that you, Roger?" And at the same time the sound of the key turning in the lock.

Roger? Who was Roger? The name, at the moment, meant nothing to him. "Yes, I'm Roger," he said, but it is doubtful if she heard him, for the words came out grumblingly, and anyway she was opening the door as she spoke; the next instant a flashlight shone on him, on his feet first—"I suppose we're being silly," she was saying, "locking up this way. But—" and then the light shot up quickly and shone on his face.

And again he was walking. He walked in, and she gave way before him like butter. She didn't say a word, but he could see, even without looking at her, the fright in her face—he could *feel* it, like an aura—and as he saw it and felt it he could feel his own anger rising.

"I just thought I'd drop in," he said. It was something he had thought of while crossing the dunes, and it came out easily. He walked past her, right into the living room, and then, after a second of hesitation, she followed.

"Yes. Yes, Richard," she said. She was thoroughly frightened, he could see that. "So I see." She looked pale, and her face was pinched, as if she were trying to hold it together. In the kitchen there was a noise of water running from the tap and an occasional shuffling of crockery that told him that someone—was it Elinor?—was washing the dishes.

"I have a right to, all right," he said.

And then suddenly she seemed to get command of herself a little. "I don't know about rights, Richard," she began.

"I do!" he cried. But things weren't going the way he had wanted them to. He was getting into an argument, and that was one thing he didn't want. And yet he couldn't stop; he had to tell her it was all her own fault, it was she that was to blame for what he had to do.

"I was the first to come out here," he said. "I found this place. I found it, do you deny that? And then you take it, you take it over. You take me over, too. Or you did, or you tried to. But you couldn't, you found you couldn't, not even with setting your own daughter onto me, and all the rest of it. So you couldn't, and you drive me out; you just take it and you drive me out. Oh, don't think I didn't know what you were up to, Florence. Did you think I didn't know? But if you think you can manage that—" He stopped. There was more that he wanted to say, much more, but he stopped. Most of all, he wanted to see them both together.

"Where's Elinor?" he demanded. She should be there to hear this, too.

Florence had been staring at him. She had been listening, all right, so hard that she had to wait a second to answer. "She is in the kitchen," she said, and then she paused again; it was as if she was trying to figure out just what she wanted to say. She was being very careful of him, all right; very careful, and it was funny to watch, and it pleased him. "My point is, there is no reason to get excited," she said.

"Excited!"

"Exactly. There is no sense in it, Richard, really. Sit down, won't you, please?"

He could let his rage rise a little. "Are you trying to tell *me* what to do?" he demanded.

"No, of course not, Richard. No one is trying to do that. I simply meant that, since you've come—well, I'm glad you came." She had to swallow a lot when she talked, he noticed; it was as if her mouth was dry. "And since you did come I just wanted you to sit down and, well, talk things over. No one drove you out, you know; that is just your imagining. And there is no sense at all in the way you are acting now; just no sense at all. As I told Louisa—"

"Louisa!" Richard felt his heart give a leap. "Is she here?"

"No, of course not, Richard; she's in New York. But I talked to her; there are such things as telephones, you know. I talked to her this morning. And she is coming out. She may come out tonight. And when she does we can all sit down and—"

At this point there was an interruption. There was a bounding step on the porch—not Louisa's step, either; this had the soft, thudding thump of bare feet or of feet in sneakers—and then Florence said something that Richard didn't understand.

He had turned partly away from her in the direction of the sound, but he saw the beam of her flashlight spring out suddenly, aimed toward the porch window, and again he felt trapped; there were signals, there were machinations going on all around him. . . . At the same instant, a voice, a boy's voice from outside, called, "Hi, folks. Here's the U. S. Marines to the rescue. Can I come in?" Richard found himself standing pressed against the living-room wall by the side of the door.

He was standing beside the door and the porch door outside was opening, and it was odd, a minute before he couldn't have said where he'd put the ice pick or even if he had it with him. But it was in his hand now, and ready. He was standing by the door, and he had a glimpse of a young fellow coming through: it was a kid of about sixteen, in shorts and a jersey, and the shorts wrinkled in front so that they looked shorter even than they were, and the legs long and tanned and a little knob-kneed in the way that kids' legs often are. He was carrying a flashlight and a model sailing ship and he had something else wrapped in a bundle under his arm, and his face was a face that Richard recognized only later as belonging to one of the Simmonses.

He came in, and the ice pick came down. (Until then, Richard had only meant to face the boy down, to send him kiting home where he belonged, but the act was its own justification; the ice pick came down.) It came down and met flesh and then instantly bone. It hadn't hit in there hard enough.

And, of course, there must be no witnesses. Richard saw the boy's face, long and thin-nosed like all of the Simmonses, turned toward him in startlement; the bundle dropped, spilling. . . . One thing that he saw was a toothbrush, dropping. And then the ice pick went up and down, up and down, mechanically, as the boy's back turned slowly, hunching away from him; beneath the jersey, striped brown and white, he could see the flesh jerking and shuddering, and the tiny black rents in the cloth, and the legs slowly folding, and then after that it was easy.

For he followed him down, striking, striking, striking, striking, striking, striking. (This was one trap he was ready for.) "I will not, I will *not,*" he kept saying, and it came to him that the boy had said something, too. It was a groan, or a plea, or something. "Oh, no. Don't. Why do you? Hurting?" Something like that.

But it was too late for anything now. The boy was lying on his face on the floor. He had been crawling and then he had simply collapsed, and the bundle revealed itself to be a pair of pajamas, now crumpled half under him; the sailboat and flashlight were off to one side and the toothbrush was just beyond his head, and as Richard looked down at him he saw one leg drawn up as if to crawl one step more, up and up till the knee was pressed almost against the belly.

There was no blood, that was one thing. It had been easy, and he realized that this was one thing that till now had been worrying him: whether he could do it or not, if he could really go through with it. And he had been, he had been able to, even with a stranger. . . . The room looked the same; there had not been any noise, or no noise that he could recall, and the furniture was the same: the big rocker and the ancient Morris chair that nobody ever sat in, and the willowy, billowy sofa, the stand-

ing lamp and the glass-fronted bookcase loaded with nobody's
books, in the corner. Florence was still there, too; she hadn't
moved an inch, but her whole body seemed to have sagged and
her mouth was literally hanging open. She was scared now, all
right, he took notice.

"I will *not* have any interruption!" he flung at her, and then
Elinor was standing in the doorway that led into the kitchen.
She had two cups of coffee in her hands and she hadn't dropped
them; she still held them, but they were slopped to the point
where half the coffee was in the saucers, and she too was
staring at him; it came over him suddenly that maybe she too
was frightened. He knew now, when he saw her, that he didn't
want to kill her. He wanted to save her; killing was easy, he had
learned that, and killing Florence would be easier still, but there
was something, he didn't know what, but something else he
must do with Elinor.

He hadn't thought things out half enough, he saw that. He
hadn't even shaved; he had forgotten, or he had done something. He hadn't brought his razor down from the city—that
was it; he had left it in his room on Third Avenue—and he
turned suddenly, fiercely, on Florence. "And you do this to me!"
he screamed. "Do you see what you drive me to?"

Florence screamed. He was lifted across the room, and his
fist went out and back, and she sprawled into the Morris chair.
And next Elinor. He saw the coffee cups drop, both together.
"No. No. Richard," she said, and struggled senselessly with him,
with *him,* for an instant; he felt her flesh twist and give under his
hands. But he was gentle with her. But he still wanted them to
be together.

"You stay there," he said. He pushed her into a corner, and
because they still were struggling he knocked over the lamp as
he did so. "Oh, I'm sorry," he said. "I won't hurt you, Elinor.
Don't you know that, Elinor?"

She fell into the corner, beside the bookcase. "I really don't,
you know," he told her. He meant that he really didn't want to
kill her, but there was a force alive within him, and he had no
idea if she had heard him. He had her head between his hands
as they fell and it snapped back under his pressure; she stared up

at him, lax and limp and her legs spread out, and then when he let go her head fell forward and slumped and she seemed to have fainted.

And there still was Florence. Something, simply something, had to be done about Florence.

This time, Florence's time, there was blood. Getting up from Elinor—for he had fallen with her, and it was a little revolting, touching flesh that he had thought about so long, so long, and finding that flesh limp and unresponding; and then pushing himself up again—he glanced quickly about the room.

He was looking for a weapon, for something, for anything. There was the ice pick, there, over there by the other one, the boy. But Richard didn't want that; it had been used, it had done its part; it belonged to the boy, the other.

He didn't want it for Florence; he wanted something else, and he stared about the room desperately, at the lamp, at the straight-backed chair by the window and the bookcase top where there were always odds and ends but now only a basket of Florence's darning and a flashlight but no weapons, no weapons; and at the rickety round center table where the books and the thick yellow peasant-pottery bowl that belonged to Louisa, but again no weapons—and then he realized he couldn't wait too long or search too much. Things were happening. Everybody was coming to life again. It seemed that killing demanded constant attention.

There was Florence. She had opened her eyes, but blindly, dazedly, and there was a kind of pale, somber, preoccupied glaze on her face that made her look heavy and ominous, like—somehow—a school principal steadying herself for action; she had put both hands on the arms of the Morris chair and she was trying, awkwardly, heavily, doggedly, to get her weight in control and lift herself from the chair.

Elinor ... And the boy! With a horror that struck deepest of all, Richard realized that the boy had stirred too. He wasn't dead. He had stirred. He had turned. He had turned on his back, and one hand, the left hand, was clawing weakly at the front of his jersey, where still no blood, or hardly any—only the slightest staining—appeared. The face showed no pain.

But there was life there, and as long as it was there Richard dared not turn his back on it. He stepped over, and—this time with real revulsion; it was a duty to be done, it was an obligation—again the little slice-tearing sound, and the needle-thin, sliding acceptance, and the soft, almost imperceptible jellylike quaking running all through the body, and the clinging withdrawal.

And still there was Florence. This time, it was hard. This time, Florence's time, there was blood. This time, really, it was killing.

She was erect when he turned, with her shoulders crouched and the old heavy head hanging, and she was swaying as if something other than her own bones and body were holding her, and she was mumbling something; she looked monstrous, as he looked up at her.

She looked huge, unpredictable, menacing, and almost in a defensive gesture, as he still knelt beside the boy's body (and the body still twitching painfully) Richard reached for the pottery bowl on the table and flung it at her, and it splashed against her face in fragments and vanished, and then her face showed through again, blind and stubborn and blood-streaked now, but still leaning and looming toward him; for an instant he felt she was about to plunge down on him and crush him, and—really, to defend himself; things were getting out of hand, it was like a war—he picked up a chair and swung it at her.

And still Elinor . . . But it was like a war. Coming across the dunes, he had had the same thought, for a moment; just as he had started out for the cottage, and after the tension before and the calmness after, it had seemed it was like a war, like those wartime movies, where one moment (the moment before) you saw the soldier standing taut and fretful, sweating; and then next (the next moment: the moment after) he was walking—gunflashes and death and the suddenness and noise of destruction all around him, and still, walking—slowly and confidently, released, relaxed, forward into the battle.

Now it seemed he had been plunged, though, into the battle itself. The gun-flashes were nearer, and suddener; the squirm of death was around him, and so was the enemy. He was beset by them, he was surrounded (and somewhere there, too, Elinor) and the flashes had a strange effect on him; they came more regularly, they came and went, shutter-like, like a light through shutters; and sometimes, in the flashes, he saw, and then sometimes he didn't, and sometimes what he saw was repeated. He saw the bowl bursting, yellow, like a sunburst, and then the trickles of red; and then Elinor, where she had fallen; and the yellow again, splattering, and the loose, wrinkle-webbed flesh of Florence's face hooking through it. He saw the chair smash and knew it was vulgar.

Like a bar-room brawl, that was what it was; like a brawl in that place in Port Jeff. And he had wanted to have it transcendent, a removal of evil, a moving upward into good. He had wanted one thing, and it was she still who was forcing another; even in her death she was trying to degrade him, and at the thought of this all his anger flared up, and his determination—for it did take determination; he knew that now, and it was something he hadn't known till now.

He had killed, and he was killing again, and meantime it was the lights going off and on that bothered him, and the feeling of hugeness and smallness that went with it, and the feeling at last of could he stand it much longer?

He saw and he didn't see. He saw her eye, Florence's eye, near, wide open, protruding, as choked-looking as the feeling of chokedness his fingers had fastened on her throat, and at the same time immediate memories came between; it was hard to know, really, what was happening. There was a moment when he found himself flitting. He was in the kitchen and then in the corridor, and before that he knew he had been in the bathroom upstairs; he had a towel in one hand and a stocking in the other (by then everything was weapons) and the only thing he found himself thinking of was that the whole thing would have been easier if he had only brought the rope; from the very beginning the whole thing could have been calmer, simpler; he could quite simply have tied them both up, he could have talked to them, he could have told them.

And at the same time he knew he was wrong, for the rope was for Elinor, and he was occupied now with Florence; and anyway he hadn't brought it, except that there it was, come from somewhere. But anyway, it was too late now, for the towel was in place (for it was the towel), but his hands were needed, too, though the whole thing was beginning to revolt him: the damp, slippery flesh (how that woman had sweat!) and the eel-like thick feel of the old woman's neck that his fingers had seized and could not now let go of, and the body that kicked and clawed and contorted, but always with his grip as its pivot; and his grip, and the pivot, the one solid stationary thing in the whole turning room, the one thing that he had to hold onto.

And he held. It was horrible at first, and then it was a test, and then it was duty, and the one way he knew he could relax was that the body grew heavier in his hands, so heavy he could hardly hold it, for now suddenly he realized that it was his strength alone that held it; the Morris chair had been over-turned, and the table; he was on his knees and half-embracing the awful woman; he had been dragged down again (were they all in league against him?) and in a sudden accession of rage he banged her head sharply against the floor a few times. "No shamming now, damn it! No shamming!" he said sternly. But it was clear that this time there was no shamming.

And then Elinor . . . And then frittering. There were fritter-ing, skittering, flittering things he did too, that he smiled about afterward, only afterward he couldn't remember them all, only glancingly, for the lights came and went, on, off, on, off, like a shutter opening and closing, or like those times on the stage, when they turn the lights on and off fast, and it makes people look like an old-fashioned movie.

Or like impulses, and even walking off across the dunes, afterward, he could feel the lights driving him. The surprise was, was Elinor. She had died, quite simply, sitting there in the corner; she must have twisted her neck, or he had, when he had (or had he?) shaken her, or had he? Anyway, it was all crooked now; she had died, she had deaded herself, and it was sad, too; she neither answered nor stirred, and he had planned other things for Elinor. But she had died, she had wasn't it demised? And sorrow, because wouldn't it be sorrow?

Sorrow it was, she was dead. Love had killed her, let love

gild her memory, or the bloody-wreathed stake—"bloody-wreathed" would have been better than whatever it was he had written, if he had thought of it in time to write it—and for a while he wrung his hands over her, even though even then he could see it was right, what had happened, since it had happened.

He thought of Elinor constantly as he walked off across the dunes. "You will live again, Elinor. I promise you," he had told her. But she hadn't heard, and he knew it, and he thought that if only he had planned things differently . . . Now, he wasn't sure. Perhaps one needed the voice to give the impulse direction. . . .

There had been one moment, too, he remembered, when he had looked about the room in incredulity, at its calmness and its disorder, at the chairs overturned and the glass-fronted bookcase still glittering, at the lights burning down, and the bodies. "Time. Weariness. Sorrow," he had thought. "The things they make a man do. Or try to. Because if you're sharp enough, really sharp enough—" That had been when he was leaving, and on an impulse he had run upstairs to Elinor's bedroom and, searching, had gotten a little ribbon bow to bind her hair; and then searching again, had found a skirt for her and, delicately, straightened her shorts-clad legs and draped it over her carefully; it was the way she would have wanted it, he thought. And if life did come to her again . . .

He thought of Elinor constantly, walking across the dunes. And Louisa. It was an impulse, bright as day, that had sent him out of the cottage, and now Louisa almost brought him back again. Hadn't something been said that she was coming down tonight? Or was it tomorrow?

Tomorrow, probably, he thought shrewdly, and anyway, what he had done was right; he was outside, where he could pounce; he could watch, he could wait; he could pounce. . . .

Yet, without really thinking, he kept walking, and as he walked all the things that had happened dropped gradually behind him. They had happened, but they were becoming past; they were becoming no more than a story that would have to be told to become a happening again, and though he knew well enough that you couldn't tell it to just anyone he knew too that there were people who would be honest and understanding.

He could tell it to Chub, for instance, and he *would* tell him, when he saw him. Or Louisa: perhaps that was what Louisa had been saved for, if he decided in the end to save her.

Or that old woman who ran the grocery store at the cross-roads. He had been brusque with her, and unjustly so, the other time he had seen her, but now he found himself thinking of her with sympathy and affection. There were people all over the world that one could be friends with, that was the truth of it; if one just wanted to make the effort. And he was free now; he could go anywhere.

The only thing was, he was so tired.

Summer is calm, too; summer is peacefulness, and the peace and the calm too grow goldener as the end of summer approaches. That, of course, is before the cold weather comes, and the storms and rains of autumn; but there's a time when the turning-point between the two seasons is marked only by a slight edge in the air, thin as silver and silver bright: it comes only in the mornings, and, if you are camping out—and what fools they are who give up camping too early!—adds a zest to the mere act of waking that carries you cheerfully into the day.

And if you are tired, too—well, if you are tired, it can conquer tiredness. You can lie in the bright, pale sun-glitter, with the still-ness and calm all around you, and you can narrow things down, bring them closer, closer—till the world is no longer the worlds of the sun and the sky and the sea; you can narrow it down, till it's no longer the dunes and the cottages on the dunes and the cities beyond them, nor is it even the nearest dune's edge: you can narrow it down till it's only you. You can lie for hours, half-somnolent, dreaming, with nothing outside or beyond you at all—except perhaps the fine grainy feeling and slight whisper of a handful of sand as it dribbles through your fingers, or the flash of the sun as it makes tiny swords, momentarily, of the few spears of grass waving just beyond your arm's reach.

You can lie for hours, while the sun and the silence soak in, just playing with the sand, scooping sand up and dribbling it into mounds and then smoothing the mounds out and dribbling again. . . .

Calmness comes with the dawn, in summer, but as the long dawn-shadows grow slightly shorter and the sea begins to stir, you stir too. You get up, perhaps, and fold your blankets, because after all order is order, and though you haven't started thinking yet, really—though you still hold your own world within you— you remember vaguely that you are going some place, or you were thinking of going. Though you know that the water may be a little cold at this season you start down to the beach for a swim. . . .

They found him there, on the beach, having sighted him moving out from his hollow onto the dunes, and after the first surprise and the resentment of seeing so many men running toward him—state troopers and policemen too, six or seven of them, and all with guns—Richard met them quite calmly, quite peaceably.